# RESCUE ME

# RESCUE ME

CHERRY
ADAIR

LORA
LEIGH

CINDY
GERARD

St. Martin's Paperbacks

This is a work of fiction. All of the characters, organizations, and events portrayed in this novel are either products of the author's imagination or are used fictitiously.

RESCUE ME

"Tropical Heat" copyright © 2008 by Cherry Adair.
"Atlanta Heat" copyright © 2008 by Lora Leigh.
"Desert Heat" copyright © 2008 by Cindy Gerard.

Cover photograph © Shirley Green

ISBN: 0-312-94842-5
EAN: 978-0-312-94842-9

Printed in the United States of America

St. Martin's Paperbacks edition / July 2008

St. Martin's Paperbacks are published by St. Martin's Press, 175 Fifth Avenue, New York, NY 10010.

10 9 8 7 6 5 4 3 2 1

# Contents

Tropical Heat    1

Atlanta Heat    111

Desert Heat    225

# TROPICAL HEAT

CHERRY
ADAIR

# ONE
*Huren*
*Congo Basin*
*Central Africa*


THE BRILLIANT LIGHTS OF the operating room glinted off the scalpel being held to Dr. Elizabeth Goodall's slender throat.

Flat on his belly in the main air-conditioning duct directly above them, Sam Pelton aimed his Sig Sauer between the soldier's expressionless eyes. The state-of-the-art, multi-million-dollar operating room wouldn't have been unusual if it had been in a large hospital in a major city anywhere in the world. But this OR was smack in the middle of the jungles of Central Africa.

"Obviously I was brought all this way for a reason," Beth was saying a little desperately. "Just tell me *why*. There's no need to threaten me with the scalpel." When she got nothing more than a blank stare, she dragged in a deep breath, held it, then let it out slowly. "Who's in charge? You?" she asked the guy with the blade.

*Yeah. I'd like to see the asshole in charge, too,* Sam thought, watching them through the small holes he'd pierced in the metal duct. This top-secret compound, deep in the Huren jungle, belonged to President Sipho Nkemidilm. What was so damn urgent that he'd had a prominent physician kidnapped from a bustling metropolitan hotel and flown thousands of miles to his hidden compound?

Something big. The compound was crawling with heavily armed, camo-clad soldiers. More of them than had been reported here a week ago. It didn't bother Sam that there were twenty trained soldiers in residence. Twenty to one weren't insurmountable odds. He had an arsenal of weapons on him, and a heavier pack, fully equipped, concealed several clicks away in the jungle. Another smaller pack was hidden just outside the compound. He was loaded for bear, with the skills and determination to use either his weapons, or whatever else was at hand. Whatever it took to expedite this rescue mission.

One of the men shoved a handful of blue fabric at Beth's midsection. It drifted to the floor as she made no move to accept it, and instead, glanced around the brightly lit room without moving her head. "Does *anyone* here speak English?" she asked with admirable calm.

They didn't. Or pretended they didn't.

Her red-gold hair, pulled up in its customary simple ponytail, was disheveled, and her amber freckles stood out in sharp relief on her pale skin. Her eyes flickered between the man holding her at blade-point and the three stony-faced, AK-47-wielding soldiers flanking her.

Two more uniforms were stationed at the door. A seventh man, presumably the anesthesiologist, stood hunch-shouldered and mute at the head of the operating table, clearly trying to make himself as unobtrusive as possible.

Wasn't going to save his sorry ass. Sam was ready, willing, and freaking able to blow the place to smithereens at the first opportunity. Once he had Beth. Once she was safe. Dropping down now, guns blazing, while personally satisfying, might get her killed. That was a risk he wasn't willing to take.

The son of a bitch with the scalpel at her throat would be the first to die.

They'd snatched the wrong doctor. *His* doctor, goddamn it. At least that's what Sam believed. Beth was a general practitioner, and while he, and the entire town of Brandon, Montana, thought she was extra special, as far as he knew she didn't have any more skills than the several hundred other GPs in attendance at the symposium she'd been attending in Cape Town. He suspected the tangos thought they'd snatched plastic surgeon Lynne Randall. And the second they realized their mistake, Beth would be dead.

And before they killed her she'd be begging to be dead *faster*.

He had to get her the hell out of here *sooner* than ASAP. People said Sam Pelton didn't have a nerve in his body, that ice water ran in his veins. But right now he was as scared as he'd ever been. Everything was different about this op because Beth was in the center of it.

Scalpel-dick jerked his head, indicating that one of the men pick up what Sam presumed were scrubs. The pulse at the base of Beth's throat pounded her stress level, yet she still refused to accept the clothing. Her sangfroid was remarkable. But that was Beth. Always cool, calm and collected.

*That's it. Keep your head, sweetheart. I'm right here.*

Ignore the scalpel indenting her skin, Sam told himself savagely. Ignore the way her fear, and the stark white lights, leeched all the color from her face. Ignore the smudges under her eyes. Ignore the rapid pulse hammering in the hollow of her damp throat.

Ignore, God damn it, the fucking scalpel pressed to her carotid.

To do his job, he had to block Beth from his mind. Since he hadn't been able to do that for the past two years, it wasn't easy. He managed to do it anyway.

She swallowed hard, and the scalpel left a razor-thin line of blood on her neck. Right where Sam had been craving to kiss her for months. And that was the *last* fucking time he'd resist the impulse to kiss her. As soon as he had her out of here, and it was safe enough to do so, he was going to kiss Beth like she'd never been kissed before. To hell with restraint. To hell with waiting.

Instead of freaking out, she reached up and gently tried to push the man's hand away from her throat. With the slight shift in angle, the thin blade cut a red line between her thumb and forefinger. She cried out, making a big production so all the soldiers could see the blood.

Christ. Had she done that on purpose?

There was much frantic debate in Hureni as they tried to figure out what to do. Her injury clearly scared the crap out of them. They'd wanted to scare her, they had no problem cutting her in small increments, but the injury to her hand had them in a panic. Beth had called their bluff.

She curled her fingers tightly into her palm, then cradled her bleeding hand against her chest. Blood stained her skin, shocking and redder than any blood Sam could remember. Maybe because Beth's skin was so pale. Hell. Maybe because this was Beth. *His* Beth.

Using every bit of control and all of his training, he clenched his teeth until his jaw ached. He might not be killing any of them, but he was counting the minutes and choreographing every move.

"I'm not resisting," she said, her voice, to someone who had studied her for months, slightly uneven. "I'm not fighting. There's no need to hurt me again. Call whoever's in charge and we ca—"

Her words were cut off with a choked scream as the man grabbed her hair, using her sassy ponytail as a handle, yanking her head back, leaving her arched throat naked and vulnerable.

Light glinted off the blade as he yelled his displeasure, his angry spit splattering her face.

Sam's heart did a double tap as the scalpel carved another thin red line on the smooth skin, this time her cheek. *Three goddamn strikes and you're out, dick. Cool it*, he told himself, almost jumping out of his skin with the need to act.

*Now*.

But his training told him that while the guy was cutting Beth, the cuts were small and not life-threatening. Not to Beth. To the guy making them, it was a death sentence. The son of a bitch wasn't going to kill her, Sam rationalized, sweat beading his brow. The grunt with the scalpel wasn't high enough up the food chain for one thing, and for another, someone had brought a doctor here for a specific purpose. Hopefully he'd find out the who and why before Scalpel-dick got any more aggressive with that blade and he was forced to kill him sooner rather than later.

Intel had reported that Nkemidilm wasn't in residence. He was off with his troops fighting the Mallaruzi on Huren's western border. Huren was also in the middle of a bloody, and extremely violent, civil war. The body count was sky high. Nkemidilm was a megalomaniacal sadist and was fighting with damn well everyone in *and* out of his country. He'd trained in Russia, his army carried American-made weapons, and he had absolutely no regard for human life. His allies were no better.

The cold air blasting around Sam did nothing to

cool his temper nor did it dispel the fear churning in his gut as he watched the tableau beneath his hiding place.

Nervous perspiration made Beth's creamy skin look dewy, touchable. They'd let her remove the jacket to her black pantsuit, and her long-sleeved pink blouse was half untucked, sticking to her skin and smeared with dirt and blood. Even mussed she was sexy. She should be back home in Montana in her small clinic, dispensing suckers to damp-eyed kids and wearing the all-encompassing white coat of her profession. And giving him a hard time.

He'd tried talking her out of attending the medical symposium in Cape Town when they'd "accidentally" bumped into each other at the bank two weeks ago. South Africa was a country in flux. Not safe for tourists just yet, and counted as one of the most dangerous places in the world. Yet in spite of, or because of his warnings, she'd gone anyway.

Who'd taken Beth, and what the hell did they want with her? No. Not *Beth*. Dr. Lynne Randall. All Dr. Randall, safely sequestered in a local safe-house, could tell them was that Beth had gone upstairs to pick up some notes for her. Beth had been snatched moments after entering Randall's room.

Thank God his people in the Cape had been smart enough to squash the story from the press. None of the bad guys knew they'd kidnapped the wrong woman.

"If no one in charge is coming, then I'm—"

One of the soldiers answered in Hureni. Sam didn't speak the language, and clearly neither did Beth.

Just her eyes moved as she addressed the anesthetist standing across the room. "Do *you* speak English?"

He gave her a blank stare and her attention returned to the man with the blade at her throat, who was still yelling at her. "I have no idea what you're saying," she told him crisply, raising her voice just enough to get his attention. Her hand must have hurt like hell, but she wasn't paying it any attention.

Scalpel-dick yelled louder, inches from her face. Louder didn't mean she could comprehend him any better.

The door opened and he shut up like a tap being turned off. The rest of the soldiers in the room snapped to, straight-backed, weapons at the ready-attention. Sam already had the Sig aimed at the potential new danger.

His heart skittered.

*Shit.*

*The Butcher.* Tau Thadiwe.

The terrorist was currently on every country's Capture Dead or Alive list. Six feet seven inches of solid muscle, with skin the color of dusty ebony, and currently dressed, unselfconsciously, in a short white hospital gown. Flip-flops snapping on his enormous feet, he strode into the room surrounded by a phalanx of soldiers.

If anyone was worse than Nkemidilm it was his

old friend Thadiwe. The two men shared an alliance that went back to their covert training days in Russia some thirty years ago. The counterterrorist group Sam worked for was aware that Thadiwe was responsible for doing a little extracurricular work after his and Nkemidilm's basic training ended. Torture was both Thadiwe's specialty and his passion, and he'd educated Huren's leader in the fine art of persuasion until both men were feared and revered for their sadistic skills.

The man was an amoral psychopath. Not only was he chillingly good at what he did, he relished his work.

Speculation had been rife about his whereabouts for months. And here he was. Deep in the jungle where no one would think to look. Thadiwe and Nkemidilm had done a damn good job keeping their friendship off the radar. They hadn't been seen together since 1996.

"Dr. Randall, thank you for coming," Thadiwe said in unaccented English. Sam didn't know if he felt better or worse getting the confirmation that they'd snatched the wrong doctor.

Thadiwe approached Beth but didn't extend his hand, nor did he instruct his men to stand down. Suddenly he noticed her still bleeding hand. Hard to fucking miss since the left side of her pink blouse was stained red. The tango scowled.

"I wasn't aware that I had a choice," Beth said dryly. "Please tell this man to put the scalpel down. I'm no threat."

Thadiwe turned on the man beside her who still had the scalpel at her throat.

*Move, Beth. For fuck's sake, move out of the way.*

Without a word Thadiwe pulled the HK out of the holster of the soldier next to him and shot his man point-blank in the face. Beth flinched, jumping back as blood and brain matter spattered the area. She moved directly into Sam's line of fire.

For several stunned seconds nobody moved, then, his eyes on Beth, Thadiwe snapped his beefy fingers. One of his men rushed to hand him a handkerchief, which he used to wipe the blood off his face. The white gown he wore now had red polka dots all down the front.

Sam now knew who, and he had a pretty good idea why. He prepared to fire. *Move, Elizabeth!*

"My apologies for the manner in which you were transported here, Doctor." Thadiwe wiped his hands, then tossed the bloodied cloth aside. "My men tend to be zealous in their interpretation of my instructions."

Beth's shoulders were stiff, and she was barely breathing. It was almost better not being able to see her face. Sam wanted to curve his hand reassuringly around her vulnerable nape.

"What is it you expect of me, Mister—?"

"Tau Thadiwe," he said, signing her death warrant. Whatever surgery he wanted Beth to perform on him, he had no intention of letting her live afterward. "Prepare yourself to do facial reconstruction immediately, Dr. Randall."

"There's nothing wrong with your face," Beth told him after a brief pause. "I can't imagine why you wa—"

Thadiwe backhanded her. She staggered, but quickly recovered. Too quickly. Goddamn it, a fraction of a millimeter more and Sam's shot would have taken off the top of her head. The tango's handprint was a livid red mark on the curve of her check. "What—?"

"Unless they are in reference to the procedure or my health, no questions."

Sam shifted the muzzle of the Sig the necessary fraction of an inch to aim at the parallel lines between Thadiwe's eyebrows. *You're about to die of lead poisoning, asshole.*

The need to take out the tango made Sam's entire body itch. He was ready to drop him right there. Right now. Beth chose that moment to shift, blocking his shot again.

*Move to the left a few inches. Come on, sweetheart. Just a couple of inches.*

"You are here to do my reconstructive surgery. You're the best. That's why I ensured you would attend the symposium in Cape Town."

"*You* were the secret benefactor that paid L— my way to Cape Town? I don't know who you are, but there are easier ways to schedule surgery than kidnapping the doctor."

"Not *just* a doctor. *You*, Dr. Randall. You are the preeminent facial reconstruction plastic surgeon in America, are you not?"

Beth still blocked the shot. *For Christ's sake, don't tell him who you are,* Sam thought, wishing to hell telepathy was one of his skill sets.

"I'd be more receptive to your request if you'd made an appointment," Beth said coolly, and Sam breathed a silent sigh of relief. Smart girl. He shouldn't have underestimated her.

Thadiwe clicked his beefy fingers, and one of his men handed him a large manila envelope. He rooted around inside to find what he wanted, then handed her several photographs. "This is what I want my new face to look like."

She glanced at the pictures, her ponytail brushing the pink, blood-speckled collar of her shirt, then said smoothly, "I can't perform surgery without extensive lab tests, X-rays—"

"The lab tests were done last week, as were these X-rays and photographs." He handed her the envelope. "Everything you need is here."

Her ponytail jerked as she looked up at Thadiwe. "Surely you don't expect me to do it *now?*"

"I wouldn't have brought you here otherwise."

"But this type of surgery has to be done in stages. Over several months, surely you kn—" Clearly he *wasn't* aware of how long the procedure took. "As you can see, I have a deep cut on my dominant hand," she told him calmly, holding out her injured hand. Beth was left-handed, not right. But she was playing every card she had. "Obviously performing any type of surgery now is impossible."

"Yet you will manage, Dr. Randall, or I will not hesitate to kill you."

Beth blinked and curled her injured hand toward her body. Thadiwe moved closer, and Sam's finger rested against the trigger, in case the son of a bitch made a wrong move. "I can't."

"You can." Thadiwe slowly ran his finger over the creased frown in Beth's forehead. "And you will. Your husband leaves for work at six-fifteen. He drops your baby off at Apple Tree Day Care. I have your mother's home address in Hollywood, your brother's too—congratulations on his wife's pregnancy. And your grandfather, well, it would be a shame if anything happened to him at the nursing home . . . In other words, Dr. Randall, if you fail to cooperate fully, I will have your entire family slaughtered by morning. All it will take is one phone call."

Sam's mouth tightened. Even though this wasn't Beth's family Thadiwe was threatening, it was Lynne Randall's—a doctor who was guilty of no more than being the best in her field. Beth's friend.

"Leave my family out of this. All right. You give me no choice. Your surgery will take upwards of twenty hours." She pulled out some of the paperwork, then took a moment to scan the information.

"You have high blood pressure." She glanced up at Thadiwe. "I appreciate your state-of-the-art OR, but what happens in the event of an emergency that I can't handle alone? We're in the middle of the jungle, hundreds of miles from anywhere." Her hand was leaving bloodstains on the manila envelope, and it made Sam crazy to see her hurt when he was right there and should have been able to protect her. Even from herself.

"There are dozens of factors to consider. A reaction to the anesthetic. Clotting issues that could cause excessive blood loss. Underlying, undiagnosed pre-existing conditions. Even though you've been treating your high blood pressure, there's still a possibility that you'd stroke out from the stress such a complex medical procedure will put on your body. Especially since you insist on having several procedures done at once. It's risky. Very risky."

Sam's estimation of her b.s. ability went up. The type of surgery Thadiwe wanted would take half a dozen procedures over the span of several months, not hours. Beth was playing along, *and* buying time.

"How close is the nearest hospital with well-trained emergency room staff and a competent cardiologist?" she asked calmly as she flipped through Thadiwe's paperwork.

"An hour by helicopter. You'd better not make any mistakes, Dr. Randall. If anything goes wrong, if I should come to any harm while under your scalpel, my men have instructions to torture you. You will die in agony and very, very slowly."

Her head jerked up. "And you think that threatening me will scare me into doing a better job?" she demanded, letting her annoyance leak into her voice.

*Annoyance.* Not fear. "I'm a surgeon and bound by my own ethics to do you no harm. But to do that, I'll need to rest first. I've been kidnapped at gunpoint, and tied hand and foot for six hours. I'll perform your surgery in the morning if you give me your word that afterward I'll be returned to Cape Town in good health. Do we have a bargain?"

Christ, she sounded cool. Everyone in the room knew the second Thadiwe got what he wanted she'd be dead.

"I'll need post-operative care."

"Kidnap a nurse," she said dryly.

"I'll give you two hours to rest and study my file."

"That's not enough time. My God, you want every bone in your face rearranged. Do you honestly think that studying your X-rays and photographs for *two hours* will be sufficient time? *I* would never allow an exhausted, ill-prepared surgeon to do major surgery on *my* face."

"You're the best in the world."

"Be that as it may, I'm not *at* my best *now*. And you want the best when it comes to *this*." She held up one of the photographs. "Give me ten hours, and I'll—"

"Two hours."

"No. You might as well save time and kill me now, then go and kidnap another facial reconstruction specialist." She thrust the envelope at his massive barrel chest. "But you know, and I know, Mr. Thadiwe, that long before you find anyone else of my caliber, *I'll* be ready to do your surgery. You kidnapped me because I *am* the best. Don't be stubbornly foolish enough to rush me. You'll have the face you want by this time tomorrow night."

Thadiwe glanced at the $200,000 Girard-Perregaux watch on his thick wrist. "I'll give you six hours."

"Eight. I'll be ready."

"Seven."

Beth said nothing. Silence throbbed between them. Finally the man caved, and he nodded. "Not one second past seven A.M."

Sam eased his finger off the trigger.

# TWO

A CALLUSED HAND CLAMPED over Elizabeth's mouth, waking her with a heart-pounding jolt. *What the . . . ?*

One of Thadiwe's guards?

God forbid, Thadiwe himself? Chills of pure terror chased over her skin, making the fine hairs on her arms and the back of her neck stand up.

She hadn't meant to fall sleep, but half an hour after she'd come to the room, the lights had suddenly gone out. She'd fought exhaustion and lost.

The man whispered something, but she couldn't hear him over the thundering in her ears. Cold sweat replaced the tropical heat of the room as she struggled to break free of the strong gag of his fingers. Whoever he was, his hand covered half her face, making it hard to drag in a breath. What air she could suck in smelled of clean male sweat mixed with the chemical stink of insect repellent. He could be any one of the guards.

There'd been two stationed right outside her door when she'd tried to leave the room just before the lights went out. But this wasn't one of them, not unless he'd taken a shower recently. It didn't matter who he was, she'd been scared long before *this* guy had shown up. Afraid that the guards would add rape to their list of duties.

Elizabeth fought harder.

"Shhh. Promise not to scream, and I'll take away my hand." The rough-edged voice, low and elusively familiar, was now only a few inches from her face.

*In your dreams, pal.* The second she was free, she was going to scream until the entire household came running. And *then* what? She didn't think it likely that Thadiwe would come to her defense— although he might shoot the rapist.

Elizabeth nodded to indicate compliance, then sucked in a breath in anticipation.

"Damn, you give stubborn a new meaning, woman." His whisper was laced with humor as his lips replaced his hand, covering her mouth, which was open, ready to yell. "It's me, Sam," he said hoarsely against her parted lips before the warm slickness of his tongue entered her mouth. His lips molded hers. His fingers tangled in her hair, holding her still as he kissed her. The kiss wasn't violent, or aggressive. But it was—*hungry* in a controlled way that puzzled her.

He was a good kisser.

He tasted— Was she out of her mind?! She tried to shut her mouth against the sensual invasion.

"Ow! Shit, no biting."

With a palm to his bristly jaw, she shoved his face away from hers. The only Sam she knew was—"Sam *Pelton?*" she asked incredulously. Pushing her hair out of her face with her injured hand, she winced as she sat up.

He—*Sam*—crouched beside the bed. "Yeah. Don't scream, for God's sake."

The room was so dark she couldn't see her hand in front of her face. It was weird hearing Sam's voice *here*, and she considered the possibility that she was dreaming. She'd had plenty of dreams about Sam in the last few months. Most of them erotic. His presence was so out of context she couldn't make any sense of it, and sitting in the pitch dark whispering made the disorientation complete.

She was probably hallucinating. That was the only explanation. Sam had been a constant presence in her life for months. A constant frustration. She'd seen him around town so often that she'd wondered if it was coincidence, fate, or maybe low-level stalking. But not Sam. He was a complete gentleman at all times, even when she'd dropped subtle hints after her divorce was final.

Either he didn't get subtle or he didn't want her. It didn't matter, the end result was the same; her simmering lust for him went unnoticed and unsatisfied. Which was why, she supposed, images of his tall, muscular body haunted her sleep night after night.

It also explained why she'd be hallucinating about him now, when she was probably only hours from death. Thadiwe didn't strike her as a stupid man. He'd eventually figure out she wasn't Dr. Randall, if he hadn't done so already.

She leaned over to turn on the bedside light, hoping the power was back on, but before her fingers reached the lamp, Sam clamped a hard hand on her wrist, startling a small yelp out of her constricted throat. He didn't feel like too-safe, too-controlled Sam in the dark. He felt dangerous, and edgy, and a little scary.

"I took out the generator." His warm breath stirred the hair near her ear, which made her shudder reactively. So he'd been the one to plunge the compound into darkness. No wonder Thadiwe's soldiers had been freaked out. She'd heard them running in the corridor outside her room as they tried to figure out what was happening.

Elizabeth rubbed her wrist as she pictured Sam's face with its bold, blunt features and dark eyes that gave nothing away. He wasn't handsome, but he was somehow compelling. Maybe because she sensed that what she saw wasn't who he really was. She'd always been fascinated by the way he moved with a controlled strength and an edgy awareness that was almost predatory. She'd never been quite able to figure out what made him tick. Although she'd spent many nights trying to figure him out.

Not that she wasn't grateful to have him here, odd as that was, but he was sure to be even more out of his element in a rain forest than she was.

"What are you *doing* here?" she demanded in his

general direction as she got off the bed. This went beyond being neighborly.

"Rescuing you."

*Talk about the blind leading the blind.* Her pounding heart sounded like thunder in her ears, and her rapid pulse made her hand ache.

"Thank God. But how did you know I *needed* rescuing?" While she clearly needed help, Elizabeth didn't want Sam involved. She didn't want his death on her conscience.

"We'll talk about it later. First, take this doxycycline." Sam placed the antimalarial capsule in her palm. "Water." He held a flask to her mouth. Elizabeth took the pill and swallowed.

The flask was removed. "Strip." His voice deepened as he wiped a drop of water from her lower lip. Since she was licking it off at the same time, her tongue encountered his finger. A frisson that had nothing to do with fear spiraled deep in the pit of her stomach. They both froze for a heartbeat. His warm breath fanned her temple, and the heat of his body seeped through the thin, damp silk of her blouse.

While she'd love to have heard those words last month, or even yesterday, Sam's timing was off. "*Strip?*" Tempting as the request was, she blinked back her good sense. "Sam, are you insane?"

"You can't go out in the jungle dressed as you are. I've brought you a change of clothes. Hurry and change. I want to put medication on your cuts, and get you sprayed with DEET before we head outside."

With no antibiotics, she'd made do washing the

cuts as best she could using the water supplied with her meal tray. An open cut in this climate could spell trouble. That almost made her laugh. How much more trouble could she be in?

Elizabeth could tell from the location of his voice that Sam was standing very close to her. But she hadn't heard him move, which was a bit unnerving. He was well over six feet tall, so he'd be towering over her own five foot, five inches. The adrenaline rush hadn't left yet, and her blood still thumped frantically in her ears. He was still disconcertingly close. She swayed in his direction, and his hands shot out to circle her waist. "Steady."

She flushed and locked her knees. "Sorry. It's really disorientating being in the dark like this." Her lips tingled from their shared kiss. She never would have guessed at his passion; he kept it well hidden.

"Are you afraid of the dark?" he asked.

"Of the entire situation."

"Yeah, well, I'm here to take care of that."

The tile floor was warm and slightly sticky under her bare feet, and the overhead fan barely moved the thick air as she stood there, trying to decide what to do next. "My shoes are somewhere. If you can break off the heels, it'll make running possible. Better than bare feet anyway."

"We need to bring them with us, but I brought you a pair of boots."

She locked her knees to prevent her body from swaying toward him again. What she wouldn't do right now for a reassuring hug. But Sam wasn't a touchy-feely kind of guy. He never wore his emotions on his sleeve. At least not that she'd seen. Which was too bad, because she'd been attracted to him from the moment they'd met. Not that she'd ever given him any indication of it. They were neighbors. Friends in a way. She didn't want to rock that boat.

"Here, let me help you," he said softly, sliding his hands from her waist to the front of her blouse. The backs of his fingers brushed the upper swell of her breasts as he efficiently unbuttoned her blouse before she could protest. His movements were quick, but the feel of his warm fingers stroking all the way down the center of her body made Elizabeth short of breath. Insanely she wanted him to palm the weight of her breasts and relieve the ache in her peaked nipples. She wanted him to kiss her, and touch her, and do all the things she'd dreamed about doing with him.

"You can keep on your underwear," he said softly, not sounding as breathless and heated as Elizabeth felt. "Everything else comes off." His slightly callused fingers cupped her shoulders, then pushed the blouse off. The blouse fell to the floor behind her with a soft whoosh. Her cheeks went hot even though she knew he couldn't see her any better than she could see him. The temporary spurt of adventure that had brought her to Africa didn't extend to Sam seeing her half naked. Him Tarzan, her Jane. Not. She enjoyed the armor of clothing.

"What did you bring for me to wear?" she asked curiously. She couldn't begin to imagine Sam picking out a woman's clothes. Unless it was something slinky in red from Victoria's Secret. "A loincloth?"

"Better." His hands went to the button at the waistband of her black silk pants; the graze of his fingers against her skin made her draw in her breath. "Get these off—" As he spoke, he unzipped and tugged, and before she could protest that she was capable of undressing herself, the smooth fabric fell down her legs like water, leaving her in nothing but a thong and a blush.

"Okay, step into the feet first."

She let Sam guide her movements for two reasons: one, she couldn't see, and he clearly could; and two, she enjoyed the feel of his hands on her. "Are you wearing night-vision goggles?"

"Yeah, but I can close my eyes if you like." His voice was tinged with laughter. "Shy, Beth?"

"Not usually, no. But I'm not an exhibitionist either." The fabric felt odd, but she obligingly placed her bare feet where he positioned them as he knelt in front of her. His warm, damp breath fanned her bare stomach as he leaned forward to pull the tight fabric slowly up her legs and hips. Elizabeth rested her hand on his shoulder for balance.

He nuzzled her tummy, by accident, or design, she didn't know. She tried to ignore the fluttering in her belly and the heavy rush of her blood. *Down, girl.*

After her ex, Rob, had told her he was leaving,

she'd wanted her world shaken up. She'd wanted *adventure*. *Excitement*. She wanted, darn it all, to *live* life instead of hearing or reading about it. She was sick and tired of safe and predictable. Both in men and in her life. Rob had been safe and predictable. Until he'd turned unpredictable and run off with his Internet honey.

Well, Elizabeth had wanted a wild fling with someone inappropriate, too. Someone who made her blood race, a man who could make her breath catch. She wanted one of those high-octane, alpha males she loved reading about. She'd thought Sam fit the bill to a tee. Unfortunately, he was clearly not interested in *her*.

Which was why, against all sane advice, she'd gone to the medical symposium in Cape Town in the first place. *Yeah*, she thought dryly. *Look how well that turned out.*

He palmed her ass, resting his face against her belly as he ran his fingers lightly across her behind. He inhaled deeply. "God, you smell incredible. Lemon and musk. I could eat you right now."

The feel of his exploring fingers, and the scalding heat of Sam's breath against her skin, was making her so hot Elizabeth had to bite her lip to prevent crying out. "Cool your jets, sailor, we're in deep shit right now. I'm presuming by *rescue* you mean remove us from this place as fast as possible?" She tapped his shoulder to get his attention, and was appalled at how disappointed she was when he removed his hands from her ass and his mouth from her stomach. She cleared her throat and took a small step away from him. "What's this? Some kind of bodysuit?"

"Made out of one of the toughest man-made fibers invented."

"Sam, I'm going to die of heat enclosed in this rubbery stuff. Let me put my own clothes back on, and—"

"LockOut will maintain your body temp at ninety-eight-point-six degrees. It'll also keep the bugs out. Lift your chin—" He zipped her up all the way. The fabric was lightweight and not that uncomfortable, even if it did cover her from neck to toes.

"Boots." He slid each foot into a boot, then laced it. "How's that feel?"

She stomped her feet. "Perfect." How did he know her size?

"Give me your hand." Cradling her right hand in his large palm, Sam applied a topical liquid antibiotic, by the smell of it, then, after waiting a few seconds for it to dry, covered the wound with a Band-Aid. "That should do it. Let me know if it bothers you. I can give you a shot."

She'd give herself the shot, thank you very much. But it was good to know he had medical supplies should she need them.

The salve felt cool, and the topical numbing immediately took away some of the pain. "Thanks," she whispered. "The only thing I had was cold water and the granular sugar they brought me with a meal."

"Sugar?" His voice came up from knee level,

and she wondered what he was doing, and if he was about to touch her again. Her entire body tensed in anticipation. But by the sounds, he was gathering her clothes. Then she heard a zipper slide, then after a few seconds slide again.

She forced herself to take nice slow easy breaths. "Decreased the bleeding, promoted clotting, and when push came to shove, the only thing I had to discourage bacteria."

The scalpel's penetrating cut had left a fairly deep gash, ripe for anaerobic bacteria. In this hot, steamy climate even a small open wound was a concern. "How did you know about the cut?"

"I was watching. That was a hell of a brave thing you did. Letting that asshole cut you like that."

"It didn't stop his boss from demanding I do the surgery anyway. Besides, I'm left-handed."

"Yeah. I know. That wasn't the point; it must hurt like hell."

"Less painful than that guy cutting my throat. I shocked him just enough to make him nervous about trying to cut me again. What are you doing in Africa?"

It was the last place she would've imagined running into anyone she knew. Especially Sam Pelton.

A teacher in a war-torn, third-world country in the middle of a jungle. Sam appeared to be an intelligent man, but she couldn't imagine what the hell he was going to do to protect the two of them from gun-toting soldiers or a rain forest alive with four-legged predators.

Apparently God had a sense of humor.

"Sam, what *kind* of teacher ar—"

"Later," he told her, still speaking so softly she could barely hear him. "Hurry."

She was all for hurrying. "They brought me in by Jeep. I think I can find my way back to where it's parked—"

"We're walking out. Through the jungle, then down-river. I have a chopper waiting to fly us out of Huren."

The chopper sounded good. "That's crazy. Why walk when there are perfectly good vehicles—"

"I pushed one of their Jeeps a mile down the road, then hid it. The rest are disabled. When they discover you've left, they'll assume you drove out. They'll spend time fixing their vehicles so they can give chase. By the time they get around to doing that, you'll be well on your way home."

He sounded like he knew what he was talking about. From what she'd seen when they'd brought her here, Thadiwe's compound was surrounded by impenetrable jungle. The narrow dirt road had been heavily guarded when she'd been brought in. Elizabeth had no reason to presume that it was any different now. "How did you even manage to ge—" *Get past the guards? Get into my room?* Those were just the more immediate questions. She'd leave the biggies—like how he'd known where to find her—for later.

He silenced her with two fingers pressed against

her lips. She nodded. His fingers lingered a second
or two, then withdrew.

"Really, Sam, I think we should—"

He took her hand unerringly in the dark. "I can't
wait to hear what you think. *Later.*" He led her across
the small room to the window. She tugged at his
hand, trying to turn him toward the door instead of
the practically hermetically sealed window. "Bars."

She'd been examining them when the lights had
gone out.

"Not anymore." A trace of amusement laced his
quiet voice.

She wasn't sure which shocked her more, the
satisfied laughter she heard in his voice, or the fact
that he'd removed the entire window. She'd never
seen Sam smile in all the months she'd known him.
Not once. And he was the least likely handyman
she'd ever met. But there'd been three strong, one-
inch thick vertical metal bars on the small window,
and also an insect screen bolted to the outside of
the frame. She knew. She'd inspected every inch.

She tried to imagine Sam yanking out the window . . . It didn't compute. Yet somehow he'd done
it, because as they approached the opening she could
smell the fetid greenness of the jungle and feel the
thick, hot, syrupy air against her skin. She shivered.

"Insect repellent. Close your eyes," he said before
applying a liberal dose to her face, neck, and hands.

She could've put the stuff on herself, but she enjoyed the sensation of Sam's big hands running

gently over her face and neck. "Thanks." Mosquitoes could give one anything from an annoying bite to parasitic sleeping sickness. She was in enough trouble as it was.

Taking her hand, Sam's fingers tightened around hers, his hand cool and dry against her damp palm. "I'll go first then help you down."

Bracing one hand against the wall to orientate herself, Elizabeth listened to the rustle of animals in the undergrowth and the susurrus of leaves moving in their passage. To say that she didn't want to venture into the jungle, in the dark, was an understatement.

But it was the lesser of two evils. Still, she had the terrifying feeling that she was jumping from the frying pan into the fire.

"Climb out," Sam's voice was pitched so low she felt rather than heard it. "I'll catch you."

She didn't need help climbing out of a window three feet off the ground. What she needed was—*daylight*. A tank that could cut a swath through jungle. A *bazooka*, or some other weapon that would—

What she *had* was a teacher. Had Sam brought a gun with him? Did he even know how to *use* the damn thing if he had? But even if he did have a weapon, it wouldn't be much help out here where the least dangerous animals were panthers, lions, and other carnivores. Thadiwe's men were heavily armed, and more dangerous and determined than any of the denizens of the jungle.

Thadiwe hadn't gone to all that trouble to kidnap

and transport her to give her up without a fight. He'd send his men after her the second he realized she was gone. Beth considered and reconsidered the rock and the hard place. Either or. If she went with Sam, she had no doubt whatsoever that they'd be caught. And Thadiwe's retaliation would be swift and violent.

The dangers of being recaptured would mean sure death. Not only for herself, but for Sam as well. And she was damned sure that Thadiwe would make their deaths slow and excruciatingly painful. If she stayed, there was a chance that Sam would return in time to prevent her death. Yet staying meant she'd be forced at gunpoint to perform a surgical procedure she wasn't qualified to do. After which, she was pretty damn sure, they'd kill her anyway.

Either way, the end result would mean her death.

Damn it. She didn't have the luxury of time to debate the pros and cons of how quickly she was going to die.

Stay or go?

How were they going to find their way out of the jungle without help? Beth had no doubt that her captors knew every tree and leaf in this jungle. She and Sam wouldn't get very far before they were caught and forcibly returned to the compound. How much better off was she now than she'd been five minutes ago? Two of them, against God only knew how many armed soldiers.

"Stop overanalyzing," he said, his voice pitched so she could hear him. "Trust me."

She did trust him—and his ability to lead her out of this mess. Teachers were leaders, weren't they? A little. Maybe? Hopefully. Yes. He'd managed to track her to the middle of who-knows-where. Might as well go with his misguided but appreciated need to be a hero. Sam had no idea what he'd let himself in for. Knowing that squeezed her heart inside her chest.

Having him here, while it was terrific not being alone, was just going to get them *both* killed. "Go and find help," she whispered. It made sense for Sam to go and get reinforcements. One of them had to be practical. "I'll stall Thadiwe again in the morning." Practicality had its dangers, and now that she knew rescue was at hand, she wanted to get away from here so badly she shook with it. But it made more sense to lull Thadiwe and his men into believing that she was getting ready to do what they wanted.

Sam just had to return *fast*.

"Get your pretty ass out here, Doctor. *Now*."

She hesitated. Unlike her sister, Kess, who made split-second decisions, and was rash to the point of foolishness, Elizabeth spent a lot of time weighing her options. She was a Libra, after all.

"Do it, Beth." It wasn't a request.

Fatalistic, she threw her legs over the sill, then slid into Sam's waiting arms. The footing was unsteady, and she realized she was standing on the barred window, frame and all.

His hands closed around her waist. "I've got you."

Blindly reaching out, she grabbed onto Sam's forearms to steady herself. He didn't feel skinny, or flabby, at all, she thought, surprised when his rock-hard muscles flexed under her fingers as she teetered. She tried to picture those muscles beneath one of his gray suits, and couldn't.

"Good girl," he murmured, as he slid his arms around her waist. "There's just one more thing before we go."

*Oh, God.* "What?"

"This."

He'd kissed her twice. Once a few moments ago, when she'd had no idea who the hell he was, and once, in broad daylight, in her office at the clinic. A mind-blowing, knocked-her-socks-off, *fabulous* kiss, and then—he *left* for a month with no word. Kess had told her to stop mooning over a schoolteacher and go find a cowboy. Or a bronco rider with great hip movement. Or an astronaut whose kisses would take her to the moon. *Kess* wouldn't wait for a guy to make the first move. But Beth wasn't her sister.

Sam spread his large hand across her lower back, bringing the other up to cup her face. As he brushed his mouth over hers, she eagerly parted her lips. He touched his tongue to hers, and Elizabeth's heart thudded hard as he sucked it into the hot, wet cavern of his mouth. *God. This is crazy . . .* She stood on tiptoes to wrap her arms about his neck and draw his body flush against hers. The thin fabric of whatever they were wearing was almost no barrier at all.

His abs pressed hard against her aching breasts, and the ridge of his erection nudged tantalizingly against her mons. Elizabeth's breath hitched.

Blank. Her mind went completely blank. She couldn't even think as she blocked out everything but Sam, and kissing him the way she'd imagined kissing him for months. A sigh of pure pleasure escaped, as Sam tasted the inside of her cheek, then ran his teeth along the edge of her teeth before sucking on her tongue and making her almost sob with the pleasure of it.

A bird screeched, and Elizabeth flinched out of the sensual spell. There were a dozen different kinds of birds perched in the trees surrounding them. There were snakes, and wild pigs, and other animals just waiting to have them for a midnight snack. And here they were—

His warm, wet tongue slid along the length of hers, bringing Elizabeth to heart-somersaulting attention again. He kissed her with slow, deliberate care. Hot and deep, taking her from zero to sixty between one heartbeat and the next. She tightened her arms around his neck and rose higher on her toes to bring their bodies flush at all the right places. Sam angled her head and kissed her like he'd die if he didn't. Hotter than the kiss he'd planted on her six months ago. Of course after that one he'd hauled ass and disappeared for a month.

Her husband had preferred closed-mouth kisses, if he kissed her at all. The kiss Sam had given her at the clinic had revved her engines and made her want more. A lot more. But that kiss was tame compared to this. That had been banked. This was Sam unleashed.

The stubble on his jaw was rough against her smooth skin, and a surprise. She'd never seen him anything but immaculately smooth-shaven. She'd never seen him anything other than controlled. As he made love to her mouth, his hand slipped lower to stroke her behind through the thin material. Elizabeth felt surrounded by him, engulfed in his taste. A shudder of raw desire spiraled through her, bone deep and primitive. His tongue mimicked the sex act, making her throb and ache and pant, and crave the feel of his hands on her naked body.

She went hot all over as he dragged her hips back and forth against the solid ridge of his erection. Her brain short-circuited as his tongue raked across her teeth before plunging inside again.

Somehow she'd known it would be this way. That she would fall, all or nothing. She'd spent months protecting her heart. What a waste of time.

Nothing existed beyond the two of them. Not the danger, not the past. She wanted him to lay her down right there and then, unzip her from this climate-controlled suit, and take her right there on the muddy jungle floor.

Too soon Sam placed his hands gently on her arms and pulled them free from his neck. "Hold that thought. Gotta get going."

Hold that thought? Her brain was filled with images of them rolling around on clean white sheets in a dimly lit room, and her heart battered at her rib cage like a wild beast trying to tear through. *Hold that thought?!*

The sounds of the jungle once again intruded.

"Okay?" At her nod, he said softly, "Let's put some distance between them and us. I need both my hands free. Grab onto my belt and hang on." He guided her fingers to the small of his back, and she latched into his wide utility belt, his body heat making her own temperature spike.

"We're going to haul ass on three. All you have to do is hang on and keep up with me. Save your questions and trust me, okay?"

*Trust* him?

Who *was* he?

# THREE

THE JUNGLE NEVER SLEPT.

Nocturnal animals, reptiles, and birds growled, slithered or chirped as they were disturbed in the darkness. Thanks to the glowing visibility of his NVGs, Sam avoided stepping on a puff adder slithering across his path. Hissing, it inflated its body in warning. Sam stamped his booted feet to hurry it on its way. The adder was highly poisonous, and while it moved sluggishly, it could turn around and strike with lightning speed.

"Why are we stopping?" Beth whispered against his left shoulder blade.

"Cross traffic." He waited until the tail of the adder disappeared. He smelled lemon-scented Beth, and sex. Wishful thinking. After kissing her it had taken a while for the cockstand to go down. He was always in an uncomfortable state of semi-arousal when she was close. Touching her, *kissing* her, had almost put him over the edge "All clear." He resuming walking.

The dense canopy of deciduous trees overhead made the swampy ground of the understory relatively easy to navigate. Still, the few small trees, man-high ferns, bushes, and snaking vines and roots made progress slow and treacherous.

So far he'd barely used the machete. Ignoring the tug at his waist, he balanced the HK MP5 fully automatic submachine gun with a laser sight in his right hand. He'd picked up the smaller pack and was loaded for anything that threatened them, from an aardvark to a zebra, two-legged mammals to everything else. Sam had absolutely no illusions about needing every bit of firepower he carried.

It was fortunate for him that currently there was a skirmish on the border between Huren and Mallaruza. The typical bands of rebels and soldiers from both sides, and soldiers for hire, were absent this far away. Usually they roamed the country, destroying everything and everyone in their path like human locusts. Looking for trouble and always finding it. And if not, making it.

Unless Thadiwe called in reinforcements, the odds were currently in Sam's favor.

Thadiwe expected his surgeon to report to his operating room at 0700. At 0701 he'd have his men fanning out to find her.

"We should go and get the Jeep you hid. We'd make better time," Beth whispered half an hour later, fingers still tucked in his waistband. Her steps didn't falter in the sultry darkness, although her quiet voice did.

"I have a boat waiting." Sam got a quick whiff of the lemon-scented soap she favored. Unlikely beneath the DEET, but imaginary or not, the lemon fragrance brought to mind every aching memory he had of Dr. Elizabeth Goodall. He'd seen her serious and professional in her crisp white lab coat at her small clinic back home. Pale red hair twirled up on top of her head in some smooth intricate roll that looked as though one tug would bring the entire mass tumbling down her back.

He'd salivated seeing her—long-legged and sexy, in jeans and a sky-blue T-shirt, that shiny red-gold hair flowing over her shoulders as she'd walked beside him to go to a movie. Then in that yellow sundress that cupped her small breasts and bared her pretty shoulders when he'd seen her with a girlfriend at that little Italian place she liked.

Jesus. She was so fucking out of her element it was surreal. Yet somehow she still managed to maintain that air of unflappability that her patients were used to seeing.

She was so delicate, so earnest. He'd spent a year and a half pussy-footing around her, biding his time. He was ready for Beth. She wasn't ready for him. Not then. She was as beautiful and fragile as a jungle orchid. It had been love at first sight for Sam. He'd decided she should be surrounded by children; he'd pictured her, a baby—his—at her naked breast. He'd never felt this alien blend of lust, love, tenderness and fear for any woman in his life. He wanted her with an intensity he'd never felt for any woman. Ever.

It was damned unsettling, he thought, shoving aside a six-foot-long palm frond. He'd gone way past *unsettled* by the unexpected mixture of emotions he'd felt for this woman from the start and directly into determination and a strange kind of peace.

A loud croaking sound, followed by a guttural *rurr*, *rurr*, *rurr*, sounded several feet to the left.

"What do you think that is?"

"Colobus monkey. He's been following us for a while." Sam could see the little guy's bright, inquisitive eyes as he swung by his tail from a nearby branch, waiting for them to move on.

"As long as it isn't a damn bird," Beth muttered under her breath, making Sam grin.

While a portion of his mind was aware of every small movement in the foliage around them, and his ears engaged in IDing every noise, a small compartment of his brain was reserved for flashing memories of Beth.

According to her patients she was an excellent GP. And sweet. And inordinately kind. And compassionate. And attentive. Everyone in the small Montana town adored Dr. Beth.

Sam had taken one look at sweet Dr. Beth's marmalade-colored hair, creamy freckled skin, and big brown eyes and fallen for her like the proverbial ton of bricks. He'd wanted to strip her and count every freckle. Unfortunately, five minutes after meeting her he'd discovered she was married. Fifteen minutes after that he'd gotten an earful from Traci at the diner about the idiot she was married to.

They'd married while both were in med school. Beth and Rob were more like friends than lovers, which Sam found good to know. Rob was a nice guy, Traci told him. Too bad he'd fallen in love with a woman he'd met on the Internet. Dr. Beth was being really decent about it and doing what she could to expedite the paperwork to get it over with as quickly and quietly as possible.

Damn good thing. Because Sam didn't poach on other men's territory. Not that he thought for a moment Beth would do anything hinky behind her husband's back, even if she were tempted.

Sam's thoughts had nothing to do with sweet, or kind. The second he'd seen her, his thoughts had turned carnal. Primitive. He wanted her hard and fast. Hot and sweaty. Slick and slippery. He wanted to have her on the counter at the bank. And on the hood of his car, on the floor of the only hotel in town. Hell, he didn't think that they'd make it to a bed the first few times.

He'd moved into a condo a few blocks from her house and waited for the divorce to be final. One look at Beth, and he hadn't been capable of staying away. Hadn't, God damn it, been able to think of much else. He imagined her naked, having her on her desk in her cramped little office at her clinic two doors down from the bank. He pictured her small high breasts, and imagined that her nipples would be a soft delicate pink, like her lips.

"You have reinforcements, right?"

She was as tenacious as a bulldog and her lack of faith stung. "I'll take care of you, don't worry." He was alone in this. It wasn't a sanctioned op. He'd come on his own. Beth was a personal matter.

"That's sweet, Sam."

*Sweet?* She didn't exactly exude confidence. And why should she? As far as she was concerned, he didn't know one end of a gun from the other. Eleven years in a private army guaranteed he knew how to use the MP5. He also knew some interesting, and painful, tricks with a machete.

"But what'll happen if you're bitten by a snake?" she continued, slightly breathless now that she was on a roll. "Or eaten by a lion?"

Jesus. "Odd are against it." He'd better stay hale and hearty. She stood zero chance of survival alone in the jungle. Less than zero if she was returned to Nkemidilm's compound and the man who waited there.

He used the muzzle of the MP5 to flip away a curious, and highly poisonous, bush viper hanging from a limb in their path. It landed almost noiselessly in a thicket of vines before slithering into the underbrush. There'd be time to think about Beth's delectable body later. Right now he had to get them both the hell out of Dodge before Thadiwe's men caught up.

"How much longer?"

"Couple of hours." Give or take. He could almost hear her brain working as she digested the information.

"Don't you think I'd be better off going back and waiting for you to bring in some help?"

He heard her nervousness. So much for trust. "No, Beth, I don't." Sam made sure his barely-a-whisper was implacable. "We're meeting a guy with a boat. Don't worry. I'll get you out of here in one piece, I promise."

He stopped, and she stepped right against his back, letting out a little huff of surprise. "There's a three-foot high log in our path. I'll go first then help you over."

Sam flung a leg over the mossy trunk and dropped down on the other side. Beth's breathing was a little fractured. Fear. Tucking the machete into the sheath strapped to his thigh, he leaned over the log, extending his hand. Not that she could see it in the crack under dark. "Give me your hand."

Blindly she held it out. Grabbing hold of her wrist, Sam gave a little tug. "Up and over. Straddle the log, then slide down on this side."

Her cold fingers felt ridiculously small in his. Her chilled, sweaty skin told him she was scared out of her mind. Despite that, she was keeping up and not falling apart. Not yet anyway.

He gave a little tug to help her up, then watched as she flung both legs over to his side. "Right here," he told her when she hesitated.

She slid into his arms. "Tha— What's *that*?"

She was pressed against his semi-erection. "Don't worry," he told her dryly. "I'm not going to have my wicked way with you. Not here anyway."

She smothered a laugh. "Not that. *That*."

That. "It's an MP5 submachine gun."

She put her hand on his chest, the smile still tilting the corners of her mouth. Sam wanted to kiss her in the worst way. This time he resisted.

Not the time. Not the place.

"Do you know how to use it?"

He huffed out a laugh. "Yeah." The fact that her body was still flush with his didn't exactly make his thinking process crystal clear. Taking her hand, he stepped back. "Know that outfit just outside of town?"

"That private military place?"

"Counterterrorist training site, yeah. I work for them."

"You—*work* for them? I thought you were a teacher?"

"Tactical instructor. I train special ops in weaponry for high-risk environments."

"Thank God." Beth gave a small laugh, her relief evident and heartfelt. "Better than I'd hoped. My highest expectation was that you excelled at playing paintball."

"I wouldn't trust your safety to anyone less than one hundred percent competent. If I didn't think I could handle the situation, rest assured, I would have sent in someone who could."

"Oh, God, Sam. I'm terrified out of my mind."

"It's warranted, sweetheart. You're in a bad spot. But this time tomorrow you'll be on your way home, I promise."

"Adventure isn't all it's cracked up to be." Beth slid a hand around his waist and leaned into him. "I couldn't have made it past the guards. And frankly, since I have zero sense of direction, I'm not sure how far I would have gotten if I'd managed to steal a Jeep and drive out. How far is the closest town?"

"Village? Ten miles or so. A real town? With transpo? A hundred."

She shuddered, and his arms tightened around her. Not romantic with a semiauto in one hand, and a machete strapped to his leg. But he'd take what he could get, when he could get it.

"I could have died here without anyone knowing."

"*I* knew." Only because he'd been called by one of the Cape Town operatives minutes after Beth had been snatched from the hotel. When he'd asked that they keep an eye on her, Sam hadn't specified just how closely he'd wanted her watched. Close enough not to be kidnapped would have seemed logical. To him anyway. Thank God they knew who to notify.

Sam had someone following the kidnappers' trail while he'd jetted halfway around the world to retrieve Beth from her captors.

"Thank God," she said with utmost sincerity.

"Ready?"

In answer she took hold of his belt, and Sam moved out.

"That OR was state-of-the-art, and equipped for anything and *everything*. I can only imagine how many millions of dollars it cost to install that way out here in the middle of nowhere."

"*Could* you have done it?"

"*Nobody* could have done it in his time frame. Interesting that he targeted Lynne Randall, but didn't research how long that procedure would take. And to answer your question: If I'd had to perform the surgery I could have done it, I suppose. But not well. The last time I did that sort of thing was during a five-month rotation in med school. Plastic surgeons—goods ones—are part practitioner, part artist. I can't even draw a stick figure."

Sam chuckled. Thadiwe was a butt-ugly individual already. He didn't see how anything could make him look *worse*.

"Fortunately you won't be doing any surgeries. You'll be out of the country before he realizes you've gone."

"From your lips . . ."

Sam had already extrapolated Thadiwe's location to the next action. Without Beth he'd find another doctor. Somewhere. Right now Sam was the only one who knew where the son of a bitch was located. He'd have to return and take him out. But first things first.

Get Beth downriver by boat, then drive her the ten miles to the waiting chopper. Get her on board and on her way to Cape Town where a private jet waited to return her to Montana.

"How soon do you think they'll come after us?"

"Long after we're gone." No point anticipating the worst. He figured he had until daylight to reach the boat Desi was bringing to a preassigned location. They'd be cruising down the Congo River before Thadiwe's men realized she'd escaped. Three hours. Tops.

They needed five.

# FOUR

A GORILLA, SOUNDING ODDLY doglike, barked in the distance. A warning? Or was the primate merely heralding daylight?

While it was still oppressively dark, Sam could almost feel the rapid approach of morning as the animals started to stir. Soon they'd be moving toward water. There was an elephant trail somewhere around here he knew from his earlier trek in. Walking on that open trail would save time, but it also meant encountering animals who had the same idea.

Mosquitoes and gnats, flies and other insects didn't give a damn if it was night or day. They swarmed and dive-bombed them as they walked. The gorilla barked again, and this time it was answered by its mate. Beth stepped in closer to him, her fingers tight on his belt.

He chuckled.

"Good grief, Sam," she whispered. "How can you laugh at a time like this?"

"I've finally got you where I want you."

"Kidnapped and running for our lives in a rain forest?"

"Alone. Without distractions."

"Boy, you live a crazy life if you consider this a place without distractions."

"No ex-husband. No clinic. A few tangos and a few plants are nothing."

She laughed. "A *few* p— Crazy man."

"The divorce was final a year from last week, right?"

She didn't say anything for several seconds. "How's that relevant?"

Sam held aside a branch, tugging Beth under his arm to clear it. Instead of replacing her hand on his belt, he shoved the NVGs out of the way on top of his head and turned around to curl her into his arms. "Plenty enough time to get over any lingering regrets or Monday-morning quarterbacking about your marriage." Screw resisting. Having Beth this close in the steamy darkness was like waving crack under an addict's nose.

Resistance was futile.

He'd held off for a full year. He was done waiting for her to catch up. Sam brushed her lips with his. She kept her mouth firmly closed. Lifting his head, he said softly, "Put your arms around my neck and open your mouth."

"Mosquitoes," she mumbled, tightlipped.

He chuckled. "Tongues are mosquito-free zones," he assured her, nibbling at her now parted lips, which were firm and warm and tasted like promise. He tightened his arm around her waist until her body was pressed flush against his. Hell, she felt good. Better than good. Imagining them both naked, Sam closed his eyes and savored the moment while around them the darkness seethed with life. And death.

He drank Beth's sigh and deepened the kiss, sweeping his tongue into the warm recesses of her mouth. The first stroke of her tongue against his sent a shudder down his spine. His body went from a gentle, bearable simmer, to a full-out boil.

Sam kissed Beth the way he'd wanted to from the first time he'd met her. Full throttle. No holding back.

Burrowing his free hand in her hair, Sam tilted her head back while he feasted on her mouth. Her arms slid around his waist, and she hugged him to her with the same ferocity he was feeling. Sam raked his teeth across her bottom lip, and she made a low sound of need as his tongue tangled with hers.

A macaw swooped between the branches over their heads, squawking loudly. Beth pulled away with a high-pitched shriek.

Hardly flattering.

Sam tightened his arm around her waist, feeling the thump-thump-thump of her heart against his rib cage. "Keep it down, sweetheart. It was only a bird."

"Sorry," she muttered. "It took me by surprise. I hate birds."

He brushed a kiss to the top of her head and

hugged her more tightly. "You hate— How can you hate birds?"

"They're like rats with wings." Her entire body shuddered.

The place was a minefield of venomous snakes, flesh-eating animals and warring tribesmen, and she was afraid of *birds*? Sam shook his head. "Better get used to them." He pulled the NVGs back over his eyes. "There are over a thousand species in the rain forest. You'd better not scream every time you see one."

Good thing she couldn't see the hundreds of birds perched in the trees surrounding them. Three curious round-faced chimps had been keeping pace with them, swinging from branch to branch, their eyes gleaming white in Sam's NVGs. Now they stopped to watch, tails and fingers wrapped around branches.

"You couldn't be more out of your element if you tried." Sam resumed walking. The wet, muddy ground and vegetation underfoot made walking exhausting. Add to that her stress, and fear, and she needed a break. A break he didn't have time to give her. A moment or two kissing would have to do as both a break and a distraction.

He waved away a swarm of tiny moths dancing inches from his face and hoped Beth wasn't spooked by everything with wings. "Remind me again why coming to deepest, darkest Africa was a cool idea?"

"Adventure." This time her voice was dry, but it held a faint thread of nerves.

*Adventure,* for God's sake. He didn't remind her that he'd pointed out all the dangers inherent in going to one of the most dangerous countries in the world. And South Africa was a cakewalk compared to Huren. "You're lucky you weren't killed. Next time you want goddamned adventure, take me up on *my* offer."

"Which offer was that? A ride on your motorcycle? Or the ride on *you*? I don't consider sex an adventure. Sorry, Sam, but that can't compare with *this* experience. Other than in both instances I'd be sweaty. Possibly panting."

"I'm insulted," he said, amused as hell. She'd be panting and sweaty, all right. He couldn't wait. "You find sex boring, do you?" A statement like that from a woman, especially *this* woman, was like waving a red flag at a bull.

"It's pleasant," she muttered, damning one of life's greatest perks with faint praise.

"With *Bob* it was pleasant."

"Rob."

"Because you weren't that into each other."

"We were married."

"Sex between two people who want each other more than their next breath can be explosive."

"I'll take your word for it. I've taken life far too seriously up until now. School, school, and school. Opening my practice, building my practice. Long hours at the clinic— I've been living life in black and white. I *want* a little Technicolor." She sounded resolved if not enthusiastic.

"Admittedly not as much Technicolor as being kidnapped at *gunpoint*, but something a few notches down from this would suit me just fine."

Sam vowed she'd have as much Technicolor as she could handle. Soon. "What does your family think about this wild idea you got about coming to Africa?"

"My sister's been in Mallaruza for a couple of months, and loves it. I thought starting out slowly by going to Cape Town would give me the flavor of Africa. I also wanted to experience the people and different culture—"

"You were kidnapped and taken to a country even more dangerous than the first."

"Thank you for reminding me. I'm already scared out of my wits. I bet my sister would love every insane second of this. *Kess* isn't scared of *anything*."

"Then she's a moron," Sam told her bluntly. He hadn't met Beth's sister. But she sounded like a flake with a death wish to him. He had no idea why Beth was so determined that she could or *should* match her sister's rash behavior. Especially when she didn't have the stomach for it.

"So you're the sane one, and she's the wild one?"

"I'm the boring daughter, and Kess is the bold one. She's always taking exciting vacations, which is why I wanted to do something bold for once."

"But why Africa? With your love of Italian food, why not Italy?"

"I'm saving that to go with—"

"With?"

"Somebody."

"Who?"

"I don't know yet," she said, sounding cross. "Someone special. Probably my sister."

Liar. If she were going to go with her sister she would have done so already. "Why didn't you go with your husband?"

"He liked American vacations."

"Yeah? How many of those did you take together?"

"We were too busy going to med school and starting the practice. There are plenty of places in the States where you can learn new techniques. Plenty of places that are exciting and different. Didn't have to be Africa."

"Didn't have to be. But was."

He set a grueling pace to make up time. When necessary, he slashed a path through the vegetation with the machete. Gnats and mosquitoes swarmed around them, heard but unseen in the dark. He'd made sure that every inch of exposed skin was covered in DEET, but the chances of getting bitten anyway were high.

Thank God she was able to keep up, her hand a small, hard ball of a fist clutching the back of his belt. He'd always wanted Dr. Goodall's small hand down his pants, Sam thought wryly as he shoved a large leaf out of the way, then held it so it wouldn't lash back. This wasn't what he'd had in mind.

He was aware of her every breath as she trudged along behind him. He was pushing it, trying to put as much distance as he could between them and the compound before they realized she'd flown the coop. Trying to get to the river. Trying not to give her the tongue-lashing she deserved for coming to a war-torn country in the middle of fucking *nowhere* to prove a point that wasn't even important.

A rustle in a nearby shrub made him turn his head just in time to see the horizontally striped butt-end of an okapi. The deerlike animal, closely related to a giraffe, darted through the underbrush unleashing a troupe of chimps, who chatted and screeched their annoyance at being woken.

A glance up at the jigsaw puzzle pieces of charcoal-colored sky now visible between the tree canopy told him dawn was on its way. Once the sun rose, the animals would be in search of food and water, making them even more alert to predators. Which was precisely why Sam had set up the extraction point at the most likely spot they used to drink.

The original plan had been to arrive hours before the beasts of the jungle came down to the river. Letting the activity of the animals mask their departure. So much for *that* plan.

Changing strategy as he walked, Sam decided that he'd park Beth somewhere upriver, and go down and get the boat on his own. He'd move faster and could, if necessary, misdirect anyone on their tail.

They *would* come after her. Thadiwe had worked too damn hard to get a physician here. He wasn't going to let Beth go without a fight.

Well, Sam wasn't going to give her up without a goddamned fight either.

"How did you know where to find me?"

"I know people in low places." He didn't bother mentioning that he'd almost puked with fear when those people had informed him who had snatched Beth.

He'd come to Africa to bring her body home.

# FIVE

SAM HAD SAID IT would take three hours to get to the river. Surely they'd walked for longer than that? While Sam moved through the stygian darkness with a lithe, powerful sure-footedness, Elizabeth's calves and lungs burned, and her skin itched despite the temperature-regulated suit. She was damn sure Kess wouldn't be huffing and puffing, mentally begging to stop so she could sit down and rest. No, her sister would be leading the way. She might not know where she was going or how to get there, Elizabeth thought with a small smile, but no one following Kess would know it.

The only reality in Elizabeth's world was her grip on Sam's belt as she stumbled blindly in his wake, stubbing her booted toes on roots and vines. And while she could easily picture him in her mind's eye, that image didn't in any way gel with the man who'd come to rescue her. With the man who'd kissed her so passionately it had made her blood race through her veins and her heart hammer.

She hated not being in control. And she hadn't been in control of her own fate from the moment she'd been snatched from Lynne's hotel room.

"How's the hand?"

It throbbed, but that was to be expected. "Okay."

"Tell me if it isn't. Don't try and be brave. An infection here can kill you."

"I'm a doctor, Sam. I know. Thanks to you, it's f—"

Suddenly his palm covered her mouth. Elizabeth gulped down the reactive scream, but felt it vibrate in her chest as he whispered against her ear. "Shh. Company."

She froze. Oh, God. She hadn't heard anything out of the ordinary. If walking in the pitch dark through a rain forest filled with snakes and monkeys and more birds than anyone could imagine could be considered ordinary.

"Down." He tugged at her arm, bending low with her. His voice was so muted it was almost more a feeling than a sound. His arm brushed hers and she realized he was removing the pack from his back. She heard a soft thud as it landed on the damp ground next to her. "Know how to fire a gun?" he whispered, his lips against her ear.

Elizabeth shook her head. "I sew up holes in people, not make them."

"I'll give you a crash course."

She shook her head again. A tiny thrill of adrenaline swirled in her belly. A big believer in self-defense, she'd spent too much time in the ER to actually pull a trigger. Or so she thought. Life or death.

Despite her refusal, Sam wrapped her non-sliced hand around what was clearly a big gun. A very big, very heavy gun. Her fingers closed around the ribbed stock. It felt weird, foreign. "I'd rather *you* take it," she whispered back urgently. It was only as she flexed her stiff fingers that she realized just how tightly she'd been gripping his belt.

Sam positioned her fingers, his touch playing havoc with her good judgment. "Won't need it. Safety's off. Point and shoot. Fires eight hundred rounds a minute. You won't miss. When I come back I'll whistle like this." He whistled a sweet, sharp, incredibly realistic bird call. Elizabeth hoped to hell no birds came to see who was calling them.

"Wait—you're leaving me?"

Screaming sounded more humane than aiming a gun and taking a life. The scream was again building in her chest. She tamped down the fear. She needed to think rationally and be alert. Being scared right now wasn't an option. She eased into a slightly more comfortable crouch by millimeters.

Now she heard them. Footsteps. Leaves rustling. Breathing. She wanted to plead with Sam to hunch down with her, to wait until whoever it was passed. But she knew he'd be proactive.

He brushed a quick kiss across her nose, light as a butterfly's wing. "Stay low." One second he was right there, the next he was gone. She knew he'd left, not because he made any noise, but because she could no longer feel his presence beside her.

"Be careful," she mouthed.

The raucous sounds of the jungle closed in on her, as did the oppressive darkness. She'd outgrown her fear of the bogyman in her closet long before her tenth birthday, but this darkness scared the bejesus out of her. The dangers here were very real. And imminent.

Crouched uncomfortably in the thick, inky darkness, Elizabeth waited, her heartbeat sounding like thunder in her ears, her jaw clenched to prevent crying out every time something crawled over her bare hands, or some creepy critter brushed her face. She tried not to imagine what that was sitting lightly on her cheek, or what the weight was on the instep of her right boot. She bit off the scream that surged up her throat as a bird shot out of a nearby shrub as if catapulted. Dragging in a shuddering breath, she held it until her heart settled down. She was dammed if she'd have a freaking heart attack because a *bird* flew past her.

Better than thinking about men tracking her with guns, mile-long centipedes, poisonous ants, poisonous frogs and, of course, a multitude of poisonous snakes.

The only thing she had between herself and all

those dangers was Sam Pelton. The thought was so wrongly comforting.

FIVE MEN. CAMO. NVGS. AK-47s. Well trained. Cautious. And definitely tracking their missing doctor. There was no other reason for their presence. No nearby villages to pillage, and Sam doubted they were hunting for bushmeat. Thadiwe was too sophisticated to eat the local flora and fauna, and the compound was miles from anywhere. No. It was Beth that Thadiwe's soldiers hunted.

Damn it to hell. He'd miscalculated, and they'd discovered her absence, and the hidden Jeep, hours before Sam thought they would. Removing the KA-BAR from his tac belt with his left hand, Sam circled around, slipped in behind them. Matching his steps to the man bringing up the rear, he maneuvered up close. With no warning he brought his forearm around and beneath the guy's chin. Pulling him back and off balance, Sam struck directly up, into the man's kidneys. It was a quick, silent death, the pain so intense the man couldn't scream before he died. Sam caught the soldier as he soundlessly collapsed against him, and lowered the body quietly into the bushes.

Sam wiped the bloodied knife on the man's shirt. One down, four to go.

Killing the soldier had taken all of three seconds. Didn't bother Sam right then, but later he'd remember why he'd gotten out of combat and into the training side. But for now he had absolutely no compunction killing as many people as it took to keep Beth safe.

He took the second and third guys out the same coldly efficient way as he'd done the first. The fourth and fifth might have been slow on the uptake, but the second they realized that they were under attack they got with the program and both rushed Sam at once.

Good. No weapons fired to draw the attention of any other hunters. The first guy came at him in a flurry of well-trained arms and legs. Sam blocked the first blow with his forearm, then swiveled to kick out at number two, who had come in from the side, his AK-47 raised to fire. Kicking out, Sam got rid of both man and weapon. The second guy went flying, striking a tree trunk with a hollow thud that set off a flock of birds in a screeching flutter of wings, ghostly through the NVGs. A group of chimps shot out of the lower branches, screaming annoyance as they swung from branch to branch.

Bending his arm, Sam used a chopping motion from the elbow, his entire body weight behind the edge-of-the-hand blow to the first guy's throat as he came at him full tilt. His hand made a satisfying connection just below the enemy's Adam's apple. The guy gagged and dropped.

The other soldier was already up on his feet and charging back for more. With a feral smile Sam side-stepped the punch to the jaw, grabbing his opponent's wrist with one hand, and pulled him off balance. With the other hand he yanked off the guy's NVGs, then melted into the high bushes to his right. The man came blindly after him. Sam stayed dead still.

The man turned in a circle, scared now, babbling God only knew what. Sam came up on him from behind, wrapping his left arm around the guy's neck, bearing down on his throat in a Japanese stranglehold. One arm across his throat, the other on his shoulders, his palm on the back of the man's head. Pulling him backwards, Sam pressed the guy's head forward.

The guy tried to grab his balls with his free hand. The LockOut suit gave him no handhold.

Sam straightened and gripped the front and back of the guy's head, then gave a quick twist. It had been a while since he'd last heard a neck breaking at such close quarters. He hadn't missed the sound. Sam tossed him aside as he heard a loud scream of fear. The scream was cut off mid-note.

*Beth.*

ELIZABETH FLUNG HERSELF INTO Sam's arms the moment he came through the trees. It was barely light, but she could see him well enough, and God, was she happy to do so. "Oh, Jesus, Jesus," she said hoarsely into his throat, her heart pounding so hard she was sure he must hear it. "I'm sorry, Sam. This giant pig-like *something* came at me, and scared the living crap out of me. I promised myself I wouldn't scream like a girl and distract you no matter what, but it ran right into me before I even knew it was there . . . Sorry, I'm babbling."

She looked up at his face. He'd removed the night-vision goggles, and they'd left a red mark across the bridge of his blade of a nose. He was several days past a shave, and the dark shadow on his jaw made him look wicked and disreputable. The sheen on the front of his black bodysuit Elizabeth easily identified as blood. She stepped back, her gaze tracking across his body for signs of injury.

"Are you—?" The matte black bodysuit hugged his muscular torso so that she could see the sharp definition of his taut pecs and cut abs, and the long length of his muscular legs, and the bulge, somehow flattened, large, and protected by something. She pictured his penis tucked neatly inside. Her body tightened and her nipples ached.

"Am I?"

Her gaze shot up to his face, and her cheeks felt warm. "Hurt. Are you hurt?"

"I teach advanced survival skills to highly trained counterterrorist operatives for a living. I'm excellent. Thanks for asking." He grinned, a flash of white teeth in his tanned face. "Did your run-in with the pig give you any nicks or cuts?"

"I scared him as much as he scared me," she muttered, searching his face. She didn't need to ask him if he'd taken care of whomever had been following them. Seeing Sam in his warrior gear, knife belted to his thigh, the big gun, his dark hair damp with sweat, his eyes glittering as if he had a fever. . . .

Good grief, if he'd looked like this back home, she would have jumped his bones at the first opportunity.

She gave him a more assessing look. "How did they catch up with us so fast?"

"Obviously someone went to your room to check on you after I cut the generator. They'll send more soldiers when those guys don't check in." He picked up the big gun and his pack. "We need to make tracks," he said, threading his arms through the straps. "Easier now that it's getting light. Drink some water as we walk." He handed her the canteen, and Elizabeth sipped enough water to moisturize her dry mouth.

"How many men were there?"

"Only five."

*Only five.* Sam didn't seem to be concerned that those men might still be following them, so Elizabeth presumed they were incapacitated. In this part of the world that could only mean dead.

"I counted seventeen soldiers at the compound. If they realized that I didn't take the Jeep, do you think they'll send all of them after us? Maybe we should double back and *really* steal a Jeep. What do you think?"

"First of all there were twenty soldiers. And no. We're not doubling back. By now Thadiwe has probably called in some of his pal Nkemidilm's people. Right now we have the advantage. Until they find those five guys back there, they won't know you aren't alone. They think they're hunting a lone woman, unprepared for this environment. That's a good thing, and to our advantage. Those guys didn't have radios or any communication devices on them.

Stupid. But hey, I didn't train them. So to communicate they'd have to have gone back to base. We have a little breathing room."

He tilted her face with a finger under her chin. His hard mouth curved into a smile. "You look like hell."

"I'm perfectly aware of what I must look like," she said ruefully. While Sam's rugged face was bug-free, she must look like the Creature from the Black Lagoon. She'd never been vain, but right now she was grateful she didn't have a mirror. God only knew what critters had glued themselves to the repellent on her skin.

He removed a cloth from his pack, and applied it—dry—to her cheeks. "This must itch like crazy. Close your eyes. Let me get rid of the bugs at least. Grab the DEET—it's in the left side of the belt. Yeah, open it while I get rid of your passengers."

Elizabeth stood still while Sam cleaned her face, then reapplied the chemical to deter the bugs. She wanted to kiss him, but knew they had to keep going if they wanted to get away free and clear.

The blackness of the night had lightened to a deep olive green. Now murky lime-green shafts of light seeped through the dense tree canopy. It felt as though they were walking through algae-filled water. The bodysuit did an incredible job keeping her body temp normal, but her head was exposed to the thick steamy heat and perspiration tickled her skin and attracted insects.

The jungle was a living entity surrounding them; the smell of dead vegetation and wet earth seemed to seep into Elizabeth's pores. The noise level was higher now than it had been earlier, and she'd long since given up trying to identify everything making such a racket. Monkeys, insects, large and small animals. And her own breathing. Every time a bird called, she flinched. Not only did she hate birds, she discovered she wasn't that crazy about snakes, bugs, or mosquitoes either. Being in a rain forest wasn't exactly the best pick for a first time Grand Adventure.

An adventurer she wasn't. Just because she wanted to be fearless and daring didn't mean she was hardwired to be so. She'd leave the adventures to Kess and concentrate on her fledgling practice instead.

If she made it back to Montana alive.

# SIX

ELIZABETH BUMPED INTO SAM'S back as he came
to a stop midstride. She came around to stand beside
him. They'd reached the river. Thank God. The water was the color of bad pea soup. Brownish green
with unidentifiable lumps of vegetation floating on
the surface. The air smelled, not unpleasantly . . .
*green*, and a little like overripe fruit. Small trees and
thick brush crowded the sloping banks. House plants
Beth grew in little pots in her condo would thrive
and flourish to gigantic proportions here.

A thin, bright yellow snake S'ed on the surface of
the water, while dragonflies, their iridescent wings
shimmering in the sunlight, swooped and dived over
their reflections, and tiny emerald-green butterflies
swar-med en masse over the bank. A pair of inquisitive otters sat on a nearby felled tree trunk watching
them.

That was the *pretty* part of the river.

On the bank a crocodile—at least seven feet long,

lazed in the sun, and four submerged hippos, small ears twitching, lay like enormous boulders several hundred yards upstream in the center of the river where the water was deep. Both species moved like greased lightning in the water.

And there were birds. *Everywhere*. Big and small. They swooped, they dove, they fluttered and they perched. They squawked and chirped and tweeted and generally freaked Beth out.

Here the sunlight wasn't being filtered through the trees, and buttery early morning light sparkled on the murky green surface, while the diaphanous dragonflies danced between the long reeds and grasses lining the muddy bank. If one didn't know that the jungle pressing against its serpentine shoreline was filled with birds and creepy crawlies, it would be an idyllic picture.

She stared at the pod of almost submerged hippos. One lifted its head, its ridiculous small ears pivoting as it called a guttural *ba-ho-ho-ho* in a low bass. Hippos were said to be the deadliest animal in Africa, but it was hard to imagine, watching them clustered together like giant rocks in the slow-moving water, that they could actually run faster than a human on land. It was unlikely they'd attack without provocation, but Elizabeth moved closer to Sam and his nice big gun.

"Shit."

"What's wrong?" she asked, dry-mouthed, waving away a dragonfly as it dive-bombed her hair.

"Desi isn't here with the Zodiac."

Elizabeth looked out across the murky surface.

The whole expanse of the river looked emptier and more dangerous without rescue close at hand. "Maybe he went up or downriver."

"This is the extraction point. We're about fifteen minutes late—but he should be here waiting."

"Are you sure he's coming? I told you we should have gone back and stolen a Jeep."

"He must've gotten delayed. He'll be here."

"How long do you think we'll have to wait?"

Sam glanced around, clearly assessing the area. "Until he gets here."

Well, duh. "What are we supposed to do in the meantime?"

"Sun's up. The animals will be down to drink any time now. We need to get out of their way."

"Do we dodge them and say excuse me? Do we walk, or do we have to figure out how to levitate?"

"We're going to climb that tree over there and stay out of their way. It's a good lookout point, and you probably could use a rest 'round about now."

"And a shower, and a thick juicy steak."

"Sorry. No shower, no room service. How are your tree-climbing skills?"

"On a scale of one to ten, one being the least? Zero. I've never climbed a tree in my life. Not since I watched Kess being hauled away in an ambulance after falling on her head. It looked like too much trouble for that amount of pain."

"I won't let you fall, I promise. Come on, this looks like a good tree hotel."

The enormous tree was relatively easy to climb

with Sam's help. The branches were as thick as her entire body, and vines made convenient toe- and handholds. She moved as fast as she could to prevent critters from taking a toehold on *her*. Sam found a fork about ten feet off the ground that hung almost directly over the water and eased the pack off his back onto one of the wide branches. Opening it he removed a circle of a similar fabric to their suits, but instead of black, this was a camouflage pattern that blended well with the surrounding vegetation.

"A Frisbee?" she teased, leaning against the trunk as she watched Sam work.

"When we play, sweetheart, it won't be with a toy." With a flick of his wrist the circle flipped and writhed into a small dome-shaped tent. "Voilà! Your room is ready." Placing the small tent to rest on the V of the branches, he quickly pounded a few pegs into the branch to support the little structure, then unzipped the entrance. "Take your boots off, drink some water and try to nap."

"Where are you going to be?"

"Backtracking to be sure we won't have any surprise guests. Stay inside the tent and zip the door closed. You'll be able to see out pretty well, and it'll keep critters out. Our ride should be here shortly. Even if you see Desi and the Zodiac, stay put. I won't be long. Oh, yeah. One more thing."

Sam gave her a quick, hard kiss.

"I really enjoy your one more things," she told him when they broke apart. She wanted to keep him safely by her side. "Come back and say it again."

"I have more than one 'one more thing,' sweet-heart. Climb in, I'll be back in an hour."

SAM RETURNED TWO HOURS later. He'd managed to contact Desi on the SAT phone he'd retrieved from the large pack he'd hidden the day before near their rendezvous point. The other man had been detained in a village some twenty clicks down river. "Detained" meant Desi had encountered a young woman whose father was off fighting on the border. Desi was Mallaruzi and he was, apparently, usually pretty dependable. Unless he ran across a pretty girl. Sam warned him away from any other pretty girls and set up a new extraction time for 1200 hours. He then jogged almost halfway back to the compound without seeing evidence that there were more soldiers following them.

They'd come. Eventually.

But for now there was nothing more pressing than being with Beth and convincing her that she liked being with him, too.

After checking the perimeter for any sign of men, he rapidly climbed the tree and unzipped the front flap of the small tent. Inside was dim and relatively cool. Beth was asleep, her head resting on her outstretched arm. How the hell had he managed to keep his hands off her for a year and a half? Just looking at her made his heart beat faster, and not even his intense training could control the speed of his pulse. It was like she was the one specifically made for him, and his body recognized its mate.

Sam removed his boots before he crawled in beside
her. It was a tight fit, which he didn't mind at all.

He lay like she was, one arm outstretched to support his head as he faced her. Merging his fingers
with hers, Sam enjoyed the simple act of holding
her hand. Hers was so small, and soft, and incredibly *female* clasped in his large rough palm.

She was perfectly relaxed, her slender body con-
forming to the thick branches supporting the floor
of the tent. He scanned her face, so perfect in repose
and just inches from his. She was prettier when she
was awake and her features animated; asleep her
beauty was more subtle, but just as heart-twisting.
Her beauty was deceiving. She looked delicate with
her pale, freckled skin and amber-colored hair. But
she was as tensile as steel. Sam touched a finger to
the dark sweep of her lashes, dyed, she'd told him
once unselfconsciously.

He trailed his finger over her cheek, then brushed
it gently over the sweet curve of her lower lip. She
smiled without opening her eyes. "What's the
scoop?" she asked, her voice thick with sleep.

"Desi's been held up. He'll be here in a few
hours."

She opened slumberous sherry-colored eyes.
"What will we do with ourselves for two hours?"

"More like three or four."

"That long? Just the two of us in this little tent?"
She brushed his hair off his forehead, then stroked
his forehead with the pads of her fingers. Her touch
traveled like wildfire through Sam's blood. She

shifted so that her hips aligned with his. Nothing between them but two thin layers of LockOut and an erection that had started eighteen months ago.

"I hate being bored, don't you?" she whispered, tracing the creases beside his eyes, then the shape of his nose, then trailed down to Braille his mouth, her touch soft as air.

Sam tugged at the zipper at the base of her throat and started easing it down inch by slow inch. Her pupils dilated. "Intolerable," he told her, his voice thick.

"Any cards in that pack of yours?" she asked, her hand tangling with his as she started pulling the zipper down on his suit. The backs of their hands brushed as their movements mirrored one another. Each zipper parted, one tooth at a time.

"Nope." He bent his head the few inches separating them and skimmed his mouth over hers. Her lips parted and she welcomed him inside. She tasted . . . like heaven. Everything Sam had ever wanted was right here in his arms.

Beth touched his lower lip with the damp tip of her tongue, making Sam's breath snag in his chest. He pressed his advantage and licked back, tasting the sweetness of her mouth as if he'd never kissed her before. After waiting so long for this, he didn't want to rush it. Tamping down the primitive urge to take her without fanfare, he kissed her tenderly, with all the pent-up longing he'd been suppressing for a year and a half.

He kissed her lingeringly, succulently, enjoying

the hell out of the tastes and textures of her mouth and the increasingly urgent sound of her breathing. Beth reciprocated, her cool fingers stroking his face, ratcheting up his need for her even more.

She broke away, panting slightly, a flush riding her cheekbones. "I suppose teaching me to fire one of your guns will draw a crowd?"

"The four- and two-legged variety." He used his thumb and pinky to spread the two halves of the deep V apart to expose the velvety roundness of her breasts. Small and plump and absolutely perfect. Her nipples were the same pale coral as her lips, and already hard and responsive, just waiting for him to taste them.

She spread her fingers on his chest, kneading the muscles, then slid her hand across his pecs to his nipple. "Swimming is probably out of the question?" she asked as she rubbed a thumb over the sensitive peak.

He pinched her nipple, making her moan low in her throat, then she reciprocated, doing the same to him. Sam gritted his teeth at the sweet sensation and used his wrist to push her zipper down another few inches. "Leeches."

"Nasty." Above their heads her fingers tightened in his, as her free hand wandered randomly over his chest, combing through his chest hair, making him crazy. She licked the seam of his lips, then whispered in a sultry voice, "Wanna play doctor?"

# SEVEN

"GOD, YES." HIS VOICE was husky, his eyes dark with desire. Elizabeth thought his hand shook a little as he gently touched her cheek. "You be the patient first. I've waited too damn long to see you naked. And if you put your hands on me now I'll go off like a rocket."

"How long?"

"Eight inches?"

Elizabeth laughed. "How long have you wanted to see me naked?"

"Eighteen months, six days, and nineteen hours."

"That's almost as long as we've known one another."

"It's *exactly* as long as we've known one another."

Her nipples pebbled and ached. She wanted him to touch her so badly. She'd imagined his touch on her breasts, dreamed erotic dreams where Sam kissed her body everywhere. She wanted that. She wanted him. "Why didn't you say anything?" she asked, pressing her hand over his where it curved around her breast to show him how she wanted him to touch her. He didn't need instruction. The pressure, the pull and caress, were perfect. He kneaded and stroked until her breath caught.

"You were married." He bent his head to take one eager nipple in his mouth, then sucked hard enough to make her moan. She speared her fingers into his hair to hold his head there.

"Then," he said huskily, trailing his tongue across the upper curve of her left breast. "You were talking divorce." His teeth surrounded the nipple, teasing and tasting until Elizabeth's hips came up off the floor. It was hard to draw in a breath.

"Then you *got* the divorce." Sam pulled the zipper down on her suit as far it would go, then skimmed his hand down her belly. His fingers slid beneath her skimpy blue cotton panties to touch her. "Then." His voice was thick as she shifted to allow him access to her wet heat. He slipped two fingers inside her, and Elizabeth's breath snagged. "Because I'm such a far-thinking guy, I waited a full, *interminable*, year to be sure I wasn't going to be your transitional lover."

She reached down and urged him to exert pressure where she needed it. "Rob and I had a very amicable divorce." It was hard to think, let alone try to talk. "I—I— Deeper. Yes, like that . . . Ahhh— I didn't *need* a t-transitional guy. But, oh, God, Sam, I

wanted you too. From the moment I saw you." He
withdrew his hand, and for a moment Elizabeth lay
there stunned. "Don't stop!"

"Gotta get naked. Now." He finished unzipping,
then pulled the tight-fitting fabric off his shoulders
and down his body.

After a shaky start, Elizabeth struggled out of
hers too. And the only way she managed that was
taking her eyes off Sam's cut abs and the swirls of
crisp dark hair on his tanned chest. She wanted to
lick him all over.

"I must admit," she said, sitting up to yank down
the legs—pretending that they were having a normal
conversation only so that they didn't jump each
other's bones instantly—"that—" God, they were so
ready for each other that she wondered if they might
jettison off the branches supporting the tent. She was
in such a hurry to get naked, her hands shook.

"When my husband told me he'd met someone
else I was hurt." She kicked the entire black suit off
and turned to see him watching her, his dark eyes
gleaming in the false dusk inside the tent. Elizabeth
placed both hands on his chest and pushed him onto
his back. She followed him down. Using him like a
very hard, not particularly comfortable, mattress. It
was sheer bliss feeling his skin against hers.

"Not a gaping-wound hurt," she told him, nibbling a path from his throat to his chin, while his
large hands skimmed down her back. "Because,"
she licked the curve of his lower lip, "we didn't
have that kind of passion. But hurt that after I'd

worked so hard to make our marriage work, he'd gone off and found someone else." She opened her mouth over his and found his tongue. She felt as though sparklers fired off in her blood.

While she kissed her way to his ear, he scooped her hair off her neck and started tasting the tendons there, making her shudder. "Then you walked into the clinic that day in the middle of all my personal drama and I forgot everything."

Elizabeth's mind went blank as his tongue traced an erotic path up the side of her throat and then swirled inside her ear.

"A-all that testosterone, a black eye, your arm bleeding. And even though I thought you'd been in some skanky bar fight . . ." She smiled at his growl of mock outrage.

"I thought you were the hottest, sexiest man I'd ever seen."

"Yeah?" he whispered directly into her ear.

She shuddered. "Oh, yeah." It had been lust at first sight. "I thought you weren't interested." Struggling to make sense of her failing marriage, building a new practice, and paying off monumental med school loans, Elizabeth had been broadsided by her visceral and blatantly sexual attraction to a stranger when her life was already in an upheaval. She'd put Sam away to think about late at night. And think about him she had. With the way her life was going at the time, she was almost relieved that he hadn't felt the same immediate attraction that she had. If both them had felt the same way, she imagined that it would have been impossible not to act on it. By his apparent disinterest, Elizabeth had managed to stay true to her marriage vows, however tenuous they'd been.

Her brain was fogging. Sam flipped her over. It wasn't easy; the tent was barely big enough for the two of them. He leaned over her, his fingers tangled in her hair, his gaze hot, his thumb making lazy circles at her temple. "That kiss I planted on you six months ago didn't give you a heads-up?"

"It gave me *pheromones* and *blood pressure* up," she assured him, tracing the curve of his smile. Even though her body pulsed and throbbed, and she was wet for him, their lazy, we-have-all-the-time-in-the-world conversation was drawing out the finish unbearably. "But that was the only indication that you even knew I *existed*."

His fingers skimmed up to cup her breast where it plumped against his chest. Elizabeth shifted to grant him access to her nipple. He squeezed it this side of exquisite pain, then stroked his thumb over the erect peak. The sensation shot directly to every nerve center in her body.

"You didn't notice I was practically stalking you?" he demanded, kneeing her thighs apart.

"I *did* notice that you were pretty much everywhere I was, yes. But you never came over and talked to me. Never asked me out. You kissed me once and then I didn't hear from you again. You disappeared for a mon—"

He slipped inside her. Hot and hard. "Ah. You noticed."

"Wait. Don't move," she begged, the sensation too strong, too sweet. She wanted him so much her heart ached with the need. Here he was, this man who had set her pulse racing for what seemed like forever. Here he was, Sam Pelton, with his hips spreading her thighs wide and his warrior eyes gleaming as he looked down into hers. Yes Yes YES!

"Of course I noticed." She tried to speak around a pant as she started to rock her hips against his. "One minute everywhere I looked there—*ah*—there you were, then you kissed me like there was no tomorrow and *disappeared* for a month. It was enough to . . . give . . . a girl a freaking . . . complex."

His penis flexed inside her, and Elizabeth moaned, then bit him on the shoulder. The pleasure he was giving her was indescribable, both sharp and sweet. Her body tightened unbearably around him as he threw back his head, the tendons in his neck showing in sharp relief.

"I was out of the country on an—op." Sam pumped his hips and Elizabeth made a soft appreciative sound in the back of her throat, stroking her hand down his back, then digging her nails into his hard butt cheek as he hit his stride. "And I was waiting— I'm trying to draw this out, sweetheart. But I'm going to go off like Vesuvius in about a second if you don't stop moving under me like that. Lie real still— I was waiting the year out."

She couldn't keep still, everything they did pushed her higher and higher, until Elizabeth didn't know where she stopped and Sam began. Her internal muscles contracted around his penis buried deep inside her. His hands were gentle as he stroked her back and her behind in strokes that he *maybe* thought were soothing, but were instead making her crazy with lust, love, and need all jumbled together.

Sam's body was a furnace above hers, sweat gluing their skin together as Sam skimmed his hand down her side, then touched her intimately where they were joined. She shifted slightly to give him better access, and thought, *We fit together perfectly*, then said out loud, "Yes, God yes, I love when you touch me there. Just like that. Just. Like. That." And—*I love you*.

Elizabeth loved the taste of his skin, loved the scrape of his jaw against her breast, loved the smell of him. Loved the satiny feel of his tanned skin and crisp hair beneath her marauding fingers.

"I figured after that— Hmm." She bit his earlobe, and he groaned his pleasure, so she did it again. She felt his desire, and it doubled her own. "I figured that you weren't following me at all. It was a string of co-coincidences. You took my dormant libido from stalled to overdrive, then—poof. You were gone. When you came back it was as if that kiss had never happened. I knew you weren't *shy*, so I was convinced you just weren't that into me."

"Make no mistake," he said, his voice raw with

emotion as his thrusts became more aggressive, as if he couldn't wait another second.

To hell with trying to postpone this. Elizabeth was just as eager. She needed it *now*. "Do it *hard*," she told him, wrapping her legs around his narrow hips and locking her ankles in the small of his back. She wanted to devour him, and set her open mouth on the thundering pulse on his throat.

"I was into you. In every way a man can be into a woman I was in . . . to you." He plunged deep, sending them both over the edge in a shower of sensation that lasted a long, long time.

SAM KISSED HER SHOULDER. "Our ride's here."

"Hmmm." She stretched, then wrapped her arms around his neck. "I thought we had a late checkout." She took a little nip on his lower lip. "How'd you manage to get dressed without waking me up?"

"Special ops training. Up and at 'em, sweetheart. We have a reservation at another hotel. One with a soft bed, and no roommates."

"Woohoo."

Her smile zinged through Sam's bloodstream like liquid sunshine. Wanting to make love to her again wasn't an option, unfortunately. He was looking forward to making love to her for hours on end with no interruption, and without being distracted by listening for the bad guys.

Their time would come to laze in bed all day. This wasn't that day.

Looked like they were going to get out of here in one piece. *If* Thadiwe's men weren't smarter than the average chimp and had managed to elude him. *If* they got downriver unscathed. *If* the hidden chopper hadn't been discovered and sold for parts. None of those things would have fazed Sam before. Having Beth with him changed everything.

"Here." He handed her the DEET. "The mosquitoes are having a freaking convention out there."

He slid toward the tent opening and yanked down the zipper. "I'll wait outside to give you room."

"Stay. I love being in tight quarters with you."

Living in a one-man tent with Beth sounded damn good to him too, but he shook his head. "You'd never get dressed." He had to kiss her one more time. Supposed to be quick, but she threaded her fingers through his hair, and held him for a kiss that turned him inside out. He'd never been much of a kisser, but Beth made him a convert. Reluctantly he brought the kiss to an end. "Don't take long," he told her, loving the way her eyes lost focus when he kissed her. "We have to make tracks." He crawled out onto the limb to give her room to dress, but left the flap up so he could watch her.

She shot him a sassy smile, and drew the Lock-Out over her body like a seasoned stripper.

He dragged his attention away from her rosy breasts and scanned the jungle around them. Thadiwe's men would be getting close. Sam had gone out forty minutes ago to reconnoiter while Beth slept. Just because he hadn't encountered any more soldiers didn't mean they weren't out there. Thadiwe's minions had plenty of time to realize that five of their men hadn't returned. Sam had a persistent itch on the back of his neck. He never ignored his intuition. It was gained by experience.

"Can we frame the tent when we get back home?" Beth asked, coming through the opening feet first. She looked sensational in the tight black LockOut, her bright hair disheveled around her shoulders, her pretty eyes alert as she finished pulling the zipper up to her throat. Sam ran his gaze unobtrusively over the cut on her cheek and the two on her throat. No sign of infection. Then he slid his hand under her hair and pulled her to him for a quick, hungry kiss.

"Nah." He smiled into her eyes. "We'll pitch it in the backyard and use it for our annual family vacation." He waited for a reaction, but didn't get one. His gut clenched before he reminded himself that Elizabeth was good at masking her thoughts. He wasn't even sure she'd heard him, as a parrot, blue and yellow wings spread, screeched overhead. She flinched, and he wondered what it would take to get her over her fear of birds. One thing for sure, he didn't have time for it now.

He'd already pulled out the support pegs on the tent, and it was a simple matter to collapse the fabric and stuff it back in the bag. He held up her favorite silk blouse, the pink liberally spattered with dried brown blood. "I needed to bring your clothing so they'd think you'd worn it out of there." He held the shirt up in a wad. "Want to try and save this?"

Beth shuddered. "No thank you. I might never wear pink silk again."

"I'll bury it, and the rest of your clothes, then. Ready?"

"As I'll ever be." She scooted on her butt as far as the trunk, then stood to climb down to the ground. It was hotter than hell. Hot and steamy. Her cheeks were a delicate rose, and Sam thought that pink wasn't so bad.

She smiled. "I'll be fine not seeing the color green for a while. But I'll miss the tent."

# EIGHT

"*MBOTÉ! MBOTÉ!* BOSS-MAN," DESI called with a shit-eating grin as he paddled a decrepit-looking pirogue up to shore. He looked ridiculously like a young Denzel Washington, and wore ragged cut-off cargo pants, and a royal blue vest with red and yellow house cats printed on it. Around his clean-shaven head he'd jauntily tied a gray and green striped necktie. The entire ensemble would make a damn fine target for anyone on shore. As if he hadn't a care in the world, Desi jumped out of the boat in thigh-deep water and dragged it closer to shore.

"What happened to the Zodiac?" Sam asked. He suspected he knew. Desi had sold it, and everything in it, to the rebels for a pretty penny. He'd then probably spent the "mbongo" he'd gotten on his new lady friend. "I need . . ." Desi looked pitiful and mimed eating. "*Koliya.* Yes?"

The guy was a strapping thirty-year-old in no danger of starving. "Hell, no. The Zodiac wasn't yours to sell." Desi gave him a blank look. "Never mind." There was no point arguing. "Let's go."

Sam tossed both packs into the middle of the boat.

"Ever paddled a canoe?" he turned to ask Beth. "Desi and I will be rowing, but it wouldn't hurt for you to know how. Just in case."

Just in case? Elizabeth resisted turning her head to scan the jungle surrounding them for snipers. "I've done the rowing machine at the gym, so I can probably handle it."

She demonstrated her technique for Sam, practicing in the air while he adjusted her left-handed grip just a fraction.

"Try that again— Keep the oar as vertical as possible. Good. Okay, let's do it." She started to cross to the water, but Sam put his hand on her arm. "No point in us both getting our feet wet. Here, I'll carry you." She expected a fireman's lift, but Sam swung her up in his arms.

It was a silly romantic gesture, one she loved. God help her, Elizabeth thought, shocked by the re-alization. She loved *him*. He'd proven that he *wanted* her. But that was lust. Did the concept of love even cross the mind of a man like Sam? She seriously doubted it. He wasn't hardwired that way. Yet he'd mentioned a shared backyard. She wondered if that was just a throwaway remark or if he actually meant they had a future together. "You Tarzan," she joked, looping her arms around his neck.

He lowered her into the small canoe while Desi

held it steady. "Hang on to me as you put one foot in . . . now crouch down, grab the gunwale and transfer your weight before putting the other foot in."

She did as he instructed, without mishap, thank God. The sun, straight up and broiling hot, beat down on her unprotected head. Without a word, Sam leaned over and withdrew a black ball cap from one of his packs and placed it on her head.

The boat barely seemed big enough to hold three adults and Sam's heavy packs.

Sam flung a leg into the boat and shot her a smile as he carefully lowered himself behind her. "We're going to get out of here in one piece. I promise."

First the hat, now he knew how scared she was. "Are you a mind reader?" she asked over her shoulder as she adjusted the cap to better shield her eyes.

"I'm a student of Dr. Elizabeth Bennett Goodall. Okay, Desi. Let's get the party started." The two men started paddling in slow easy strokes that took them out to the middle of the river.

Her heart did a little zig-zag at Sam's response. "What's my favorite color?"

"Purple."

"What's your favorite food?"

"Same as yours. Italian."

"Favorite ice cream?"

"Vanilla. Yours is Rocky Road. Keep to the middle of the river, Desi. Better chance of being seen, but less chance of encountering most of the wildlife. Watch out for hippos." Elizabeth presumed he was talking to her and not their guide. "They're vicious and fast. And don't put your hands anywhere near the water. Snakes and crocs."

"I didn't even want to put my hands in the Thames when Kess and I went on that river cruise last year. Believe me, I'll keep my hands to myself. This water looks alive with every known parasite and creepy-crawly known to man." She wasn't sure which was scarier, the critters she could see or those she couldn't.

"Can you swim?"

"I'm *not* getting in the water."

"Brace your feet on the sides and bring your paddles in and lock them. There's white water ahead."

"White water?"

"Rapids."

"That was rhetori—" Her words cut off with a scream as the small, narrow pirogue slewed sideways in a froth of white water. She grabbed the gunwale with both hands and braced her feet as best she could. Hadn't she been the one craving adventure? The adrenaline spike was pure fear.

"Dig deep and hold on!" Sam yelled over the scaling thunder of the water. The boat pitched sideways, going down at a steep angle. "Forward paddle—hard!"

The men's oars weren't in the water because they were riding on air. It was electrifying. Terrifying, but heart-thumping exhilarating. Elizabeth hung on for dear life, and lifted her face to the diamonds of spray jettisoning around her. If she was going to die, she was going down with a fight.

The boat came down with a bone-jarring *thump*. Trees and bushes went by in a blur of greens and browns as they shot downstream, slewing sideways, bumping and jostling as the unruly water tossed them from level to level in untidy increments. Down the rapids almost on their nose, then jolting them backwards until she was practically in Sam's lap.

"Hang on. There's more," he shouted.

Elizabeth noticed. There was more white water, all right. Lots more. The water frothed high over the sides of the pirogue, drenching them all. Maybe instead of being exhilarated she should be praying. She tried it, but her breath caught as they glanced off a submerged rock and literally went flying. Down, down, down, over the rocks and debris that swirled and tumbled down a series of cataracts.

"Hold on! Hold on!"

*Thump, slam.* Into a flume where the water raced around a sharp bend, then dropped seven or eight feet over a ledge. Elizabeth's breath caught, and her heart stayed in her throat as the boat tipped and swayed with the force of the thrashing, churning water tossing them around like a child's toy.

She was too scared to close her eyes, and too terrified not to. This made the roller-coaster rides she'd taken as a kid pale into insignificance.

They landed with a bone-jarring skid, then slid backwards over a short drop.

"Catch your breath," Sam told her when they seemed to have dropped into a pool of calm below the rapids. The little boat bobbed a bit, then glided through the water. "You've got about ten minutes before we hit the next set." He placed his hand on her shoulder. "Enough adventure for you, sweetheart?"

Elizabeth turned her head to smile at him through the water dripping from her hat brim and off her lashes. "It's freaking terrifying. But I'll remember this for the rest of my life. How did you make it upstream?"

"Pottage— Ah, shit. Desi, *haul ass*. Now! Go. Go. Go!"

Elisabeth's heart leapt into her throat again. Now what? She spun around to face front. "What— Oh, my God."

Thadiwe's soldiers, guns pointing right at them, lined the banks. The three of them in the boat were sitting ducks.

# NINE

KNEELING, SAM PADDLED AS fast as he could. In the front of the pirogue, Desi's hands and arms glistened, a chocolate-colored blur as he dug his oars into the water, pulling the boat with him. Thadiwe's men were firing round after round. Thousands of birds, in hundreds of species, were catapulted out of the trees by the noise. Squawking and crying out, they flew in a tidal wave of multicolored beating wings up into the sun-baked air.

Sam felt a burn zing across his upper arm. It didn't slice through the LockOut, but he felt the sting. Ignore it. Pull. Pull. *Pull.* "Beth. Get *down.* Lower, damn it." Bullets crisscrossed overhead, cutting through the water, or ricocheting off nearby rocks. Beth's cap went spinning over the side, and Sam's heart fucking stopped in his chest. "Beth?"

She was bent over, her head on her knees. "I'm okay. I'm okay," she shouted, her voice muffled.

Thadiwe's men had chosen well. The river not

only curved blindly right after the rapids, it also narrowed to just a few hundred feet wide. It would then be impossible to miss the boat or its occupants. To return fire, Sam would have to stop rowing. Right now he wasn't stopping for anything, or anyone. Speed was going to save their asses. Speed. And luck.

The soldiers were running downstream, trying to keep parallel. Fortunately the bank was littered with thick vegetation and it wasn't a smooth run. But it was damn well impossible to dodge that many bullets.

The pirogue swept under a low-hanging branch where a leopard was sunning itself, its amber-spotted body sleek and lethally beautiful. The cat raised its magnificent head, and its muscles flexed beneath its glossy fur as the boat flew beneath the branch. "Stay where you are, Spot," Sam warned. That's all they needed: a pissed-off cat in the boat with them.

"Take it, Desi," Sam yelled, waiting for Desi to adjust his strokes to make allowances for Sam taking his hands off the oars. The second Desi was rowing on his own, Sam pulled out the MP5 and returned a blast of fire. Two men went down, splashing into the water. Eight hundred rounds a minute had a lot of stopping power.

He chambered another $9 \times 19$ mm Parabellum ammunition cartridge. Thirty rounds left a lot of holes. He was counting on it. The roller-delayed blowback mechanism of the weapon fired from a closed-bolt position. When the trigger was pulled, the bolt was already locked forward against the cartridge, which reduced the amount of mechanical movement, improving accuracy. And Sam needed every advantage he could get.

He got another man in midair, as the guy tried to vault over a log. Two more who'd chosen wading in the thigh-deep water lapping the shore rather than the obstacle race that was the bank. Sam got them both in one sweep.

He saw the alternate view of the leopard's tail or head or streamlined body as it ran behind the soldiers, stealthy and well hidden in the brush. It was keeping well back, but hauling ass, ready to pounce should a man fall behind.

Sam knew they had maybe a minute or three before the next set of rapids. Not as steep as the first, but navigation would require both his strength and concentration. The river narrowed substantially right there, and the drop was perhaps twelve feet in a hundred-yard stretch. There wasn't a chance in hell the soldiers would miss them at that range. Sam's heart raced with anticipation as bullets strafed the water beside the boat. Several hit above water, striking the pirogue but missing *them* by fractions of an inch.

"What can I do?" Beth shouted, still doubled over.

"Nothing!" Jesus. She was enough of a target as it was. He didn't want her sitting up to take stock of the situation. "Stay down!" He returned fire. Got another raze on his shoulder, hurt like hell, but again, didn't cut through the LockOut. The bullet hit the inside of the boat, inches from Beth's back, making Sam's heart leap into his throat and lodge there.

A small chunk of wood flew off, hitting him just above his eye. Blood trickled down his face, blinding him to the left. Shit. He wiped his face on his shoulder, then fired into a group of four men clustered on a jut of land just ahead. The soldiers went down like bowling pins.

A four-course meal for the giant croc that had slipped into the water a few feet away on their arrival and now turned back in a lash of tail and jaws to collect.

Sam saw Thadiwe immediately. The tango towered over his soldiers by a good eight inches and stood, legs spread, arms akimbo, as his men aimed their weapons at the approaching boat.

Sam shifted the submachine gun, centering the sight between Thadiwe's close-set eyes. "Here's that facial reconstruction you wanted so badly, asshole."

Thadiwe's head exploded like a watermelon.

Excellent. Saved Sam a return trip.

The soldiers leaped into action as another croc whipped its head around as the man's body crashed into the tall reeds, half in, half out of the muddy water. The white spume flung up by the croc's frenzy turned crimson as he dragged the tango deeper into the water.

The soldiers tried to make up for their inattention by firing off a barrage of bullets willy-nilly. Their enthusiasm was admirable, but their aim sucked, even at this close range. Most of the bullets missed their target by several feet. Sam happened to glance in Desi's direction as a bullet sliced through the man's upper thigh. The injury was deep, and bled. A lot. The other man faltered for a moment, then attacked the water with his oars like a man possessed as the soldiers gauged the target better and started narrowing the gap between hits and misses.

ELIZABETH SMELLED THE FAMILIAR metallic scent of blood over the fruity/muddy smell of the river. *Sam.* She lifted her head just enough to see that it was Desi who'd taken a hit. He was rowing like a madman. The oars sliced through the water, sending up sprays and droplets that sparkled in the sunlight. On either side of the river, men in uniform were running as they fired their weapons. The noise was horrendous. The soldiers shouting, animals screaming, the thrash of the narrow boat moving rapidly through the choppy water. And birds. Flying about wildly, their cries adding to the cacophony.

None of that mattered to Beth right then. Desi's wound was life-threatening. He was losing too much blood, way too fast. She grabbed the smallest of Sam's packs, which rested between her feet.

"Stay down, for God's sake."

"Desi's been hit. What do you have in here that I can use— Ah. Thank God." Sam's kit contained a new device she'd only read about. A "Wound Bullet." An ingenious closure device.

Hauling the pack with her, Elizabeth scooted on her butt toward Desi. The boat rocked, and all of them yelled out at the same time. She felt for the distal pulse at Desi's ankle. Weak. But he reacted at her touch, which was good. His skin was warm. Also good.

While she knew it must hurt like blue blazes, it was an uncomplicated wound. No major arterial or bone damage. But his leg looked like minced meat. She'd never used a Wound Bullet, but she'd read the articles in *JAMA*.

"Beth, get your ass back here and stay down."

"In a minute." She wasn't about to take cover while Desi was losing blood just two feet away from her.

"Now, God damn it!"

Staying as low as she could, Elizabeth quickly swabbed the wound as she tried to remember everything she'd read about the mechanism she was about to use. The closure device consisted of a metal shaft within a cylinder through which standard sutures were threaded. "Okay. Let's see how this thing works."

She understood the basic principle. Brilliant, really. By turning the internal shaft with the use of a simple tool, Elizabeth inserted it into the wound and applied tension to the surrounding tissue. She maintained the pressure by periodically tightening the sutures. Because the tension was evenly distributed, approximation smoothly followed the natural contour of Desi's leg. The gaping, bloody wound slowly closed. Wow. Sam had some *very* cool toys. Blocking out the noise, she pretended that bullets weren't flying around them. Finding a pressure dressing, she covered the incision as best she could; his leg was wet, and she had nothing to dry it with.

"He'll live," Sam yelled, sounding seriously pissed. "Get your head down. Now."

*Okay. Okay.* She got her head down.

"Rapids coming up," he said, almost redundantly since the little boat was slewing and bouncing and boomeranging off rocks and the water was frothing, splashing around them. "Hold on," he added also unnecessarily as Elizabeth rose independently of the boat, then landed on her butt with a thunk that jarred her teeth.

Desi was bleeding through the bandage, but she couldn't do anything about it. All she could do was hold on. And pray.

She unsnapped the oars beside her and dug them into the water. Behind her Sam cursed.

BETWEEN THE THREE OF them they managed to run the rapids without tipping the pirogue. And without being killed. By some freaking miracle, they outraced the enemy and ended up in calm water with not a soldier in sight.

All in all, a damn good day as far as Sam was concerned. They dropped Desi off at the small rural hospital near his village, then borrowed his brother's, brother-in-law's, sister's, aunt's truck to get them to where Sam had left the helicopter in a small clearing just outside the village.

"You can fly this thing?" Beth asked, limping slightly as she crossed the soggy grass to a group of men sitting in threadbare lawn chairs nearby. The five men rose as they approached. Desi had assured him that his uncles would protect the chopper with their lives. They didn't look as though they'd had to forfeit any body parts as they greeted Sam and Beth with wide grins and handshakes all around.

Sam had retrieved his wallet from the pack, and now peeled off the local currency in payment. "*Mbongo*, thank you for protecting my chopper." He offered the money, which they accepted with bows and great ceremony. Although he knew they didn't understand his thanks, they got the gist. Money in hand, they traipsed across the weedy field to drive the truck back to the village.

"Is everything where it's supposed to be?" Beth asked, eyeing the Blackhawk sitting incongruously in the middle of a field with five ripped and torn pieces of lawn furniture, a rainstorm of cigarette butts on the dry dirt surrounding them.

"Looks good," he told her, as he did a visual scan. The rotors were intact, and the body looked untouched. "Don't worry. I'll check to be sure." He took her hand as they got closer. The black paint gleamed dully in the late afternoon sun. "How're your legs?"

"Muscle cramps. I'm good."

Yeah. She was good. And exhausted. And so fucking brave that Sam wanted to throw the little tent to the ground and crawl inside with Beth right there and then. Not for sex, although God only knew he wanted that too. But just to keep her next to his heart. The image of them lying together, in a cool dim room, held enormous appeal.

They'd have that.

And everything else.

"Yeah, I can fly this thing. Here." He opened the door. "Hop in while I do the preflight check."

He lifted her up, his hands lingering on her narrow waist for a second before he deposited her in the leather seat.

Fifteen minutes later they were airborne. And an hour later they were in the Bombardier Challenger being flown back to Montana.

The company jet was sleek and came fully equipped. As soon as the pilot reached cruising altitude, Sam released their seatbelts and took Beth to the aft cabin where there was not only a luxurious bathroom, but also a bed.

Sam turned her into his arms the second he'd kicked the door shut. "There's a bed back here." His voice was thick as he pinned her to the wall and yanked down the fasteners to get her out of the LockOut. "We're not going to make it that far." Her beautiful breasts and the slope of her belly were exposed as he bit lightly on the tendons on her neck, enjoying the way her body shuddered in response and her arms came up around his neck, her fingers fisting in his hair.

Her skin was cool and soft, so soft. Sam multitasked as he backed her into the bathroom, stripped her out of the suit, and kissed her, all without missing a beat. "I wish I were an octopus," he murmured against her mouth, freeing a hand to reach in to turn on the shower. "Then I could touch you everywhere I want, all at the same time."

Beth's eyes were filled with laughter as she helped him strip off his own suit, made complicated because he was so erect the skintight suit had to be peeled away carefully. "It's a loooong flight." She gave him a glittery-eyed inspection as he kicked the suit off each foot and stepped free. "You look like a—"

"Guy with a hard-on?" Sam hoped to God his reaction to her would simmer down just a little in a few years. It was damned uncomfortable, not to mention embarrassing having this kind of erection anytime he was within five feet of her. Especially in public. He swallowed a laugh. Christ. This was never going to end. He'd be ninety and she'd walk into the room, and he wouldn't need a walker.

"Oh, yeah." She placed both hands on his chest, and pushed him ahead of her into the shower stall, which was already filled with steam.

Her fair skin looked incredible against the glossy black tile—not that Sam was taking time to admire the scenery. His mouth went dry as lust surged and intensified to the brink of pain. He backed her against the wall, then lifted her legs around his hips as the hot spray pounded his back. Arms wrapped around his neck, Beth gave a helpful little hop, then tightened her ankles in the small of his back.

He shuddered as he entered her moist heat. They both groaned at the exquisite sensation.

"Oh, God, Sam. This feels— Feels—" Unbearable. Wonderful. Intense. His body was hot against hers; the hair on his chest abraded her breasts deliciously. Elizabeth captured his mouth in a hungry kiss, her own tongue eager and demanding, her hips moving frantically against his. She loved the taste of him, the smell of his skin. She loved the way his body thrust into hers over and over again, so that she didn't know where her body started and his began. "Harder. Harder. Harder," she urged, her back slamming against the cold tile as he surged into her with a power and heat that made her body shake and shudder.

He devoured her mouth.

The kiss went on and on. Hot and wet. Tongues, slick and in constant motion, slid and slithered in a motion mimicking penetration. Her breath hitched and caught. She made a sound in the back of her throat and shuddered with the beginning of a hard fast climax.

"Not yet," Sam muttered thickly, withdrawing a little and dragging in a harsh ragged breath, hard fingers gripping her ass cheeks. "Not." He rammed home again, biting down gently on her earlobe.

Elizabeth's back arched as her body tightened unbearably. "Yet." He pulled out, slick and hard. Hot and greedy.

He brought her to the very edge. Again and again. Prolonging the climax in a carefully choreographed dance that had her clawing his back as violent ripples wracked her body, making her pant and sweat and moan his name.

"Nownownow," she chanted, tightening her arms and legs around him as he pounded into her, the sweet torture almost unbearable.

In answer, Sam crushed his mouth back down on hers as he thrust inside her again and again. Strong and relentless, he controlled the speed and intensity of his thrusts as if he could read her body's every action and reaction.

Harder and harder. Closer and closer together, until she couldn't tell where he began and she ended.

Elizabeth opened her eyes, and Sam's were there, also open, waiting for her, consuming her with the heat of his gaze. She let her lashes fall, scared he'd see too much. *I love you. I loveyou, Iloveyou.* Blood thundered in her ears, roaring through her veins in a sweet blaze that left her shaking and needy. She held him with every well-toned muscle, inside and out, as he plunged into her like a hard-driven weapon. Hunger was its own reward and carried its own demand.

Elizabeth buried her face against Sam's shoulder, but that didn't muffle her scream as they climaxed together hard and fast.

"I'm a noodle," she gasped, her legs refusing to unclasp.

"Since we're here, might as well make use of the rest of the water." Which was now decidedly cool. It felt good on her burning skin. Sam reached for the liquid soap in a container on the wall, and started washing her, starting with her hair.

Elizabeth leaned her head against the tiled wall, eyes closed as he used his large hands to wash her face and throat, then trailed his fingers over her soapy breasts until she muttered, "No fair," and slid her legs from around his hips so she could stand. Her legs felt even more noodley than before.

She pushed the button on the container and got a handful of scentless soap in her palm. "You are a dirty, dirty boy."

"Man."

Her hands slicked down his sides, then honed in on his erection. Cupping his length, she smiled as her soapy fingers tightened around him. "All man, all the time," she agreed. "This is going to take me some time, so lean back and close your eyes. I'll let you know when I'm done."

Sam's chuckle turned into a groan as Elizabeth skimmed her lips from his chest down to his rock-hard belly as her slick fingers went to work. "Just so you know," she said, when her mouth reached the nest of crisp dark hair at his groin, "this is uncharted territory for me, so let me know if I don't do it right."

In answer Sam tangled his fingers in her wet hair. "You're doing it— Jesus, Beth!" he said as she tentatively took him into her mouth and used her tongue to make his entire body jerk satisfactorily. "Per-fec-tly."

Just before he came, Sam pulled her up, and kissed her.

"Didn't you want to—"

"Plenty of time," he assured her, grabbing another handful of soap. He skimmed his large hand down over her belly, then slid his fingers deep inside her, bringing her to a surprise, and immediate, climax before she knew it.

"Holy Mother of God. We're going to kill each other." She gasped as he withdrew his fingers and let her body sag against his as she fought to regain her breath and her equilibrium. "Give me a sec to get my breath, and then let's get out of here. I want to make love with you in that bed I didn't see in there."

They took turns washing each other, then made love again slowly, the cold water pounding on Sam's back spraying her and making her shiver deliciously.

After the longest shower in history, where the water ran cold as they ran hot, he carried her to the bed, where Sam turned the tables on her as he spread her thighs and feasted on her until she cried out mindlessly and begged for mercy. Thankfully he knew when to not take no for an answer, and drove her over the edge of an unknown precipice until her body was so attuned to his that she couldn't imagine being anywhere than right here, with his mouth between her legs, and the hum of the plane's engines throbbing through her body like an extra pulse.

Exhausted as they were, they made love again slowly. Then again, more quickly. Finally, too tired to move, they slept, curved around each other as the plane chased the sun.

THE PLANE LANDED AT an airfield Elizabeth didn't recognize, although she knew where they were. Just outside Brandon. Her stomach was doing flip-flops. This was it. Elizabeth undid her seatbelt as the small plane taxied down the runway and into an enormous hangar. "Now what?" She was talking about more than just the next few moments.

The door to the hangar closed behind the plane, and they were plunged into semidarkness just before the lights in the cabin came to life.

Sam's expression was unreadable. Back in Montana for five seconds and he was already the same old inscrutable Sam Pelton. "I'm going home," he told her, shouldering his packs and starting off down the aisle.

"Oh." Her stomach hurt, but she didn't complain as she rose to follow him. She'd expected it really. Hoped that they might have a future together, but known that was highly unlikely. Known all along that she'd only had him temporarily. The knowledge didn't lessen the ache of loss in her chest. It didn't make the prickle in her eyes go away. She swallowed the almost unbearable disappointment as she drank in the sight of his tall muscular body just a few feet in front of her as he strode toward the door to the plane which now stood open.

He paused in the wide aisle and turned around to face her again, blocking her way. Reaching out, he cupped her jaw and Elizabeth heard the *thud-thud* as the packs dropped to the carpeted floor behind him. "When I say I'm going home, I mean I'm going wherever *you* are. I love you, Beth. Have from the moment I laid eyes on you. I want to marry you. I want to take you to Italy, and make love to you in the sunshine, and in moonlight. I want babies with you. And a dog. And a garden for the kids and dogs to play in, with room for our tent. I want the whole package, Dr. Elizabeth Bennett Goodall. With you."

Heart singing with happiness, she wrapped her arms around his neck, lips curved in a triumphant smile. "I love you, Sam."

"Marry me," he whispered against her waiting mouth. "I promise you the adventure of a lifetime."

"Yes," she said when he let her up for air. "Wherever you are will be my adventure. Let's go home, my love."

# ATLANTA
# HEAT

LORA
LEIGH

# PROLOGUE

SOME WOMEN A MAN knew to stay the hell away from. It was a self-preservation thing. Survival instinct. The lone wolf that reveled in its independence and sexual freedom knew when it was staring in the eyes of a sensual trap. A woman capable of making the male animal stand up, take notice, and tremble in his military boots.

Mason "Macey" March was a man who liked to live on the edge, though. He was all about the challenge, the risk, the excitement, whether it was a mission or a woman, or a terrorist out to destroy the world. He was a man who stared out at life with a defiant snarl and dared it to take first blood.

He was a man staring at his own destruction, and he had enough sense to recognize it, and to be equally terrified and drawn to it. Like a spectator to a train wreck. It was going to be bloody. It was going to be a mess. But he couldn't look away because she had him by his soul and he knew it. One kiss. That was all it was going to take. One touch and he was going to be a goner. He was aching to touch.

Hazel-green eyes twinkled mischievously over lightly freckled cheeks. Lush lips curved enchantingly, and made a man wonder about the things that mouth could do even as it threatened the fit of his dress whites.

Softly curved, temptingly delicate, and trouble with a capital T. Messing with this woman was the ultimate insanity, but no one had ever accused him of being sane.

"You know, Lieutenant March," she drawled in a seductive Southern accent. "You could always slip out the back door. I bet the admiral won't even realize you're gone."

He stared down at her, eating up the vision of her below the neck even as he kept his gaze steady on hers. Wasn't a chance in hell he was going to let the admiral catch him leering at his goddaughter's ample breasts. The way the sapphire blue silk clung to them, held over the luscious mounds with the tiniest of straps. Her long chestnut hair fell down her back in thick soft waves, making his hands itch to touch it.

"Sweetheart, the admiral would fry important portions of my anatomy if I dared." He attempted to smile, but he was damned close to swallowing his tongue as he caught sight of those sweetly curved mounds lifting in a sigh. If he wasn't mistaken, there was a sheen of moisture popping on his brow as he fought to control the hard-on threatening beneath his slacks. This wasn't the best place to prove to the admiral that he really was nothing more than a dog panting after a pair of pretty tits, as the bastard had recently accused him of being.

He didn't pant after tits. He revered them. Worshipped them. He was nearly drooling over them. Maybe that did make him a dog.

He watched Miss Emerson Delaney smile. A playful curve of her lips that was a warning in and of itself. And beneath that silk was the faintest hint of nipples hardening.

"You know, I could help you sneak away," she whispered playfully. "Admiral Holloran is, after all, my godfather. I'll make your excuses. You aren't looking well, you know." She was laughing at him. Playfully. In amusement. But she was getting a kick out of the fact that he didn't dare piss the admiral off at this point. He'd already been busted down in rank for one misdemeanor; he didn't need to get brought down again because Emerson was in the mood to play.

"Don't do me any favors, imp," he growled.

She pouted back at him playfully. "But Macey, doing you a favor would just make my day complete. Didn't you know that?"

He snorted. Likely story. If he didn't get the hell away from her the admiral would barbecue his ass.

"Do me a favor then and find someone else to harass, kid," he told her. "I'm in enough trouble."

He caught the narrowing of her eyes as he made

his escape, quickly. Before he lost control and let his gaze drop to those incredible breasts.

Okay, so he was a tit man. He couldn't help it, and she had the most incredible set he'd ever seen.

He drew in a quick, fortifying breath as he made his way through the ballroom, the foyer, then quickly entered the silent, empty study that the admiral made available to his men during these jackass parties his sister insisted on throwing in his name. Holloran should get married or something, to a nice shy little wife who didn't like parties instead of letting his sister run his social life.

He stalked across the room to the bar, pulled a glass from the shelf, and splashed in a healthy dose of whisky as he heard the door snick open behind him. And he knew. Hell, he knew who was back there.

He tossed back the whisky. "Go back outside and play, little girl." He grimaced as he caught sight of her in the mirror over the bar. "You're biting off more than you can chew this time."

He'd known her for years. Known her and avoided her and lived in dread and in anticipation of the chance to touch her.

"I had a message for you." Her voice wasn't teasing this time, it was a chilly snap. A proper, aristocratic, holier-than-thou, kiss-my-ass whiplash of sound.

It made his dick hard. Made his balls draw tight in hunger and his fingers curl with the need to touch.

"So what's the message?" He rubbed his hand over his face before glancing at the mirror again.

She was leaning against the door, her eyes were glittering with anger, and those lush lips were tight with irritation.

She opened the little evening bag she carried and drew a slip of paper free, extending it to him as she crossed the room, then slapping it into his open palm.

Then, he made the biggest mistake of his life. He didn't just take the paper and tuck it in the pocket of his slacks. And he sure wasn't dumb enough to read it. Oh hell, no. With his free hand, he gripped her wrist and jerked her to him, shoving the note in his pocket with the other and then curling his hand around her waist and jerking her tighter against his body.

Hell. Fuck. Son of a bitch.

Those firm mounds pressed against his lower chest, her head tipped back, shock and lust brightening her eyes as his head lowered.

He was crazy. He was destroying his career, right here, with a single kiss.

His lips took hers. Like a man starving for passion, a man suddenly, forcefully aware of the hunger tearing into his gut.

And he was hungry.

Her lips parted on a gasp and he was there, his tongue stroking past them, daring her to do her worst with those sharp little teeth. Wishing she would, because then, maybe, he could find the strength to release her.

But did she bite him? Did she rack her knee into his tortured balls as she should have? Hell no, she had lost her mind too. Slender arms were suddenly wrapped around his neck, fingers plowing into his hair and her lips parting, taking him, her tongue tangling with his as a rough cry whispered against his lips.

She tasted like honey and spice and she went straight to his head. Kissing her was like immersing himself in addictive sweetness. He licked at her, his tongue tangled with hers, and before he realized the idiocy of his actions his hands were tearing at the little straps of her dress, dragging them down her arms. His lips tore from hers to travel down her neck, down the arch of her throat, heading for nipples that, as the pads of his thumbs stroked over them, tightened further.

Ah hell, he couldn't breathe, he couldn't think. He had to taste.

He lifted her against him, and set her on the padded barstool, his hands cupping those luscious breasts, lifting them to him as his mouth captured one tight, hot bud between his lips.

He'd have thought he could hold on at that point. He'd have thought that the sheer pleasure of finally tasting Emerson's tits would be enough to give him the control needed to hang on and enjoy it. And in doing that, he could find at least a single thought to remind him that he wasn't just playing with fire, he was playing with his own career.

But did he think? Thought washed away when she cried his name in that breathless, shocked voice. It ripped out of his head and left him in a reality where the only thing that mattered was her fingers tangled in his hair, holding him to her breast as he sucked at that tight nipple like a man drowning in lust and pleasure.

Sharp nails pricked at his scalp, pulled at his hair, dragged him close as she arched and shoved her nipple tighter between his lips.

Thought didn't control him now. His dick controlled him. Thick and hard and straining beneath his slacks. One hand dropped to her thigh and he began jerking that softer than soft evening gown up legs that he knew had to be softer.

This was what happened when a man denied himself. When he worked with no breaks to play. When he pushed back lust and refused to drown the hunger for one woman in another woman's body. This was what happened. Because then weakness became hunger, and hunger became a ravenous instinct that refused to be controlled.

Until the door to the study slammed open violently, causing his head to jerk to the mirror, his gaze to clash with the enraged gaze of the admiral. The admiral who cherished his goddaughter as most men did their own children.

Admiral Samuel Tiberian Holloran. Known as the

Commodore to most of the men who served under him. A tight-assed bastard where his goddaughter was concerned.

Macey shielded Emerson with his own body, her bare breasts pressed into his chest as she struggled to straighten the bodice. He felt ice form in the pit of his soul as his gaze stayed locked with the admiral's.

"My office," the admiral snarled. "Now!"

Holloran jerked the door open, stalked out, and slammed it with enough force that Macey was surprised the frame didn't crack.

Drawing back, he stared down at Emerson. Her face was still flushed with pleasure, but her eyes were concerned.

"Thanks," he snapped as he stepped back from her, watching as she dragged the straps over her shoulders, a hint of confusion, of hurt in her face.

"For what?"

"For staying away from me like I asked you to. You're trouble, Miss Delaney. More trouble than I think I need right now."

With that, he stalked from the study and headed for the office and the bust in rank he knew was coming. Hell, he'd just been reinstated back to lieutenant, and for what? So he could go right back down because he was hungry, hungry and hurting for a woman so far out of his league that she might as well be in another universe. The one woman Macey knew Admiral Holloran would kill him over. The one woman he very much feared held his heart.

Hell, he should have stayed home.

As he entered the hall, he drew the note Emerson had just given him from his slacks.

*The admiral requests a meeting, ASAP, his office. Landry.*

Hell. No wonder the admiral was pissed. God only knew when his aide had given Emerson that note. One thing was for sure, the admiral was out for blood now. His blood. And Macey knew he would be damned lucky if he survived.

# ONE
*Three weeks later*

EMERSON HAD BEEN KIDNAPPED.

That knowledge echoed through Macey's mind from the moment he received the admiral's phone call to the second he had received the information informing him of her location.

She had been taken from him. As the admiral had snapped in his taciturn voice, she had been stolen. And the admiral's blue eyes, chips of icy rage, had glared at Macey.

"You'll find her. Find her and hide her, Macey. You're the best, and that's what she needs now."

The best. Yeah, he was the best at this. Tracking, killing. The admiral had made certain his men were the best; he considered Macey one of his, despite their problems.

Now, Macey crouched in the corner of the shadowed warehouse and told himself it was all in a day's work. He would get through it because he didn't have a choice, and he would do it right because that was the only way he knew how to do things. Even when he fucked up, he always made it right in the end. Answering the admiral's call at midnight was his chance.

He'd fucked up last month. He hadn't just lost rank for messing with the wrong woman, but he had walked away from the woman as well. Dumb move. Hell, the admiral had had every right to be pissed when he demanded to know Macey's intentions toward his goddaughter. He had, after all, just caught Macey in a rather explicitly compromising position with her.

Unfortunately, Macey hadn't had the right answers, so to say he was surprised when the admiral called to assign him to the mission to rescue her was an understatement. But as the admiral had known, there was no keeping the information from him. There was no keeping him away from her. And that was besides the fact that the admiral knew Macey would give his own life to protect her.

It was partially his and the admiral's fault she had been kidnapped, after all. The remnants of a terrorist and white slavery organization he had helped to destroy were now striking back at the admiral because of his part in the assassination of the head of that organization. And the admiral's goddaughter was his only weak spot.

"Remind me to put your names on my birthday card list." Emerson Delaney's voice was soft and sweet, sugar-coated and so gently Southern it sounded ridiculously out of place here in the darkened warehouse. "What was your name again? Mo, Larry or Curly?"

The sound of flesh hitting flesh sent his blood temperature rising. Fine, she was a smartass, but that was no reason to hit her, and some bastard inside that warehouse had hit her. He would kill the bastard who had dared to touch her.

"You, Miss Delaney, are in no position to sneer." The accented voice was cold, purposeful. "You will pay for your godfather's crimes."

"Melodramatics," she seemed to wheeze. "Pure melodramatics. Is that a French flaw or just your charming personality?"

The bastard hit her again. Macey knew he was going to have to move before the bastard put a bullet in her head.

Blood was going to spill tonight, and it wouldn't be Emerson's. He'd already made up his mind that the woman was his; he had only to stake his claim and convince her of it. But first they had to get her out of here. At least he had the element of surprise. The men who had kidnapped her from her bed had no clue that their route to the warehouse had been followed.

He turned to the SEAL with him, meeting the wild blue eyes of the demon stalking behind.

Nineteen months of torture and drug experimentation on Nathan had nearly broken him. It had definitely changed the SEAL for all time, but a year later, he was holding his own. Honed, savage, a creature of rage, but holding his own.

He held up three fingers. There were three guards posted at the entrance to the warehouse. He held up two more and pointed inside the warehouse. He was getting ready to give the command for Nathan to work his way around to the other side of the warehouse when the son of a bitch held up the flat of his hand and shook his head.

Before Macey could argue, Nathan was striding around the warehouse, calm, cool as hell, and crazier than a fucking loon. Son of a bitch. Macey gritted his teeth again, grinding his molars and cursing crazy Irish men to hell and back.

"Hey, dude, I need a light." Nathan's voice was ruined, slurred as he stumbled against the warehouse.

"Get the fuck out of here," one of the guards cursed.

Macey peeked around, trained his weapon on the three guards.

Macey saw Nathan's knife gleam in the darkness a second before he buried it in a smooth, hard upward strike into the heart of the first guard. The guard gasped, gave a shudder, then appeared to stagger with Nathan's weight, taking him closer to the other two.

Three seconds later blood coated the asphalt and three French nationals, one of whom had embassy clearance, Macey had been informed, were propped up against the wall as Nathan moved into place beside the door, his demon eyes glaring across the distance.

Who needed a whole team of SEALs? He and Nathan were enough SEALs for this job. Nathan might be a tad mentally unstable in Macey's opinion, but he was a hell of a killer. And that sucked. It used to be that Nathan shed blood only when there was no other alternative. Now, he killed without mercy, with expediency. He gave nothing or no one a chance to strike first.

"Your godfather Admiral Holloran will regret his part in the strike against our leader," the terrorist was raging, as though Emerson was going to give a damn. "He and that bitch daughter that betrayed her father. Once we have her, you will be executed, your deaths viewed by millions and cheered on by the loyal followers of Sorrell."

Sorrell, the son of a bitch terrorist and white slaver they had taken down months before was rearing his ugly head again, even after death.

"Wish you luck with that." Emerson's voice was weak. "I really wouldn't expect more than a few dozen loyal hits; the rest will be for entertainment value alone. Kind of like a train wreck." Her voice was flippant, but Macey could hear the fear in it.

Nathan smiled that demon smile of his. A hard curl of his lips, the flash of strong white teeth and cold hard death. He was a killing machine now, determined to take down the last cells of the terrorist organization that had backed Sorrell. Until it was finished, he couldn't return to his own life, couldn't reclaim his wife.

Nathan gestured, signifying that they go in low,

catch the two inside off guard, and snatch the girl. Hell, it would be risky. Too fucking risky. He shook his head and began to gesture a less risky move when Nathan crouched, slammed the door open and went in shooting.

"You stupid bastard!" Macey snarled, fury and an edge of fear growing in his gut as the sounds of gunfire exploded through the night.

He threw himself into the room, rolling to the chair Emerson was tied in and tipping it over. He jerked the knife from his boot and sliced the ropes holding her wrists and ankles. The two men with her lay in their own blood as Nathan moved quickly to cover Macey.

"There's more coming," Nathan hissed as Macey checked the girl quickly for injuries.

She was glaring at him. Her hazel eyes were pinpoints of fury, the green in them nearly overshadowing the brown, glittering in a rush of anger as she snarled back at him. That was Emerson—fear made her angry. Made her snap and snarl and that was a hell of a lot preferable to tears. Could he handle tears from Emerson?

"We have to run for it," he warned her.

"You have to drag your heavy ass off me first," she panted. "Dammit, Macey, you weigh a ton."

"Move!" Nathan snapped behind him. "Here they come!"

He jerked her to her feet, ignoring her gasp, grabbed her by the wrist and pulled her through the shadowed, cavernous building at a low run.

"I lost a shoe," she gasped.

"So lose the other one," he growled, checking behind them and praying Nathan kept up rather than dropping behind to shed more blood.

That boy was going to end up getting himself killed, if he didn't end up getting them all killed.

"I'll put those on your tab," she informed him, her voice bland despite the breathless quality of it and the fear in her eyes. "You can pay for them later."

"Sure," he snarled, jerking her around another crate as the front of the warehouse erupted in curses. "I'll go right out and buy you a new pair."

"They're very hard to find," she informed him with testy patience as he jerked her low to the floor, within feet of the back entrance, and motioned Nathan to secure the exit.

"Should he be going out there by himself?" she leaned close to his ear and voiced the question. "The bad guys would cover the back, wouldn't they?"

Nathan gave the all-clear.

"Not this time. Shut up and run." He pulled her behind him, moving past Nathan as he collected the automatic rifle they had hidden in the back. He followed at Emerson's back, placing himself between her and any bullets that would have flown through the night.

Lights illuminated the warehouse and the lot in a flood of color, only a millisecond behind their rapid push through the chain-link fence that they had cut earlier. The truck was on the other side of the neighboring lot, less than a quarter of a mile and with plenty of cover. With any luck they were home free.

"I can't run like this," Emerson gasped behind him.

God, did he think "luck"? Didn't he remember that luck didn't exactly look favorably toward him, even at the best of times?

He looked back and nearly groaned. As she ran, those impressive, make-a-man's-mouth-water breasts were jiggling, reminding him of more than one night's worth of erotic dreams that he'd had concerning them.

"We're almost there." He pulled her to him, wrapped his arm around her waist, and half carried her as they snaked through the hulking, shadowed crates, equipment and vehicles that filled the industrial warehouse lot they were running through.

Nathan moved quickly ahead of them now, securing the area to the truck as Macey gritted his teeth again. Her left breast was moving against his side, a firm, erotic weight that he should be shot for noticing.

*Save the girl first*, he reminded himself.

But it wasn't the breasts that drew him and Macey knew it. It was the woman, and that was what terrified him clear down to his combat boots. The woman could take him down, and he had a feeling he was getting ready to go down hard.

EMERSON DELANEY KNEW SHE was in trouble the minute hard hands jerked her from her bed and pulled her from her home. She had been driven through Atlanta surrounded by hard, cold-eyed terrorists intent on death. There hadn't been a doubt in her mind that they intended to kill her. Just as there hadn't been a doubt in her mind that Macey would be sent to rescue her.

Tall, over six feet four inches, perhaps six five, dark brown eyes, long dark hair, and a bad-boy sexy face. He was the rebel, the troublemaker. The man she couldn't stop thinking about or dreaming about. And the one she knew would come for her.

Her thoughts were interrupted when Macey March tossed her into the backseat of the dual cab pickup, followed in after her, and gave the other man the order to drive. They eased out of the parking lot slowly, lights out, rather than tearing out of it in a scream of tires, which would have surely alerted any terrorists nearby.

The dark vehicle blended in with the shadows of hulking semis and eased out of the warehouse district and into the stream of traffic bordering it. The headlights came on then, and she wondered if it was okay to breathe yet.

She glanced over at Macey, aware that he was watching the traffic with narrow-eyed intent, his weapon held low against his thigh, his hand still pressing her shoulders against the soft leather seat, keeping her hidden from view.

"Could you pull my skirt down? It's riding up." There was a demon imp that came out every time she came in contact with the huge, taciturn SEAL.

She couldn't help it. Needling him was her favorite sport.

A large, broad hand smoothed her skirt from high on her thigh back to her knees. And he did it . . . slowly. As though he were savoring the act. *She* sure as hell was. She stared up at him in the darkness, aware of the fact that he was apparently unaffected.

"Thanks, I appreciate it." She shifted her legs against his. "Next time I get kidnapped, remind me to wear panties."

His expression tightened, as did the hand on her knee. "Don't fuck with me right now."

"I'm fully dressed, Lieutenant, so 'fucking' with you is the least of your worries at the moment."

He smiled a slow, predatory smile.

"If you don't shut that smart mouth of yours, I'll have to shut it for you."

"How are you going to do that?" she whispered back. Excitement churned inside her as he leaned over her, bringing his face closer, his lips so much closer, making her mouth water.

"By cutting out your tongue. I'll blame it on the terrorists."

She sighed with dejection. "Damn. There goes that tongue ring I was going to invest in."

A rough chuckle sounded from the driver as Macey's eyes narrowed in contemplation.

"Give me trouble, Em, and you'll regret it."

"Give me lip, Macey, and I'll bite it." She snapped her teeth back at him and was rewarded with a flare of lust in his gaze. Unfortunately, the lust came with more than she expected. It came with a wolf's grin and a knowing smirk.

"Be careful, Emerson, because I've been known to bite back."

# Two

EMERSON JENNIFER DELANEY WAS shaking. At least on the inside. She'd be damned if she would let Macey, the big, tough, larger-than-life Navy SEAL she'd always lusted over, see her shake on the outside. She wouldn't let *anyone* see her shake on the outside if she could help it. It wasn't acceptable. Good Navy children had a stiff upper lip and kept their fears to themselves. They weren't whiny babies or wimps, and if they made the mistake of being one in her family, then they learned fast the error of their ways.

So she let herself shake inside. All through the ride, while her legs remained draped over his, his large hand occasionally cupping her knees as he flicked a heated look at her.

Otherwise, he watched the traffic, kept a careful check through the back window, and talked to Nathan Malone in SEAL jargon that Emerson had only halfway learned to translate throughout her life of dealing with Navy SEALs, admirals, and various officers. Even her mother was an officer, as were her aunts on her father's side, various uncles, and cousins. Out of her entire family on her father's side, in three generations, Emerson was the only one to buck tradition and make a life and a career outside that hallowed institution.

So, translating SEAL talk wasn't easy.

She knew they were driving aimlessly around Atlanta to make certain there were no tails. Then, Lieutenant Malone was going to drop them off and report to the admiral. After that, there was something about hiding her in a cave. She hoped that was a joke, because, well, caves had bugs and bats and stuff, and she did not do bugs and bats and stuff.

"All's clear," Macey finally murmured after watching the back window for what seemed like hours. "Take us to the drop-off then head out. Clint will be straggling back into the States around daylight. Catch up with him and let him know what's going on. Kell and Reno are OOC for a few more days."

OOC. Okay, she could handle that one. Out of Country. "Admiral's gonna wanna know your location," Nathan reminded him. His ruined voice was harsh, but there was just a hint, the slightest flavor of Ireland sneaking through. She bet his voice had been a panty-wetter before he was tortured by Sorrell and his associates.

"You don't know," Macey reminded him. "Clint

doesn't know. Until I know we're secure, Nathan, I trust no one. Not even the admiral."

It was too important. Emerson was too important. And the hairs at the nape of his neck tingled at the thought of letting the location out to even the admiral.

Nathan nodded sharply as the inner city streetlights became further apart and the dimmer, more distant lights of the residential areas threw longer, darker shadows into the truck.

"Can I sit up now?" She was tired of laying on her back and staring at Macey or the ceiling. Not that Macey wasn't a fine thing to look at, but he wasn't paying any attention to her, so it made the discomfort a bit more noticeable.

"Not yet." His hand tightened on her knee again and gave her a thrill. She was pathetic, really. Creaming her panties for a shift of fingers against her knee. How low could a woman sink?

"This is uncomfortable, Macey."

"So is death." Clipped and impersonal. She hated that voice.

"Do you believe death is uncomfortable? I'd think you'd be unaware—"

"You're going to be gagged if you don't shut up." He glowered down at her.

Emerson twitched her nose. The imp inside her was shaking in fear and staying quiet wouldn't be easy. If she wasn't talking, goading or taunting, then she was going to start crying. And she really hated crying.

"Here we go." Macey jerked the door open, jumped out and grabbed her legs, pulling her across the leather seat as she jerked up in response.

"Let's go," he ordered as he gripped her waist and set her down on the sidewalk of a less than reputable residential area.

"I don't have shoes," she reminded him.

He began dragging her through a row of scraggly hedges as the pickup pulled away from the curb and drove off.

She was nearly hysterical with fear, well aware of the fact that she was in a bit of trouble. After all, terrorists didn't drag you out of a bed on the spur of the moment unless they had very bad plans for you.

She shuddered at the thought and thanked God Macey was too busy dragging her through someone's backyard to notice.

"We're almost there." His voice was low, smooth, a stroke to her shattered emotions as he led her into the thick overgrowth of a neglected backyard and into the side door of a garage.

"Where are we?" she asked as he let her go and stalked through the darkness.

A second later, flashlight in hand, he moved back to her and took her arm once again.

"Watch your step here." He led her through a maze of rusted vehicle parts before they came to the back door. He pulled aside the panel of an electronic alarm, pulled out the wires and accessed the hidden dual security panel where he punched in the security code, waited a few seconds, and reconnected the wires to the front plate before replacing it.

Dummy security plate, she thought, checking it out as he pulled her in through the door. Unusual and unexpected. Anyone who attempted to access the code, no matter the tools, jammers, or methods, would active an alarm simply by attempting to de-activate it.

The inside of the house was darker than ever, the smell a bit musty, as though it was rarely visited. There was the slide of a door, fresher air as he pulled her into a hallway, then downstairs.

Emerson tried to get her bearings. Behind her she could hear the slide of a door, then something else. A muted hum, a click, and then a burst of lights.

She brought her hand up to shield her eyes, blinking as the lights dimmed marginally.

"Sorry, I left them on full power before leaving last night." Macey stood in the center of what she assumed was the "cave."

She looked around. Across the room were a computer and server terminal, routers, secondary systems, and external hard drives. A metal cabinet held a stack of monitors that blinked up, the images showing the inside of a house. Each room and hallway was displayed and several others covered the darkness outside with infrared and heat-seeking capabilities.

Her gaze slid to Macey as he stalked to the main station, sat down in a chair she would give her eyeteeth for at work, and with his large, broad hands began a delicate series of commands over a straight keyboard.

Emerson eased closer to the command center, her eyes tracking over the electronics, both surveillance and stealth, her brows lifting at the impressive setup.

"Give me a minute to set up security and I'll show you around."

Emerson looked around and took in the small kitchen/eating area tucked into the corner beside the stairs. On the other side was an open living room with a sectional couch, plasma television with satellite reception, and a complete surround-sound speaker system. A few bookshelves. A scarred coffee table and a door that led into another room of some sort. She hoped there was a bathroom somewhere.

"Where are we?" She rubbed her hands over her arms and fought the chill beginning to invade her system.

The clock on the wall swore it was nearly five in the morning; it had felt like days rather than hours since she had been dragged from her apartment and forced into the back of a stinking van.

"The cave," he mumbled, hunched over the keyboard, his fingers working the keys with rapid motions that she would have been impressed by if it weren't for the fact that she was cold, exhausted, and standing on less than certain ground.

"I don't like caves." She bit her lip as she stared around the dark wood walls.

"Stand down, Emerson, I'll be with you in a minute." His voice was clipped again, impatient.

A frown jerked at the corners of her mouth; it had been a long night and she needed some fresh air. . . .

She came to an abrupt stop when the steps met a blank wall. Reaching out, she searched for whatever mechanism opened it. There had to be a mechanism.

"It's electronically controlled and only I have the code."

"Why isn't there a regular door?"

"It's a secured room, Emerson," he told her quietly. "No entry in or out without my command. We're on lockdown until Admiral Holloran and Nathan manage to figure this out and capture the leader of the cell of terrorists that took you from the house tonight. We're going to be roommates for a while, so you might as well come on down here and let me show you around."

"Do you have any idea when that'll happen so I can get my life back?" She watched him, feeling uncertain, off balance. Not frightened, but neither did she feel secure within herself.

"Are you going to whine over this?" He cocked his head to the side and watched her curiously. "Funny, Emerson, I didn't see you as a whiner. Come on, I'll show you the bedroom and bath. You can freshen up and get some rest."

He strode across the huge room toward the door at the far wall. Her lips parted in shock. He was ignoring her, striding away from her as though her questions were the result of a whining personality. She did *not* whine.

Her eyes narrowed to slits. "You're enjoying this, aren't you, Macey?" Each word was precise, hard.

Macey paused at the door, turned and lifted his brow.

"Oh, yeah, Emerson, I'm really enjoying this. Instead of being on the streets searching down terrorists, or covering my buddies' backs, I'm here. With you." His gaze flicked over her body. "Where I get to sit with my thumbs up my ass, deflecting your little daggers, and praying this case breaks before the March family reunion weekend in a few weeks."

She blinked back at him in surprise. "You have family?"

"I wasn't exactly hatched."

"Neither are coyotes, but that doesn't make them domesticated," she shot back sweetly. "Does your family live close?"

"Close enough."

"Just close enough?" She turned and leaned against the wall, watching as he watched her.

"Why do you want to know, Em?"

He was the only one who called her Em. It sounded good, much better, and much more feminine than Emerson. But then, her father had wanted a son, not a daughter. They hadn't been prepared with little girl names when she had been born.

"Maybe I just want to know about you." She leaned her head against the wall, somehow enjoying how he towered over her, the way he watched her with that baffled male confusion.

"No, you don't, you want to make me crazy." His voice roughened as his gaze flicked down her body again. "That's what you're good at. Be careful, it might backfire on you this time. You're damned good at making me crazy, and that should tell you something about this little deal heating up between us. You're not going to walk all over me like you do the admiral or the men you work with."

Her eyes narrowed. "I resent that remark, you know." But she had to admit she did have that habit. "Maybe I just want to find someone who can out-think me. Can you outthink me, Macey?"

"On any low country night that you want to bring on, sweetheart."

That voice: dark, husky, male. It did something to her. It soothed the anger and the fear and it made the hunger hotter, brighter, the need for his touch almost desperate.

His head lowered as Emerson felt the familiar slow burn, the rising mind-numbing need that began to fill her. It was more than arousal, more than hunger, and it went deeper than lust. She knew lust. She had felt it often enough before Macey. No, whatever it was her body decided it wanted from this man, it was unlike anything she had ever wanted from a man before.

"Maybe it would backfire?" She stared at his lips, mesmerized, feeling her lungs struggle for oxygen as adrenaline began to pump hard and heavy through her body. She had to curl her fingers against her side to keep from touching him, had to fight to keep from tasting his lips.

"Do you want to find out?" His lips curled into a smirk.

That smirk capped it.

"No, Macey, I want you to tease me over it," she informed him flippantly before turning away.

She would have walked away if he hadn't grabbed her. Again. If his fingers hadn't curled around her wrist and the next thing she knew her breasts were cushioned against his chest and his eyes were glittering down at her.

That look haunted her dreams. That gleam of lust and awareness that there was something between them that he couldn't fight any more than she could.

The instant his lips touched hers, it was over. She was trying to climb into his body, crawl under his skin as his lips moved to take hers.

God, this was one of the things she had loved about his first kiss. Forget an initiation or discovery. He knew what he wanted, sensed what she wanted, and gave it immediately. His lips settled over hers, his teeth nipping her lips until they parted, and his tongue rushed inside to claim territory that already belonged to him.

One large hand cupped the back of her head, and his arm tightened around her back, arching her to him. The height and breadth of his body, the powerful lean muscles, the confidence in his hold washed over her, filling her with an awareness of feminine weakness.

But fear struck her, hard and fast.

She jerked out of his hold, catching the look of surprise on his face as she stumbled away. She couldn't think. Instinct and reaction surged inside her. Her veins were pounding with the rush of blood that fueled the arousal.

What she just experienced was even more intense than the first kiss. More fiery, harder to control.

As she stared back at him, fighting to make her tongue work, to forget the feel of his against it. He smiled down at her with something akin to tenderness. Surprising, wicked tenderness.

"Gets hot, doesn't it, Em?" he crooned, moving toward her, his head lowered, his eyes dark.

Before she could consider evading him, his hands curved around her upper arms, his hold light, her response to his touch almost violent. His head lowered to her neck, his lips pressing against the throbbing vein pulsing just beneath the skin. The heated caress had her breath catching, her eyelids fluttering with sensual weakness.

"This isn't a very good idea." She licked her dry lips nervously, wondering why it was stronger, why it was hotter than that first kiss a month before, why it made her weaker, made her burn brighter.

He snorted as he raised his head. "No kidding. The last time the admiral caught me groping you I lost rank. Maybe you owe me for that, Emerson.

From lieutenant to junior lieutenant isn't fun and games. I should at least get a taste of what I paid for, don't you think?"

Hurt flashed inside her. "I had nothing to do with that."

He shrugged as she jerked away from him. "The admiral might have ignored that last little infraction if he hadn't caught me devouring your tits. I think that tipped the balance."

Emerson felt the flush burning in her face and the anger blooming in her mind.

"He didn't see anything." She could feel the breath strangling in her throat at the thought of what her godfather had walked in on and the lecture he had given her hours later.

"He didn't have to see." Macey's voice dropped, the arousal that still burned in his eyes brightening as his gaze flickered over her body. "The position of my head was self-explanatory. And if you don't stop pushing me, sweetheart, you're going to find my lips there again, and next time, I won't stop. Now, go shower, crawl into bed, and stop arguing with me. Arguing with you just makes me harder."

It made him harder? It was making her wetter. And if she didn't get out of this secured basement that he called a cave and away from him, then it was going to make her jump feet-first into a relationship that she knew had the potential to break her heart.

He didn't want her, he wanted her body. He didn't want her heart, he just wanted sex. And reminding herself wasn't easy when he was standing there, his jeans straining with his erection, his gaze hot and hungry. She was terribly afraid that reminding herself was going to do very little good.

# FOUR

"COME ON, WE BOTH need to get some rest." Macey forced himself to ignore the hard-on torturing him. He had his pet snake to put away before she went to bed. Drack was his defense. It hated guns, and anyone with the ability to access his cave would no doubt be packing a gun. He didn't think Emerson would appreciate curling up with a full-grown anaconda on her first night here.

Besides, there was something in her eyes that pricked at his heart, that had him releasing her slowly and stepping back. Not exactly fear of him, but there was fear there, uncertainty, innocence. And the look didn't make sense to him.

He knew she'd had lovers before, he'd made it his business to know. He knew her medical history and the fact that she had lost her virginity between the ages of eighteen and nineteen.

She wasn't promiscuous, but he knew she wasn't a prude. Unfortunately, she might be too damned innocent for the likes of him, because the things he wanted to do with her would have had a call girl blushing.

She didn't speak as he turned away and opened the bedroom door. Flipping the lights on, Macey had to clench his teeth against the sight of the huge bed across the room: plenty large enough for two people to play some hellaciously erotic games on.

*Dumb thought*, he told himself, shaking his head as he felt her move into the room cautiously.

Striding to the walk-in closet, he pulled one of his t-shirts from one of the drawers built in beneath the hanging clothes. From another drawer he pulled free a pair of his sister Stacey's cotton leggings. She was always leaving clothes scattered around the upper level of the house.

Moving from the closet he glanced at where Emerson stood in the center of the room, staring around it, resignation filling her face.

She might as well resign herself to it. Other than the bolt hole, this place was locked up tighter than Fort Knox. There was no getting in and no getting out without his help.

"Shower's in here." He moved to the door at the far end of the room, opened it, and flipped the lights on. "Towels and washrags are under the sink, fresh soap, both bar and that shower gel gunk my sister likes, is on the shelf beside the tub. Get whatever you need."

"Now you have a sister, too." She was leaning against the doorframe, looking around the bathroom with hazel eyes that were gleaming a brighter green than before. "Guess you weren't hatched after all, Macey."

"Guess I wasn't," he drawled, his lips quirking as he watched white, sharp little teeth nibble at her lower lip.

She was nervous. He rarely saw Emerson nervous, and had never seen her uncertain, until now. Seeing it in her made him want to kill. It made him wish he was hunting terrorists with Nathan and drawing their blood. It plain pissed him off that Emerson would know so much as a moment of uncertainty or fear.

He watched as she backed out of the doorway and turned to the bedroom again. Her shoulders were stiff, her head held high, and as he moved around her he caught the flicker of indecision on her face. "I want you to promise me you won't try to leave while I'm trying to sleep, Em."

"I am not stupid, Macey."

"I didn't say you were stupid," he assured her. "But you're headstrong as hell. The admiral gave the orders, sweetheart; calling him or trying to run to him isn't going to do anything but endanger your life. And if I have to stand and listen to another bastard strike you, I just might have to lose my temper."

He reached out to run the backs of his fingers over the bruise that had formed on her cheek, remembering the killing rage that had swept through him when he heard the blow.

"It wouldn't do a lot for me, either," she assured

him, pulling away from him as a flush brightened her cheeks and renewed arousal glittered in her eyes.

Oh, she was hot. As hot as he was and just as ready for bedroom aerobics as he was; she was just more cautious.

Macey caught her arm as she turned away from him, holding her steady as her gaze flashed back to his. Wide, wary, her eyes glittered like emeralds and threatened to ensnare him in a web of arousal.

"I told you this wasn't a good idea." Her breath hitched as he curled his arm around her waist and pulled her to his body once more.

He couldn't help it. He needed to feel her breasts against his chest again, needed the taste of her kiss going to his head like potent liquor.

"It's the only idea."

Her lips parted, whether to protest or meet his kiss he wasn't certain, so he took the kiss.

It was late. Weariness was dragging at both of them, but he couldn't help it; one more taste, one more touch, that was all he needed. His head lowered, his lips touching hers gently as he stared into her eyes. He didn't take the kiss this time, he eased into it, eased her into it. He licked at her lips until they parted further. He nipped at the lower curve and felt her ragged breath of response, watched her lashes flutter as her hands clenched on his upper arms.

And he felt that tight clench in his heart again, the one that had warned him years ago that Emerson's touch went deeper than flesh. Deeper than bone.

Macey could tell that she didn't know whether to push him away or to pull him closer to her. Her breathing was harsh, irregular, those temptingly full breasts moving against his chest heavily. He wanted to fill his hands with them, feel her hard little nipples against his tongue again. He wanted to devour her.

"Macey, please . . ." A whisper-soft plea fell from her lips as he licked over them, her eyes dilating, the small ring of green darkening in arousal.

Macey cupped her cheek with one hand, his thumb relishing the feel of satiny flesh dewed with moisture. He could feel her burning, heating up for him.

"I want to touch you, Em." He nipped at her lower lip. "I want to feel you silky and wet." His hand moved from her cheek, down her neck, her shoulder. Going lower, he watched her eyes, her expression, each nuance of emotion that flickered over her face as he gripped the material of her skirt and drew it upward.

She trembled in his arms, a delicate little ripple of response that fanned the flames inside his own body higher. He was burning for her. Touching her was addictive; the more of her soft, sweet flesh that he touched, the more he wanted to touch. The more he needed to touch.

As the material of her skirt cleared her thighs, Macey watched Emerson's lips tremble, part, fight to draw in air.

"Can I touch you, Emerson?" he whispered, his

fingertips running along the elastic band of her panties as they curved around the cheek of her rear.

"Macey . . ." There was protest and hunger, fear and need resonating in the tone.

"Just a little touch," he crooned, keeping his voice soft, cajoling.

Touching her meant everything. Touching her right now was as imperative as breathing.

He moved his hand around her thigh again, sliding his fingertips over the soft damp crotch of her panties.

"Emerson." He groaned her name as his forehead rested against hers. "You're wet."

Her face flushed brighter as her hips jerked, pressing her silk-covered flesh more firmly against his fingers. She wanted, she needed, just as desperately as he did.

He moved his hand higher, slid his fingers into the low band of her panties, and a groan tore from his throat as his fingers feathered over damp curls. Sweet, heated dampness beaded on silky curls, drawing his touch, his hunger, as nothing else could have.

He couldn't stop himself. He had to have more. He wanted to see her face, watch her eyes as he took more. And he did. His fingers slid into the narrow slit, parted sweetly swollen folds, and found the nectar of the gods.

"You're hot." He was burning alive in her heat. "Hot and sweet, Emerson."

Hot and sweet. Emerson stared back at Macey, fighting to breathe, to make sense of the wild sensations tearing through her. She couldn't find the strength to pull away from him this time. She felt weak, senseless, unable to process anything but the pleasure. The feel of his fingers sliding through her pussy, parting the sensitive lips, circling the entrance to her vagina.

She lifted closer, standing on her tiptoes, desperate to encourage his fingers to delve further, to slip inside her, to ease the tight knot of pressure building in her womb.

She needed to orgasm. Oh yeah, she needed that so bad. Just this once, in his arms, to know the culmination of this pleasure.

A finger slipped inside her. Calloused, firm, confident, it parted the tight muscles and sent her senses careening. Flames seared her nerve endings and she felt as though she was burning alive in his embrace, coming apart at each touch.

"This is going to be mine, Emerson," he snarled, his finger thrusting inside her, sending waves of heat and violent pleasure through every cell of her body. "You're going to be mine. You know you are."

"Macey." Her head tipped back as she fought the sensations. "You don't understand . . ."

His fingers moved inside her, fracturing her senses. But nothing could cover the feel of something . . . something smooth twining around her ankle.

She jerked, looked down. Her eyes widened. Terror ripped through her senses as a blood-curdling scream tore from her throat.

Emerson jumped as a pointed head lifted, the flickering tongue touching her bare ankle. Nothing mattered but escape.

She was screaming, screeching, trying to crawl into Macey's body, frantic to evade a bite from the biggest, most terrifying snake she had ever seen in her life.

One minute she was climbing Macey's body, the next he was cursing and they were falling. Was he laughing?

They rolled away from the too-long, too-thick reptile, but it wasn't enough. Emerson scrambled to escape. She felt her knee hit Macey's body, heard his grunt, his strangled curse. Clawing at the wood floor, she finally managed to drag herself up on the bed, panting, certain the snake had followed.

But it was gone. It was gone and Macey was curled up on the floor, his hands cupped between his thighs as something between a laugh and a groan left his throat.

"It's a snake!" She jumped to the floor now that it seemed to be gone and tugged on his arm. "Get up, Macey. It's huge. Oh my God, it's horrible."

He was laughing?

Emerson stared around the room, caught sight of the huge reptilian head peeking from beneath a chair and screamed again. She was back on the bed, staring at the chair in horror.

"Macey, get up. Oh my God. Macey, get up." The head was the size of a platter, and surely its mouth was large enough to swallow an ankle whole.

"Drack." Macey groaned, pulling himself to his knees and giving a faintly wheezing cough.

"Are you crazy?" she screamed, watching the chair carefully. "Where's the gun? Tell me and I'll get it." She was terrified he wasn't going to get off the floor in time.

"Drack." He laughed; he was laughing, for pity's sake.

Emerson stared back at him, fighting the panic, the fear.

"What the hell is Drack? Macey, please get on the bed."

He laughed harder.

"What's so funny?" she cried, still keeping an eye on the chair. "Would you please get in the bed until we can find a gun."

He straightened, bent over laughing again, then restraightened.

"You just terrified my anaconda, Em. And de-manned me all in the same whack. Hell, I bet you're related to Morganna." He laughed again, drawing her shocked gaze as his words began to register.

"You live with a snake?" she wheezed.

"Well, she lives here." He snickered, moved to the far wall, and pressed a lever.

And there it was, the biggest aquarium she had ever seen, ripples of water, foliage and flat stones displayed behind glass as Macey opened the door.

"Come on, Drack, time to go home."

Drack. The snake. The huge snake. The twelve-foot-long, at the very least, reptile slithered from beneath the chair with lazy ease and slid into the aquarium.

Once it was inside, Macey closed and locked the glass door before turning back to her with a grin.

"She watches the place while I'm gone."

Emerson sat down slowly, staring at the well-lit aquarium, certain her heart had stopped and she had died.

"She lives here?"

"Right in there." Macey nodded, chuckling as he pointed over his shoulder at the glass-enclosed cage.

"You should have left me with the terrorists," she said. "It would have saved them the trouble of recapturing me after I leave here. Because no way, no how, not in a million years am I staying here with a snake."

# FIVE

EMERSON'S SLEEP WAS RESTLESS that morning, filled with visions of a naked Macey and an anaconda twined around his body rather than her. Flickering tongue and slitted eyes dared her to touch his gleaming, muscular body.

She shouldn't have been bothered by it. She didn't consider herself innocent; sometimes she considered herself too jaded, too cynical. She had learned years ago that defending her heart wasn't easy. She wasn't like her family. The Navy, preserving honor and tradition, had meant more to them than trying to understand the clumsy, too-emotional child they had found themselves stuck with.

Her parents had been overprotective, and each time she tried to protest the restrictions, her parents had pulled the guilt card. They were trying to protect her. They couldn't work if she was constantly crying for their attention or arguing over their precautions.

So Emerson had kept her mouth shut and endured. Until her graduation from high school, until she left on her own for college and began carving out her own life.

But she had learned that those lessons she had missed as a child held her back now. She succeeded in her career, enjoyed it and the company she worked with. But interaction, allowing herself to be vulnerable, defenseless enough to allow herself to belong anywhere or with anyone, had become impossible.

Now, lying on Macey's big bed, that monster snake curled in the glass tank across the room, she admitted that she had never felt that loss more keenly than she did now.

She could have been curled against him, reveling in a fantasy come to life. Macey had starred in her most erotic dreams for nearly two years. But as she lay there, she realized he had somehow managed to situate himself into her heart.

If he were any other man that she desired, then she could have at least taken the physical pleasure he could give. If she hadn't hungered for more than just his touch, if she didn't crave more than just his kiss or the heated possession of his body.

Shaking her head, she forced herself from the bed, glancing at the bedside table and the clock set there. It said twelve, but if it was noon or midnight, she had no idea. There were no windows in the basement Macey called the cave, no way of telling if it were day or night.

She glanced at the glass cage and watched as the snake, Drack, Macey had called it, flicked its tongue out, her eyes slitted and displaying something akin to curiosity.

It figured Macey would own an anaconda. He couldn't do anything the easy way, could he?

"Well, she's awake," he spoke from behind her, his voice lazy and amused as she straightened the bed.

"Is it noon or midnight?" Whichever it was, she needed coffee before she took someone's head off.

"Noon. Sunny and in the high nineties. Weather guy said it might hit a hundred before evening. Be thankful we're nice and cool down here rather than sweltering out there."

"I like the heat."

"Yeah, I like it hot too," he assured her. "Want me to turn off the AC?"

Emerson shook her head. "Do whatever you want to as long as you have coffee."

"I couldn't live without it. I also have lunch on the stove and ready to eat. You can shower first if you like. Homemade veggie beef soup and bread. It's one of my specialties."

She straightened and stared back at him suspiciously.

"Soup out of a can doesn't constitute homemade just because you fixed it on your own stove, Macey."

She turned and caught the flash of his smile as he leaned against the doorframe, his arms crossed over his broad chest.

"Homemade means from scratch, smartass." He laughed at her. He was the only person she knew who had the nerve to actually laugh at her to her face.

"It's safe to eat?" She moved to the dresser and gathered the shirt and leggings he had left there the night before for her to wear.

"It's not safe to snarl at me when you first get up," he told her, though the vein of laughter hadn't left his voice. "Where did you come by that prickly attitude, Em? It's cute as hell most of the time, but when a man's trying to seduce you, you should soften it some."

"I do, when I want to be seduced." Her return smile was tight, but the tension whipping through her was anything but anger.

She could feel his touch. His lips on her breasts, his fingers between her thighs, and that was a very dangerous thing to remember.

"Go ahead and shower." He shook his head at her, his overly long hair brushing his shoulders as his gaze softened. "I'll put the coffee on and feed you. Maybe you'll be nicer then."

"You like that dream world you live in, don't you?" she asked him, though she had to admit she wanted to smile. It was impossible to stay mad at Macey for long. Irritated, yes. Frustrated most often. But anger wasn't an emotion she could sustain around him when he was trying to be nice.

"Hey, baby, my dream world is what it's all about." He grinned wickedly. "Want to know the part you play?"

"No thank you, I think I can probably figure that one out on my own."

She escaped quickly to the bathroom and the shower with his chuckle lingering on the air behind her. Damn him, he was getting under her skin and she knew it. It was bad enough that she had all these pesky emotions to deal with, but dealing with them while the object of them was around wasn't going to be easy.

She showered quickly, dried her hair, and dressed in her borrowed clothes before striding into the living room and toward the smell of coffee and homemade soup. If the smell was anything to go by, it was going to be delicious.

"On the stove." He was sitting at the computer, a security program working through several formulas and protocols, if the screen she managed to read meant anything.

"We had a bit of action around here early this morning sometime after we arrived," he told her as he pointed to two monitors off to his left.

A replay showed the black van had pulled up in the alley and the four men had exited it. Dressed in overalls, they had entered the backyard and began canvassing the outside of the house.

"Did they manage to get in?" She moved to the control center and watched as Macey flipped through several commands to show each view of the house.

"They didn't get in, but only because they managed to figure out the garage alarm had a false code box." He shrugged at that. "They moved back when they saw that, seemed to be checking for signs of life. They had all their heat-seeking and sound-detection devices." He shook his head as the replay followed the men working around the house with black boxes.

"Military devices?" She leaned in to look closer. "I thought they were still in the R&D phase."

"So did I," he grunted as he rubbed at his jaw and leaned back in his chair. "That means our boys have some military connections we haven't managed to pinpoint."

"Have you tried contacting anyone from the team yet?" she asked, watching one of the men, trying to pierce the shadows cast by the ballcap he had pulled low over his forehead.

He looked familiar. Something about the shape of his jaw and the way he moved made her think she had seen him someplace before.

"I'm not risking it." Macey shook his head. "Any transmissions out of the house could be tracked at this point. I have all Internet and broadband shut down for the time being. Reno knows how to get a message to me, if one is needed. Right now we're just laying low."

The monitors flipped from playback to real-time view, showing the peaceful, tree-shadowed street and kids playing in the yard next door.

"Why do you live here?" She stared at him in bemusement. "I would have figured you for a man with an apartment, not the responsibility of such a large house."

"Emerson, Emerson." He shook his head sadly. "I'm a family-type man, I told you that. The house belongs to my parents, more or less. They moved out to the farm with the grandfolks a few years back and I watch after it. I'm not an apartment sort of guy. Too many restrictions."

"Too many nosy neighbors?"

"You haven't lived on a residential block, have you, sweetheart?" He snorted. "Try block parties, someone knocking at the door at midnight to borrow a tool or to stop and chat. Old guys giving you women advice and old ladies warning you not to listen to them. Trust me, an apartment would be a hell of a lot more private."

By the tone of his voice, he didn't seem to mind the advice or the midnight visits. That should have surprised her more, she realized; the fact that it didn't worried her.

"What about you?" He swiveled around in his chair as she moved to the kitchen and the smell of coffee. "Why an apartment over a house?"

She lifted her shoulders in a shrug. "Too much room for just one person. I wanted something smaller." Too many open rooms to wander through alone would have driven her crazy, made the loneliness sharper.

She didn't glance back at him; she couldn't. Macey would see things she knew were better kept hidden, both for her peace of mind and for the state of her heart.

A heart that was rapidly beating out of control.

She hadn't missed the sexual wickedness blazing in his eyes when he had stared at her moments before. She could feel it now, his gaze roaming over her back, her butt as she fixed her coffee. She would eat later, but for now, she needed a clear head to deal with Macey.

"You don't seem to return home to Virginia a lot," he commented as he leaned back in his chair and watched her quizzically. "The admiral seemed a little put out that your parents hadn't seen you for a while."

She took her coffee to the small round table and stared back at him resentfully. She didn't want to discuss her family, but she could see the determination in his face.

"Why would the admiral mention my family?"

"He had a hard time contacting them when you were taken by those French terrorists."

"They have a life." She sipped at her coffee and tried to ignore the hurt.

"They also have a daughter," he said tightly.

"A daughter who, as you said, rarely returns home. Look, Macey, we don't have family reunions; sometimes we manage to catch dinner together if I'm there on business or they're here to see the admiral about something. We aren't tied at the hip."

"You don't have to be tied at the hip to be a family," he pointed out. "You don't seem like the type of woman who would distance herself like that from family. You're close to the admiral, but not your mom and dad."

Mother and father, not mom and dad. She shook her head.

"This is really none of your business."

"I've met your parents," he said.

Emerson stared back at him directly, keeping her gaze cool. She didn't want to hear this, but she had a feeling a family-minded person like Macey would have to see her actions in a less than complimentary light.

"They're cold as hell." He sighed. "It's hard to imagine you growing up with them. Tell me they at least loved you."

"They loved me." In their own way. Bemused, irritated, often uncertain what to do with her, but they had loved her.

His expression tightened, then seemed to clear as curiosity took over. "What was the one thing you always wanted as a child and didn't get?"

The shift in the conversation threw her off balance, had her answering before she thought.

"A treehouse." Regret shimmered in her voice because she couldn't stop it. "I wanted a treehouse."

"Your parents owned a fifty-acre estate and you didn't have a treehouse?"

"Everything had its place." Except her. She had never figured out where her place was there. "A treehouse didn't fit into the scheme of things."

"Everyone needs a treehouse," he said softly, rising from his chair and moving to her.

Before she could move or avoid him, he was by

her chair, his hand sliding into her hair, his lips stealing a quick kiss. "Don't worry, Em, one of these days, I'll give you a treehouse."

Sure he would. She shook her head and smiled at the thought as he released her and moved to get a cup of coffee for himself. She knew and understood promises and how easily they could be broken. Not just for children. She could have survived the broken promises as a child, gotten over them, gone on. But she had learned as an adult as well how easily even the most sincere promises were broken.

"I'll settle for the ability to return to my apartment. Do that for me, Macey, and you'll have my eternal gratitude."

"That and more," he stated, moving back through the kitchen to his computer. "I promise you, Emerson, I'm going to have that and more."

# FIVE

HE WAS FALLING FOR her. Three days later Macey sat hunched over his computer keyboard and tried to make sense of his own tangled emotions.

He knew he cared too much for her; hell, he had known that for the past two years. He dreamed about her, fantasized about her, and for the past two years hadn't managed to find a single woman he wanted to fuck because none of them were Emerson.

The problem was, he didn't just want to fuck her. He wanted to give her treehouses.

And now he wondered: who would take Drack? That was sad. He'd had Drack since he was a boy. Hell, he loved that cold-hearted reptile and would have laughed at the idea of giving him up because a woman was scared of him. But instead of laughing, his first instinct was to find Drack a home, because his heart, his soul warned him that an anaconda had no place within a family.

Family.

Geeze, the admiral would put a bullet between his eyes if he even suspected what Macey was thinking, wouldn't he? Or had he already suspected it?

And God forbid if Emerson should suspect. But the fact was, she belonged to him. Didn't matter what the admiral thought about it, didn't matter the price to be paid. Though he somehow suspected the admiral was a step ahead of him here.

Emerson fit him, and he was going to make damned sure she understood that he fit her too, before this was over.

And for the time being he was going to thank God that the admiral couldn't get ahold of him.

Complete communications blackout meant no messages transmitted to or from the team, Admiral Holloran, favorite friends, family, or associates of the dark and shadowed variety.

The blackout meant freedom from the admiral. He wasn't about to restrict his own freedoms, not when he needed information and he knew damned certain he was secure. And the information he was after pertained to the case; at least that's what he told himself. He had no intentions of letting anyone know he was checking out Emerson. Especially not Emerson herself.

He turned his head toward the bedroom door again, smirked, and pulled up her FBI file. Hell, who could have guessed Miss Goody Two-Shoes had an FBI file? My my my.

Picture. Stats. Hmm. No bra size, but he could guess that one.

A nice Macey handful. He looked at his hand, curled it just right, and felt his palm itch at the remembered feel of silky flesh.

Whew. Blowing out a hard breath, he shook his head and went back to the computer screen while keeping a careful ear out for the opening of the bedroom door.

Okay, FBI file. She even had a low-level security clearance. He scratched at his jaw, his eyebrows lifting as he scrolled down the screen and scanned the information. She worked for Diasonis, he knew that. The high-level programming, analysis, computer design and integrations firm was a favorite with the Bureau.

He knew her college degree was in communications, design, and integration. As he read, he pursed his lips in surprise. She was good. She'd designed several integrated programs the Bureau was currently using. Nothing compared to those on his own personal setup, but he liked to think he had equipment the Bureau couldn't touch.

He backed out of the Bureau's files before heading into Diasonis. That was a little harder. The Bureau's system was well known to him, its back doors as familiar to him as his own. Diasonis was a little more complicated.

He was working his way through the first pass when he heard the door. Damn. He backed out carefully, his fingers moving quickly over the keyboard as he exited the system, not that he'd managed to get in far, and cleared the program as she stepped into the living area.

"There's chili on the stove." He turned, tilted his head to the stove, and reactivated the virtual war game he had standing ready.

She glanced at the monitor and moved to the stove. "What time is it?"

"Nearly eight in the evening. You slept a long time, Em. Feeling rested?" He moved his player around a tree, collected a rocket launcher, and blew a tank to hell and back. A thousand points and no sound behind him.

He jerked his head around to take a quick look, and froze.

He blinked, eye level with breasts he dreamed about, covered in nothing but one of his t-shirts. She hadn't been close to him in forty-eight hours. She had maintained distance, kept a wary eye on him, and ignored most of his questions and attempts at conversation.

She had been hiding, if only inside herself, and he knew it. For the time being, he had allowed her to hide. The nice thing about his cave was the fact that sooner or later she was going to have to acknowledge him, him and the sexual tension, not to mention the emotional tension rising between them.

Two years he had waited, and she knew it. Two years too long.

"You're losing your game."

He lifted his gaze to her face, his eyes meeting her narrowed ones.

"My breasts aren't part of your game, Macey. You just lost."

A distant virtual explosion sounded behind him as she moved away. Macey sighed dejectedly and turned back to the computer. Oh well, the game was just there to hide his activities, not to actually win. He'd already beaten that sucker months ago anyway.

He swiveled around in his chair to watch as she moved across the room to the kitchenette. She was wearing one of his t-shirts and a pair of his sister's cotton sleep leggings and socks. Damn, she looked too young to be here, too young for the thoughts running through his brain.

He watched her ass as she reached up into a cabinet and pulled out a bowl. His teeth clenched in an effort to maintain control as the twin cheeks bunched and rippled when she moved back to the stove and filled the bowl with chili.

When she turned, his gaze was lifted innocently to her face as he fought every male instinct to drop his eyes to those pretty unbound breasts again.

SHE COULD HAVE HIM, a little voice reminded Emerson. How many times over the past two years had he let her know just how easily she could have him?

"So when can I get out of here and back to my life? Any news yet?"

"What's the hurry? Do you have someone besides the admiral waiting for you on the outside?"

She didn't like the tone of his voice, didn't like the friendliness in it, or the silent invitation to spill her guts to him. She had no secrets; she had no reason to feel sorry for herself.

"I have a full life." She shrugged easily.

"And an empty bed." His voice lowered, the black velvet tone stroking over her senses as he moved toward her.

"My bed is none of your business, Macey. When I want a man there, I have no trouble filling it."

And how many times had she had done that? Too few. And they had been gone too quickly.

"Why are you so defensive with me, Em?" he asked then, his tone too soft, too knowing, too sexy. "You snap and snipe at me as though I've done something to hurt you. If I have, I'd be more than willing to kiss it and make it better."

He was teasing. That playful, come-hither male sexiness that she found so hard to resist. That she had to resist. Otherwise, there would be no way she could hide the feelings she had for him. Feelings that went beyond scratching a little sexual itch while they were confined together.

"If I'm so hard to be around, why did you take this job?" she asked.

"Why did I take this assignment?" He leaned close, his lips curving into a smile, his dark eyes gleaming with sexual intent. "I took this job to finally get into your pants, Em. To get you under me, around me, and to get so deep inside you that the last thing you think about is pushing me away. That's why I let your godfather maneuver me like the good little SEAL I am. Now, answer my question. Why, Emerson Delaney, do you try to push me away every damned time I get close enough to do that?"

"I don't know, Macey," she snarled. "Maybe I don't want to join the Macey's Castoff's club. Sorry, Lieutenant, but being part of the crowd never appealed to me, and being a part of your crowd appeals even less. So why don't you stop trying to seduce me, get on your handy-dandy made-for-spying computer and find me a way out of this. Otherwise, we're going to end this little fiasco as enemies, rather than the fragile friendship I thought we had managed to maintain."

His brows lifted, amusement filling his expression.

"Do you let all your friends suck your hard little nipples in your godfather's study, Em? If you do, I think I'm going to need to spank you."

Flames raced through her body. Warning alarms were clanging through her head. But when his head lowered, his hand sliding into her hair to hold her still, feeling his lips on hers again, she was lost. Lost in the touch of a man she knew she could never hold, and unwilling to break free, because nothing, at no time in her life, had ever felt as right as Macey's kiss. Macey's touch. As belonging to Macey, if only for this moment.

# SIX

HE WASN'T STOPPING THIS time.

Macey eased over the back of the couch, keeping his lips on Emerson's, tasting the wild passion and honeyed sweetness of her kiss, her tongue, letting himself become trapped in her pleasure and his own.

This was the snare, and he knew it. A pleasure unlike any other that he had known in his life. For the first time, he could feel his lover's pleasure as well as his own, and he was trapped within it. He wasn't touching, stroking, giving pleasure in the hopes of having that pleasure returned. Hell no. Hearing her pleasure, feeling her tremble with it, the sound of it echoing in her shaking moan, that was pleasure.

He stroked his tongue over Emerson's lips, felt them tremble as he took another short, drugging kiss. He let his hands move over her shoulders as he tried to sate himself with the sweetness of her lips and her inquisitive little tongue.

But there was no sating himself and he knew it. Had known it since that first kiss.

"Come here, Em." He lowered her to the couch as her velvety hazel green eyes opened and she stared back at him with pleasure.

"Macey." She licked her lips, and he followed suit. He let his tongue run over them before taking another hard, quick taste of her.

"Don't think, baby," he whispered. "Let me touch you. Have you. Don't you know I'd beg for just another taste?"

"Macey." She blinked drowsily, sensually, her hands fluttering to his shoulders. He watched the hunger overcome the hesitancy in her eyes. "Why?"

"Because I can't fight it any longer."

"But you'll break my heart." He heard her breath hitch as his lips became distracted by the long, slim line of her neck. "You know you're going to break my heart."

He jerked his head up, his eyes narrowing on hers. "I take care of what's mine, Emerson. Every part of it. And whether you end up liking it or not, sweetheart, you're mine."

Her arms curved around his neck, and he set out to mark his territory. The primal need to possess had him by the balls now, and he had a feeling it wasn't going to release him anytime soon.

As his hand flattened beneath her shirt on the bare flesh of her stomach, a moan slipped past Emerson's lips into the kiss he was stealing from her soul. Calloused and warm, the tips of his fingers stroking her flesh had her nerve endings howling in pleasure.

They strained together, hips arching, bearing down, the thick length of his cock pressed against her saturated core as her hands curved around his back, her nails digging into the material of his shirt.

It wasn't enough, she needed to touch his flesh, needed to feel it against her. She tore at the cloth, tugging it upward to his shoulders, revealing the tough skin and hard muscles of his back. Pleasure whipped through her palms as she stroked his flesh and felt him tense tighter against her.

"Get naked," he growled, tearing his lips from hers, lifting just enough to jerk his shirt from his body, then her shirt followed. A dark, almost black patch of chest hair arrowed along his hard abs and into the band of his jeans.

Her hands tore at the belt cinching his waist, pulling it free as his hands worked on the metal snap and zipper.

She tugged at the material, pulling it over his hips with one hand as she parted the front edges, pulled the snug boxer briefs from the thick length of flesh it covered and felt her mouth go dry.

His cock was so hard and the skin stretched so tight it appeared painful. Heavy veins throbbed in hungry demand and the wide, dark crest pulsed with a heartbeat all its own, pushing a silky pearlescent bead of pre-cum from the narrow slit.

"Oh God, Macey," she whispered, desperation coloring her voice as she held the heavy flesh, stroking it, her pussy clenching at the thought of accommodating it.

She lifted her eyes along his tight abs, his heaving chest, to meet his dark eyes. He watched her as well, his expression tight, honed with hungry lust as she stroked the length of his erection.

"I want to taste you," she whispered. "All of you."

"For God's sake, hurry," he groaned. "If I don't touch you, taste more of you, it might kill me."

She wanted to smile at that. Had any man ever been so desperate to touch her? She knew there hadn't been.

She sat up on the couch, her legs between his spread thighs. She lowered her head, the fingers of both hands curling around the heavy shaft as she licked the little bead of creamy liquid from the head of his cock.

The savage groan that tore from his throat shocked her, excited her. Hands slid into her hair roughly, bunching it and clenching in the strands.

Fiery bursts of heat spread through her scalp. Her mouth opened, covered the swollen head, and sucked it in. She gloried in the strangled curse that fell from his lips. Her tongue swiped over the tight flesh, curled around it and rubbed the underside, that sensitive little area just beneath the head.

"Emerson, darlin'." His voice was rough, thick and heavy with pleasure.

He was close to the edge. She could tell by the tight length of his cock, the throb of blood beneath the flesh. The fingers of one hand cupped his balls, feeling the taut sac ripple beneath her touch.

She sucked at him firmly, finding more pleasure in the act than she ever had before. He tasted male, clean and strong, vibrant and aroused. The taste could become addictive.

As she sucked, her gaze lifted to his again. A moan caught in her chest as his eyes met hers. His lips, so sensually curved, were parted, his strong, white teeth clenched tight.

"So beautiful," he groaned hoarsely. "Keep looking at me, Em. God, your eyes are beautiful. Your face. So beautiful. Your mouth so hot, so sweet."

Her mouth was filled with his flesh, with the taste of him, the heat of him.

"Do you know what you do to me, watching me like that? Sucking my dick and staring at me as though you were starving for the taste of me?"

She felt her face flush, watching the satisfaction that filled his eyes.

"Such a pretty blush. Such a wicked little mouth."

He was fucking that mouth with slow, easy strokes. He wasn't digging in or trying to ram it down her throat. He wasn't in a hurry to release. He was letting her enjoy, letting her taste, stroke.

Pleasure. It was in her eyes. She was drowning in her own pleasure right now, finding joy in touching him, even knowing she might not know the same consideration.

*   *   *

LOVE HER HEART, HE was going to eat her alive. He was going to have her screaming in orgasm, have her begging to be fucked, to be taken, possessed before the night was over. He'd take that look out of her eyes once and for all.

He watched the head of his cock disappear into her mouth once more, bit back a curse as her mouth surrounded it, her tongue stroked it, and she sucked at it with heated hunger. Her moan was another caress, dark, rippling over the sensitive flesh and drawing his balls tighter with the need to come.

That wasn't happening. Not yet. Not nearly. First, he'd devour that sweet, sexy little body, those lush, luscious breasts. Oh yeah, he was going to gorge himself on the taste of her breasts and her sweet cherry-red nipples.

"Enough, baby." He moved to draw back.

Panic flared in her eyes; her fingers tightened on the shaft of his dick and had him grimacing with the pleasure-pain of it.

"Come here, Em." He reached down, loosened her hands and pressed her back to the couch. "It's okay, sweetheart. I just want to touch you. Don't you know how much I need to do that? Just a few minutes, that's all."

Just for the rest of his fucking life. God, the look in her eyes was killing him. Hope mixed with fear. Not the fear of physical pain, but the fear of loss. He knew that fear himself, knew how it hurt to wake up and realize that love had just been a fantasy.

Long ago, far away, when youth thought it was wise and all-knowing.

He knew better now. He knew the risk he was taking, the rewards and the possible consequences, just as he knew that he would always regret letting her slip out of his grasp if he didn't try to find her heart.

"Do you know how beautiful you are, Em?" He leaned forward, his lips feathering over hers as he touched the firm, rounded globes he dreamed about.

And he was lost. Simply lost. Oh, hell yes. Clearly more than a handful, topped with cherry-red, spike-hard little nipples and covered with a sprinkling of freckles.

"Damn, Em. You have paradise right here." He cupped the generous mounds, his thumbs flicking over the tight nipples. When an involuntary moan left her lips, he swore the sound went straight to his cock, wrapped around it and stroked.

# SEVEN

EMERSON WATCHED IN A daze as Macey's head lowered, his tongue peeking out to curl around her hard nipple. She swore she nearly orgasmed the moment it touched her.

Her hips jerked against his, rubbing the hard wedge of his cock against her core as one of his hands caught her wrists and held them over her head.

"Easy, baby," he groaned as she writhed beneath him. "Let me have you, Emerson. Just like this."

Their moans mingled as he drew her into his mouth and sucked, devoured. His teeth scraped, his tongue lashed, and heated, fiery whips of sensation wrapped around her clit. The tiny bud became more swollen, more sensitive, throbbed and threatened to explode in orgasm.

"Macey, I can't stand . . ." A desperate cry left her throat as the suckling changed, became slower, firmer, his tongue licking her nipple with relish rather than desperation.

She needed to hold back, but he wouldn't give her the chance.

And it was more destructive. So destructive that she was only barely aware of his free hand pushing at his jeans, removing them, then pulling the sweatpants from her hips and pushing them down her thighs before she kicked them from her legs.

She didn't care. She knew what was coming, knew and ached for it.

"You make me crazy," he groaned, releasing her wrists to cup her breasts, to kiss each nipple and suck it into his mouth in turn until the sensations were ripping through her body, the heat building in her womb and threatening to explode.

"Oh God. Macey. More. More." She forced her eyes open, to stare into the near black of his. His cock pressed against the folds of flesh between her thighs and throbbed against her clit.

"Not yet," he groaned. "Not yet, baby. Let me feel this. Let's see how good it can feel."

"I can't stand more," she protested weakly. She could feel her wetness coating his erection as she tried to move against him, to force him to finish it before he chained her body to his forever.

"God, you taste sweet," he muttered, his lips leaving her breasts, stroking down her stomach, parting her thighs. She watched as he lowered his head to the damp curls between her thighs. "Do you taste sweeter here?"

He didn't give her time to protest. Confident, hungry, his lips lowered to her clit, his tongue stroked it, and his groan, when it vibrated against her flesh, sent her senses reeling.

Her thighs fell further open, her hips lifted to him, and Emerson knew nothing had ever felt so good. He knew his way around a woman's body. Knew where to lick, where to stroke, how to flick his tongue against her narrow opening. How to make her scream and make her beg for him to take her.

She saw a smile flash across his face, sexy, certain, before his lips covered her clit and he sucked it with slow, torturous draws of his mouth as his tongue flickered around it. Never in the right spot long enough, just enough to tease, to torment, to cause her to writhe and to plead but never enough to throw her over the edge.

"Macey, it's too much," she cried out, her fingers twining in his hair, holding him to her flesh rather than pulling him away as she should have been. "I can't stand it."

"Not enough," he growled before he licked. "So sweet and hot, Emerson. I need more of you."

"Please," she panted. "I need you now. I can't wait."

"Just a few more minutes, baby," he crooned before licking lower.

His hands cupped her ass, lifted her, and a low, ragged cry filled the air as he buried his tongue in her pussy.

Emerson felt herself unraveling. Everything she had held safe inside her came loose and streamed toward him. She had managed to keep her heart sheltered through the flirty confrontations that were more a result of sexual tension than actual enmity. But this, she couldn't hold herself distant from this, from a pleasure that unlocked every shield she had placed around her emotions.

As his tongue thrust inside her, his groan vibrating against hidden tissue, she felt the explosion building inside her tighten further.

She couldn't fight it. She arched to him, begging, pleading, pulling at his hair until he loosened her hands and eased them up to her breasts.

"Touch them for me," he whispered as he lifted himself between her thighs and curled her fingers around her breasts. "Pleasure them for me, Emerson. Let me watch while I take you."

She cupped the heavy flesh, her fingers stroking over her nipples as Macey quickly tore at the foil wrapper of the condom he had pulled from his jeans.

Sheathed, his hands gripped her hips, pulling her closer as he nudged the broad head of his cock against the slick entrance to her pussy.

"Don't stop, baby, let me watch you play with your pretty breasts while I take you."

The hard crest wedged inside her, stretching her, sending rivulets of burning pleasure radiating from the slight penetration.

"Ah, that's a good girl," he whispered, his voice heavy, his breathing as labored as her own. "So pretty, Em. So damned pretty."

So erotic. Emerson stared back at him, working

her nipples with her fingers, feeling the alternating sensations building inside her, burning through her nerve endings.

It was sexy, it was wicked, tempting him even as he worked the thick length of his erection inside her.

"Macey. It's so good." Her eyes closed, her fingers tightened on her nipples. It was too good, too intense, too much pleasure.

"So sweet." His voice was rough as he worked himself deeper. "So sweet and tight. Hell, Em. You're killing me."

He pressed to the hilt. The head of his erection throbbed inside her, heated and heavy, iron hard, spiking the heat burning beneath her flesh now. She felt her womb clench and ripple. Her clit, pressed solidly against his pelvis, throbbed on the brink of release.

"Macey." Trembling, she fought for the orgasm just out of reach.

"You make me lose my control," he breathed out roughly. "God, Em, I want this to be good for you. So damned good for you."

Shock shattered her. Had anyone ever cared if it was good for her? If she needed to come, or if she felt the same pleasure they did?

"It's good. So good." It was better than anything she had ever known.

His eyes narrowed on her then. "Oh baby, it's about to get so much better."

She didn't think it could get better until he began to move. She expected him to take her hard and

fast, to rush to the finish line and his own release.
But Macey was a sensual demon. She should have
known he liked to play, liked to draw the pleasure
out. He had a lazy drawl, a patient way of moving,
and the sleepy sensuality in his gaze should have
warned her.

"Lift your breasts to me, Emerson," he growled.
"Lift those pretty nipples for me."

She cupped her breasts and offered the hard sensitive points to him, then screamed out her pleasure
as his lips surrounded one tight peak.

It wasn't just the hard, heated suction of his
mouth, but the thrusts of his cock, the rasp of
his pelvis against her clit. It combined to push her
higher, but held her back just enough to keep
her locked to earth rather than flying in release.

"Not yet," he bit out, moving from one nipple to
the other. "Not yet, baby. Feel good. Feel so fucking good for me."

"It's too much," she cried, trying to push past
that final barrier.

"It's not enough. Not yet."

She released her breasts to grab onto his shoulders. The sensations were too much, too violent, too
much pleasure. But it didn't stop him. He cupped
them himself, his mouth devouring first one then the
other as he began to stroke his cock inside her in a
smooth, controlled rhythm.

Each thrust, each draw of his mouth stole another piece of her mind until she was nothing more
than a creature of his pleasure. His pleasure, her

pleasure. It whipped through her, broke through barriers she hadn't known she'd erected against him and had her fighting for release, fighting him for her release.

His hoarse chuckle pushed her higher. The slam of his hips as she writhed against him, then his hard hands gripping her hips, his lips latching hungrily to her nipple and his thrusts increasing.

That was what she needed. She lifted to him, her gaze filmy. Ecstasy washed through her veins, built and burned until she was screaming his name, screaming and exploding beneath him in a cataclysm of pleasure that ripped through her body.

She heard his shattered male cry, felt him tense and shudder as her arms tightened around his shoulders and the pleasure burned through her. Like lava. Like white-hot electricity shot straight to her soul.

# EIGHT

SHE WAS IN LOVE with him. She may have denied it before the mind-blowing sex, but hours later, curled against him in his bed, exhausted and sated, she couldn't ignore it any longer.

Letting him go was going to bite. Watching him walk away, that careless smile on his face, would break her heart.

"This should be over in time for the March-Illison-Beckinmore family reunion." Amusement laced his voice. "The biggest damned get-together in the state of Georgia. We hold it on Grandpa's farm further south every year. And every year most of the men walk away with bruises from a fight or two, and the women walk away irritated and grumbling because they fought again. And everyone agrees it's the best year we've ever had."

Her head was pillowed on his chest as he spoke, though a frown edged her brow as he spoke of it.

"Sounds like a big family." She had no idea what

a big family constituted. There were no family reunions in her family, no get-togethers outside the
occasional dinner with her parents and godfather.

"One of the biggest. Over three hundred last
year." His hand smoothed down her hair, her back.
"Tents and RVs crowd the place for a full week,
and the main farmhouse is packed with sleeping
bags and overnight mattresses. Grandma March
swears every year she's canceling the next one, but
come June, she's the one making the calls and or-
ganizing it. The woman is seventy and runs around
the place like a woman half her age. She amazes
me."

"Sounds like an organizational nightmare." She
could respect someone's ability to pull it together,
but knew it had to be a pain. She just had no idea
why Macey was telling her about it.

"Every morning for a week we pile outside for a
dawn breakfast, cooked over every barbecue grill,
gas grill, and fire ring on the place. Scrambled eggs,
biscuits, gravy, sausage and bacon are heaped on
picnic tables and everyone eats like they're starving.
For lunch the tables are piled with sandwich fixin's
and pulled pork barbecue, and for dinner, good God,
fresh catfish, steaks, burgers and hot dogs. It's like a
camp for the insane." But she could hear his love for
it in his voice.

She just couldn't imagine Macey with a family
that size. She couldn't imagine anyone with a family that size.

"How do you keep everyone straight?" she asked,

confused. "Over three hundred people? That sounds more like a convention than any kind of reunion."

"It resembles one sometimes too," he chuckled. Through it all his hands stroked over her hair, her arms, her back. They were never still, always touching her.

Was it normal for him, she wondered, to want to cuddle after sex? He must be the only guy in existence who did, because it was the first time she had ever experienced it.

Hesitantly, she let the hand that lay on his chest move, to stroke over the silky hairs that grew there and enjoy the feel of them against her palm.

She hadn't imagined how much she would love his tough, hard body. The barbed wire tattoo around his left bicep, the scar on his thigh, the packed, lean muscle. Just laying against him turned her on and made her want to ignore the little aches and pains in her body and take another taste of him.

It wasn't just his body she loved, though, and that's what frightened her.

"You could go with me, you know."

Her thoughts slammed to a halt and her head jerked up. Her hand paused in the middle of the hard abdomen she had been stroking, growing ever closer to the erection stretching from between his thighs.

"Excuse me?"

"I said you could go to the family reunion with me." His eyes narrowed on her. "You'd have fun."

"I'm not part of the family."

"You're mine. That makes you family."

Emerson felt everything inside her slow to a quick stop as time seemed to take on a heavy, sluggish quality. She stared into his eyes, seeing the determination, possessiveness, and total resolve in his eyes.

"You know better than that, Macey." She had to force herself to breathe, to push back the need to believe.

"Do I, Em?"

"You should." She eased from him, wrapping a sheet around her body and moving for the doorway. "Don't make promises you can't keep. Not now. I'm not a starry-eyed teenager that needs a proposal and professions of love to excuse a little sex. You're off the hook. I won't cry on the admiral's shoulder or accuse you of taking advantage of me. So do us both a favor and don't make more out of it than what it was."

She needed her clothes, fast. She needed to shower, to wash the scent of his body from hers and get dressed.

"Do you really think I'm going to just walk away from you, Em? For any reason?" Quiet understanding. It was in his voice, in his eyes as he stood up and walked over to her. "Did you think a one-night stand was all I wanted?"

"What else am I supposed to think?" Her heart was racing in her chest, her mouth dry with a sense of panic now. "You're not exactly known for your monogamous lifestyle, Macey."

"And you still went to bed with me?" He tilted

his head, his gaze gentle as he smoothed his hands over her bare shoulders. "Why did you do that, Emerson?"

"I wanted you."

"Do you just go to bed with every man you want, Em?"

*No.* She stared up at him, mesmerized by the softness underlying the steel in his gaze. He was a SEAL; she knew what that meant. Filled with purpose. Determined. Slick. He knew how to get what he wanted and he didn't stop until he got it.

Emerson licked at her lips with trepidation. She could feel a trap, she just couldn't figure out where that trap lay.

"I don't sleep around." She tried to pull away from him and put distance between them.

Macey wasn't having it. His hands held her close to him, the warmth of his body enfolding her, making it harder to think, harder to resist.

"Then why a one-night stand with me? What made me so special?"

# NINE

MACEY FELT HIS HEART melt, right there in the underground living room. His gaze locked with Emerson's, seeing the conflicting emotions in her eyes that shadowed the rest of her features. Panic, fear, hope, and hunger. Not sexual hunger, though that was there as well, but a hunger for more. A hunger to see where the emotions building between them would go.

He knew where they would go. He knew that within the year he'd have his ring on her finger and her soul melded with his.

But he swore he could spank her for being so damned stubborn, so unaware of her own fierce heart, and so frightened of her own emotions.

"You're not answering me, Em," he pointed out, making certain he kept his hands on her. "If you don't have one-night stands, what made me so special?"

"You don't understand. It's not like that."

"Then what's it like, sweetheart?" He lowered his head, touched her lips, kept his eyes on hers. "I love you, Emerson. Do you really expect me to walk away now that I've found the woman I've searched for my entire adult life?"

He loved her? How could he love her? She was gawky, accident-prone, and she didn't know how to love. She would mess it up. Just by being her, she would exasperate him, frustrate him, until he didn't love her any longer.

"You're wrong." Her heart was racing in her chest, making it hard to breathe. "It's just sex. It's always just sex with you. Everyone says it is. All your lovers—" She shut up, her hand clamping over her mouth as a wicked smile bloomed across his lips.

"You bothered to check me out with old lovers? I'm impressed, Emerson. I really am. Tell me, how close were you to clawing their eyes out?"

So close it had terrified her each time. But she wasn't about to admit it. "You're crazy."

"I'd hate to run into one of your past lovers." He was stalking her now, drawing closer. "I know who each one of them is, where they live, where they work, and what could destroy them. If I had to meet one of them, I'd break their bones."

Her eyes widened. He couldn't be serious. It had to be a game.

"Macey." She held one hand out as he drew closer and she blinked back her own tears. "Don't. Please. I can't handle this."

"You don't have a choice, Em. You have to face it,

and you have to handle it. Because you're going to have to look me in the eye and tell me you feel nothing for me to stop this. Can you do that? Can you tell me that all you wanted was a one-night stand?"

Her lips parted, the need to tell him just that, to take the escape he was offering. But she was staring in his eyes, saw the pain in them, and the hope.

"Why are you doing this to me?" Her hands fisted in the sheet as her control broke. Years of control, the determination to never cry or ask for love again.

Her parents had always given her that vague pitying look whenever she cried, whenever she asked for hugs as a child. As though they weren't quite certain what to do with her.

"Because I won't watch you run away from me." He moved too quickly for her to avoid, pulling her into his arms before she could retreat further.

"Put your arms around me, Em." He lowered his lips to her ear as he held her against his chest. "Hold onto me. Let me hold onto you. Don't you know, when you're in my arms, I finally feel like I belong to one person rather than just having parts of me allotted out to family, friends and the Navy? When I hold you, Em, I'm whole."

"Don't do this to me," she whispered against his chest, and wrapped her arms desperately around his neck, terrified of falling.

She was strong on her own, she knew how to do that. She knew how to be alone. She didn't know how to be a part of a couple, she had proved that.

"What am I doing to you, baby?"

"You're making me weak, Macey." Tears slipped from beneath her lashes. "Don't make me weak. I won't survive when you walk away."

"I won't walk away, Emerson." He leaned back, one hand threading through her hair to draw her head back, allowing him to stare into her eyes. "Don't you know that about me? I never walk away."

She did know that about him. Everyone knew Macey was stubborn, hard-headed, and he didn't back down.

"Why? Why do you love me?"

His lips quirked. "Why do you love me?"

Because he was funny, flirty, strong and certain. Because looking at him made her soul ache and her heart hope. But she didn't say that; she couldn't say that.

"I love you, Em, simply because you're you, and you belong to me. Your heart belongs to me. I want your kisses and your touches, your laughter and your fantasies to belong to me."

They had belonged to him for years.

"Give us a chance, Em." He touched her cheek with the tips of his fingers, brushed her lips with his thumb. "Just a chance for more than a one-night stand. Can you do that?"

She would give him her life if he needed it.

"I don't know how to do this." She swallowed, the movement difficult with the emotions clogging her throat.

His smile was rough, rugged, and filled with sensual, wicked certainty.

"We'll learn together. Learn with me, Emerson. God, baby, learn with me."

The kiss took her by surprise, as did the roiling emotions that fired in his eyes a second before he took her lips. It was fiery, demanding, hungry. So hungry it seemed to feed her own hunger, to stoke it with ruthless licks, rough nips and pure demand.

The sheet fell away from her body and within seconds they were back in bed.

# TEN

DRACK WAS AN UNFEELING creature. She had no emotions, no loyalty, no sense of honor or dishonor. She didn't care what day it was, what part of the day it was, and she had no particular feelings for the creature that she shared her space with.

She knew he was strong. She knew that pitting her own strength against his wasn't advisable because he would only lock her into the cage when she wanted to be free to roam rather than giving her the freedom to come and go as she pleased.

She wasn't a thoughtful creature. She didn't think, plot, or plan. She didn't particularly care about anything but where the next meal was coming from and the occasional need to mate.

But there was one thing Drack did hate. Drack hated guns. She hated the scent of them, she hated the feel of them, and she particularly hated the nasty wounds they had once torn into her body.

She hated them to the point that even when the creature who housed her carried one, she felt nothing more than the overriding instinct to kill. To destroy. Pain was the one memory, the one instinct that held sway when she felt the vibration of the small door open in the bathroom.

That door led to dark places, places where she could depend on a source of food if she ever reached it. Not that the creature didn't keep her well fed, but she loved the hunt.

Tonight she would hunt more than rodents or lizards. Her slitted eyes narrowed, her tongue tested the air, and a hiss of rage left her throat as she butted against the glass that held her confined.

She wanted out. Why wasn't the creature who slept with his mate in the soft nest moving? He should be awakening. Didn't he smell the death moving in, the weapon held by the creature that moved into the room?

Drack watched from her glass-enclosed cage, hissed and slithered to where the door latched. Her tongue flicked, testing the air, and she smelled the offensive scent of evil.

Instinct and rage converged as she lay coiled, tense, waiting. The door would open, and when it did, she would be free. When it did, the evil that had stepped into her lair would die.

She knew it would open. It always opened. No one entered for long without detection. The creature who housed her, he would give her her chance. When he did, she would kill.

* * *

MACEY CAME AWAKE CERTAIN in the knowledge that somehow, some way, he had managed to fuck up. How had he done it? Had he set the security parameters wrong? Had a power supply failed?

It didn't make sense. He was careful, he was always careful, especially when it came to his cave. He had one main entrance, blocked by pure steel and set with enough alarms to bring down the house. There was a bolt hole, just as heavily secured, that led to a sewer drain beneath the streets and any number of manholes scattered throughout the city.

The bolt hole should have been even harder to find than the main entrance, but someone had managed to not only find it, but to crack his security as well. And that someone had managed to slip into the bedroom where he slept with Emerson.

He could hear Drack scraping against the door to her glass cage. A door that should have opened when either entrance was activated. But Drack was scraping against it, which meant she was still locked in. There were no alarms screaming through the cave, no lights flashing, no hard rock blaring. And he was defenseless.

"Come on, Lieutenant Junior Grade Mason March. Wakey wakey." Amused. Familiar. Deadly.

Macey opened his eyes and prayed Emerson would stay asleep just a few minutes longer as he stared into the shadowed face of the admiral's executive aide, Pierce Landry.

Hell, he had never had liked that weasely little

bastard. Macey especially didn't like him holding that automatic weapon to his head.

Macey sighed in resignation and hoped he could manage to get under the former Green Beret's guard for a second to reactivate security and release Drack.

The anaconda could smell the weapon Pierce was carrying, and she hated guns. Hated guns so much that Macey had to bar the few friends allowed access to the basement from carrying weapons.

"How did you get past the security?" he asked, hoping to stall, to find that window of opportunity. Unfortunately, he knew Landry's service record.

"All it took was finding the entrance; the security wasn't that hard. After all, I've read most of your mission reports, March; I've studied your file and your abilities. Reasoning your system out wasn't that hard." Pierce's gaze went to where Emerson appeared to still sleep against his chest. "You must have fucked her half to death. She hasn't moved."

Macey smirked. He could hear the vein of jealousy in his tone.

"What the hell are you doing here, Landry?"

"What am I doing here?" Landry's large white teeth flashed white in the darkness of the room. The son of a bitch, Macey had always hated that smile. "Why, Macey, I'm here to carry out my assignment," he continued. "I'm here to kill Admiral Halloran's goddaughter since you so kindly fucked up the last plan to do so."

Son of a bitch. He'd missed Landry. All these

years, all the leaks they were searching so hard for, and he had missed Landry.

"See, this is why I didn't just kill you when I stepped into the room," Landry sneered. "Where would the fun have been in that? You wouldn't have known who took the shot. Who got past your security. The admiral's golden child wouldn't have known who was smarter and better than he was."

Macey arched his brow mockingly despite the violence slowly gathering inside him. Emerson had woken too and he could feel her tension, her fear.

"You must have me mistaken for someone else, Landry. If I'm anything, it's the pain in the admiral's ass."

Landry chuckled at that, but the gun never wavered.

"He played you, Macey. He marked you for Miss Delaney's bed years ago. Though, to be honest, I believe he was hoping for a wedding ring for her rather than a romp and play between the sheets."

Macey managed to slip his hand beneath the pillows beside him to the alarm switch just below the headboard of the bed and the knife strapped to the wall. He could distract Landry, but Emerson would have to release Drack.

"The admiral's learned to accept what he can get from me." Macey tsked. "Too bad he didn't know what he was getting with you."

Macey tightened his hand on Emerson's wrist beneath the sheets, a warning he prayed she was paying attention to. When he flipped the internal alarms, Drack's cage would open. The anaconda would go for the gun. He hoped.

Macey tripped the switch. Immediately the raucous blare of sirens, screaming music, and flashing red lights tore through the room.

Landry jumped, and Macey knew the instant surprise was the only opening he would get. He tore from the bed and tackled the other man at the waist, taking them both to the floor as Emerson shot up from the bed.

Landry was strong and well trained. Macey had sparred with him on more than one occasion and had learned the other man couldn't be anticipated. He was a gutter fighter, and he was mean.

But Macey was mean too. Mean enough to slam his fist into the other man's upper thigh, his aim off just enough to distract Landry rather than curling him up in the floor.

It wasn't enough. Landry managed to roll, kick out and throw Macey back. The gun discharged, shooting wild before Macey was on him again.

"Emerson, the cage," he screamed out as he glimpsed her from the corner of his eye. "Open the fucking cage."

Because Drack might be their only chance. The gun had shot wild, but Macey could feel the sting of a flesh wound in his side and the blood saturating his flesh now.

He was wounded and it wouldn't take him long

to weaken. If they were going to survive, they just might need all the help they could get.

OPEN THE CAGE? EMERSON'S panicked gaze swung to the glass-enclosed tank that held the anaconda. Over the past days the snake had stayed hidden amid the thick plants and shallow water basin in the stone floor, but it was out now, butting against the glass, tongue flickering, slitted eyes dilated. It looked pissed. It looked dangerous. And she was terrified of snakes. She hated them. But she loved Macey. Loved him. Trusted him.

The sirens and music were blaring through the cave. Red lights were streaking through the room. It was disorienting, as she was sure it was meant to be.

She scrambled across the room, shaking, shuddering. The anaconda was huge. If it managed to wrap around Macey rather than Pierce Landry, then he would be dead.

Snakes had no loyalty. They couldn't be trained. They were driven by instinct, nothing more. It wouldn't know to attack Landry rather than Macey.

"The cage. Now!"

Her gaze swung to Macey where he struggled with Landry for possession of the gun. The other man still had it clenched in his hand, fighting to bring it around to bear on Macey.

Her gaze swung back to the snake. It was pressing against the seam of the glass door, butting against it, demanding its freedom. Emerson imagined she could feel the rage pouring from the creature.

Macey had warned her that the anaconda hated guns. Hated them so much that he had to keep them in a specially designed safe and he couldn't carry one himself within the basement because of the snake's instinctive need to kill whoever or whatever carried the weapon.

With a trembling hand she lifted the latch to the door, swung it open, and jumped aside as Drack immediately pressed out of the opening.

Drack wasn't a fast creature, but she knew where she was headed.

Pierce. Her godfather trusted him, loved him like a son. He was always extolling the warrant officer's virtues. He hadn't mentioned deceit and treason as any of those virtues, though.

She couldn't just stand here, but she couldn't look away. The anaconda was making its way across the room toward the two men struggling for the gun. Emerson was terrified the snake would go for the scent of blood rather than the scent of a weapon.

The two men were cursing, delivering hard, powerful blows even as they fought for the gun.

Emerson considered attacking Landry herself, but if he got hold of her, she knew Macey would sacrifice himself to protect her. Instead, she ran to the other side of the bed and the phone that sat at the side of it.

She glimpsed the anaconda drawing closer as she skirted the side of the bed. Had she been insane to let the creature free, despite Macey's orders? She hadn't even told him she loved him, she thought frantically as she reached the table and jerked the cordless phone from its base and began to dial.

It was ringing. Ringing. Emerson stared across the bed, watching as the two men struggled on the floor now. Macey was gloriously naked, Pierce was dressed in a black mission suit.

Macey straddled the other man, one hand locked on Landry's wrist, trying to dislodge the gun as the other hand delivered a blow to his face. Landry returned with a blow to his side, throwing Macey off as he nearly lost his grip on Landry's wrist.

They were cursing, snarling. Macey delivered another blow to Landry's jaw. When Landry's fist connected with his side again, Macey's hand broke contact with his wrist.

"Answer the phone. Answer the phone," Emerson cried out. "Oh God, where are—"

"Macey!" Her godfather's voice yelled into the line. "Secure premises. Our mole is Landry, I repeat—"

"No shit!" Emerson screamed into the line. "Get down here. Where are you? Landry's here."

A shot exploded in the room. Horrified, Emerson tried to pierce the disorienting flare of light and shadows to the two men fighting. Macey had Landry's wrist in a two-handed grip, holding the weapon, trying to turn it back on the other man as Landry's fingers tightened on the trigger again.

Macey's expression twisted savagely. Landry's

wrist turned until the gun was almost trained on Macey.

She was aware of her godfather screaming in her ear, an explosion from the front of the house, and the increased blare of sirens.

It happened in slow motion, and yet so fast she couldn't make sense of it. Macey twisted Landry's hand back just as the gun fired again. The warrant officer's body jerked, spasmed, then Macey jumped back as Drack attacked.

It shot forward, slicing between Macey's body and Landry's, her mouth opening wide, teeth gleaming to clamp over the dying man's face and twine its massive girth around his neck. Two more shots fired; the snake jerked, shuddered, but held its grip.

Voices were raised. Not her voice. Not Macey's. He was jerking the sheet off the bed and wrapping it around her as black-suited SEALs swarmed into the room, weapons held ready, lights slicing into the room.

"Get those fucking weapons out of here!" Macey screamed.

Amazingly, the six men rushed back into the living area and returned seconds later, weaponless, their gazes locked on the still form of Warrant Officer Pierce Landry and the anaconda attached to his head.

"Shit," Macey breathed out as he finished securing the sheet around Emerson. "Reno, hit the code on the alarms," he yelled at the suited men. "Shut this damned noise off."

Drack was dead and so was Pierce. Emerson could see the blood spreading out from beneath the creature and the aide's still form.

"Fucking bastard killed my snake." Macey's voice was weary, resigned.

The sirens cut off abruptly, the music and lights stilled, and bright normal white light lit up the room.

Macey was behind Emerson, his arms wrapped around her, his heart racing in his chest.

"You were shot." She tore her gaze from the death across the room as the six men stared over at her and Macey in varying degrees of shock.

The members of Durango Team were there, along with her godfather, and her godfather wasn't looking happy.

"Lieutenant," the admiral snapped as Emerson moved to check the crease in his side. "Are you going to live?"

"Yes, sir."

"Then find your pants, sailor. You're not dressed." The admiral's tone was clearly disapproving.

"No sir, I'm not," Macey growled, his voice, irritated, still rough from rage, cut through the room.

"Enough." Firm, brooking no refusal, Emerson sliced her gaze back to Macey. "You need to have this seen to."

"It's nothing," he snapped. But his lips were tight and discomfort darkened his eyes as he glared at the admiral.

Emerson turned back to her godfather. "If he loses rank again, you're going to have to deal with me. Now take care of the mess in here and I'll take care of Macey."

She bent and jerked the jeans he had worn earlier from the floor where he had tossed them before lifting her gaze to his. He still looked ready to fight.

"In the living room." She swallowed back the bile in her throat at the smell of death that had begun to permeate the room. "You can take care of Drack after I take care of you."

She led Macey back to the room, aware of the glowering looks he and her godfather exchanged. She couldn't worry about that; her godfather didn't get along with anyone, with the exception of her.

She couldn't worry about the consequences Macey might face in the short term. Because she had come to realize days before that her godfather had been matchmaking for years. In his own less-than-courteous way.

Macey would get over it. Because in a few short minutes Emerson had realized what mattered most to her and it wasn't protecting her heart.

Macey owned her heart. And he'd better be serious about her owning his, or she was going to make Pierce Landry look like a walk in the park.

Macey belonged to her.

# ELEVEN

THE MURDERING SCUM-SUCKING BASTARD had killed Drack. Macey still couldn't believe it. The snake had lived through one attack, years ago, by a burglar intent on stealing Macey's electronics.

At that time, the cave hadn't existed, the computer setup hadn't been as extensive, and Drack had been a full-grown anaconda. Macey had kept her locked in the computer room as an added precaution. Somehow, someone had gotten in and Drack had taken offense to a stranger in her territory. She had been very territorial.

The snake had taken six shots that had creased her hide deep enough that Macey had to take her to the vet for an extended stay. Drack had never forgotten the scent of a gun, or its consequences. And now, she had died because of one.

Snakes were unfeeling creatures, Macey knew that, but damn if he hadn't been fond of her.

But Emerson was safe.

He looked down at her as she knelt by the couch, the first-aid kit beside him as she cleaned the wound in his side.

"You need stitches." She pressed a thick piece of gauze against his side, then pressed her forehead to his jean-clad leg.

Wrapped in a sheet, her shoulders bare, her hair falling down her back, she was like a young goddess kneeling, beautiful and courageous.

Macey buried his hand in her hair and bent his head to hers, despite the pain in his side.

"I'm going to be fine, Em," he promised softly against her hair. "It's all over, baby. You're safe. That's all that matters to me."

She shook her head against his leg, and he realized that tears would begin falling soon. She had been brave and strong, but she would need to crash.

He would take her out of here, take her to a hotel room in town, someplace bright and romantic, where he could lay her back in bed and hold her through the night. Let her get used to being safe again.

"That's not all that matters." She lifted her head as he eased back, her expression pale and distressed, her sensual lips trembling. "I'm sorry. Macey, I'm so sorry. I should have told you . . ."

He laid his fingers against her lips. "You tell me later, Em. When we're safe. Where I can hold you."

"I love you, Macey. I've loved you for nearly two years. I love you so much that you terrify the hell out of me." Her voice hitched as his arms eased around her, pulled her against his chest, and felt his heart trip in joy.

Burying his head in her hair, Macey closed his eyes, fighting back the need to run away with her and hold her until he heard those words enough to fill his soul. But he didn't think he would ever hear it enough.

"Landry bypassed your security." Admiral Holloran stepped into the room, his voice scathing. "Emerson, sweetheart, Reno's getting you some clothes so you can dress upstairs . . ."

"There's a bathroom under the stairs." Macey jerked his head up and glared at the admiral. "She's not going upstairs until I can go with her."

"Macey . . ." Emerson's voice was edged with steel. It was the same tone his mother used on his father when she thought he was getting out of hand.

"Don't 'Macey' me, Em," he told her gently. "When Reno brings your clothes out, you can dress down here. This was too close." He touched her cheek, let his thumb run over her lips. "I came too close to losing you tonight. Don't separate yourself from me."

He saw the understanding in her eyes as Reno stepped from the bedroom, one of Macey's t-shirts in his hands and a pair of Stacey's leggings.

"Get dressed, baby," he whispered, ignoring the admiral for now. "We'll get out of here soon. I promise."

She turned and gave her godfather a hard look,

rose to her feet, and took the clothes Reno held out to her.

"Morganna, Raven, and Emily will be here soon to take care of her," Reno told him. "We have a full night ahead of us, Macey. Cleaning this up with the local cops isn't going to be easy. Your security here will be compromised further. It won't be a secret any longer."

Macey shook his head. He'd be damned if he cared right now.

He turned his head and watched Emerson disappear into the bathroom before turning back to the admiral.

"Respectfully, sir." He clenched his teeth around the words. "Don't try to take her away from me. I'll fight it."

Admiral Holloran's eyes widened, his expression stern, though if he wasn't mistaken, Macey detected a glimmer of humor in his blue eyes.

"I expect to see a ring on her finger soon," he finally snapped. "Don't disappoint me."

Macey grunted at that and turned back to Reno. The ring would be there because that was where it belonged, not because the admiral ordered it.

"How did he get in?" he asked Reno. "He bypassed every safeguard I had."

Reno glanced disapprovingly at the admiral, his expression quiet. Macey felt his stomach sink as he turned back to Holloran.

Holloran was one of the few people who knew

about the cave. He and Durango team. It was a secret that shouldn't have been uttered.

"I told Pierce about the cave." The admiral sighed. "This one is on my shoulders, Lieutenant; I accept responsibility for it."

He wasn't going to say anything. He really wasn't.

"Respectfully, sir," he sneered. He guessed he was going to say something after all. "That's hardly acceptable."

Holloran's lips pressed together in irritation. His arms crossed over his wide chest, his expression darkening.

"It worked out," he snapped back. "I won't be chastised by you, Lieutenant, remember that."

"Like hell! With all due respect, Admiral, your decision sucked, endangered my woman, this team, and the operation you ordered. Chastising you is the last thing I want to do."

He wanted to plant his fist in the other man's jaw.

"I want to know how we managed to miss Landry when we took this terrorist cell's leader down," Reno said.

The question from his commander had Macey turning and drawing in a hard breath as he fought to push back his anger.

"Landry managed to stay under the radar." The admiral sighed again. "He was a deep-cover mole. With the death of their leader, Sorrell, that particular cell lost its driving force. Landry wanted blood in retaliation. He messed up when he went after Emerson. It was only a matter of time before I figured out I had a spy in my own camp. Very few people were aware she was my goddaughter, rather than just a friend's daughter. On my team, only Landry knew."

And Landry would have known the admiral would figure it out after the terrorists had left the note in her apartment that they had taken his goddaughter and would kill her in retaliation for Sorrell's death.

"Yeah. Might have all worked out great if Landry hadn't known about my place," Macey snapped, glaring back at the admiral as his fists clenched.

Unfortunately, the admiral's lips twitched as that glimmer of humor returned. "Hit me and she's going to be mad. You ever seen her mad, March? I have, son, it's not comfortable."

"And I nearly lost the chance to see it," Macey fumed. "Next time you want to play patty-cake with my secrets, sir, remember this. The next time you endanger her life, you'll deal with me. And doing mad isn't my way. I do blood."

"And I do a baseball bat on stubborn male skulls," Emerson announced as she left the bathroom. "Now, can we wrap this up so I can get some real clothes on and finally get some sleep?"

She was swallowed by his t-shirt. Her legs covered in dark bronze leggings, her hair falling around her face like mussed silk, she looked like a queen to him.

She moved to Macey, gripped his arm and pulled him back. He looked down at her, his heart softening, his soul—damn if he didn't feel his soul turning to mush at the sight of her pale face and her tired smile.

"Just hold me," she whispered as his arms surrounded her and the sound of police sirens filtered from the open entrance outside. "Just hold me, Macey."

He held her, ignoring the amusement in his friends' gazes and the admiral's scowl. He held on tight to what was his and thanked God she was safe.

His Emerson was safe and right here, in his arms, where she belonged.

# EPILOGUE

THERE WERE OVER THREE hundred people at the family reunion. There were dozens of tents in every shape and size scattered around the large farmhouse. There were bunks in the upper level of the barn and every kind of barbecue grill in existence set up beneath a covered wing off the barn. The floor of the huge shelter had been set up with dozens of picnic tables of varying sizes, and huge serving tables lined the wall.

It was an organizational nightmare, and Emerson was loving every minute of it.

Macey's parents and grandparents had welcomed her into the family with hugs and bright smiles. Brothers and sisters, cousins and aunts and uncles had all taken their turn at making her blush and hugging her fiercely.

There were so many people they could have made their own town, and their personalities, temperaments and smiles all made her feel welcome, if a little overwhelmed.

Macey was chafing at the restrictions, though. His grandparents had placed her in a small bedroom between their room and his parents', and gave Macey strict instructions to steer clear of it after she went to bed.

The pressure was wearing on him, she thought in amusement on the third day. He'd already been in two mass brawls with too many of his cousins, and sported his bruises with pride. The lot of them were rough, ready to fight, and always good-natured after trying to break each other's faces with powerful fists.

She'd tended his split lip, bruised ribs, and the wound that he had broken loose on his side. She watched as one of his cousins, a nurse, repaired the stitches that closed the wound while he glared in irritation over the inconvenience.

He was unlike any man she had ever known, even other SEALs. She knew why he had excelled in the SEALs now. A mission would be child's play compared to butting heads with the other males in his family.

And she belonged to him. She might even belong with this strange, crazy family because rather than feeling like she was drowning amid them, their easy acceptance and laughing friendliness drew her in instead.

"We gotta get out of here."

Emerson smiled as Macey's arms surrounded her

from behind and his lips moved to her neck in hungry kisses.

"Stop, Macey could catch us!" She laughed as he growled.

"Macey has already caught you." He turned her in his arms, staring down at her, his dark eyes filled with laughter and arousal. Heavy arousal. He was a man skirting the edge of his control.

"Do you know what these shorts are doing to me?" His hands skimmed over the snug, low-rise shorts, smoothing over her butt and upper thighs. "They're making me crazy."

But his eyes were on another portion of her anatomy. They were gazing in rapt attention at the smooth mounds of her upper breasts as they peeked from the top of her light blue cotton shirt.

Her nipples hardened instantly, pressing against the thin material of her bra and showing through the shirt. He groaned low in his chest. "We're getting out of here." He grabbed her wrist and pulled her away from the shadow of the house toward the four-wheelers parked at the edge of the yard. Grandmother March did not allow four-wheelers in her yard.

"Where are we going?" She laughed as he gripped her waist and set her on the back passenger rack attached to it before swinging himself onto the front.

"Away from the mob." The smile he flashed back at her was filled with happiness, male appreciation, and more than a little lust. "A hidden place."

He started the four-wheeler and with a shift of

power they were bouncing through the field that surrounded the house amid the hoots and catcalls of his male cousins and knowing smiles from the female ones.

She should have been embarrassed. There were possibly three hundred people who were going to know in a matter of minutes that Macey had made off with her for some fun sex in the sun. Somewhere. But she wasn't embarrassed, she was invigorated, energized. She could feel the emotions she had given free rein to grow inside her, filling her, pushing away the loneliness and lighting those dark places with happiness and a sense of freedom.

It was hard not to enjoy the freedom Macey gave her. The freedom to touch him, to revel in his arms surrounding her and the love growing between them.

Two weeks. It had been two weeks since Pierce Landry had tried to kill both of them. Two weeks since Macey had bulldozed his way past her shields to steal her caution and replace it with hope.

Her arms tightened around his waist as they entered the treeline and began moving deeper into the thick forest that covered the March property. She had forgotten how many hundreds of acres the senior Marches owned, but it was vast. Once a thriving cattle farm, it was now rich farmland warming beneath the sun and cool forests shadowed with secrets and a mysterious sensuality. She could imagine living here, hearing the birds sing every morning, watching the deer graze on rich, lush grass as rabbits scurried to and fro.

Maybe she wasn't the city girl she thought she was.

"Here we go," Macey called out as he parked the four-wheeler under a strand of thick trees.

"And what is this?" She kept her arms wrapped around his waist, leaning her head against his shoulder as she breathed in the scent of him and felt her hunger rising.

"Look up."

She looked up and her eyes widened in surprised pleasure.

"It's a treehouse." Her smile widened at the size of it. It was built between two huge trees, the lumber weathered with age, but not with rot. It looked sturdy, natural. A part of the trees that surrounded it and comfortable with its surroundings.

"Come on, I want to show you."

Macey helped her from the back before swinging from the four-wheeler himself and leading her around one of the largest trees where a ladder had been folded down.

"It's gorgeous," she breathed. She had always wanted a treehouse, but hadn't had a tree when she was younger to build one. It always seemed like such a cozy idea, the thought of the trees embracing a small shelter that embraced her. And now, Macey had one. "How long has this been here?"

"Since we were boys," he told her. "Up you go. We checked it out earlier this morning for squirrels and stuff. It's nice and safe."

Emerson glanced back at him as she moved up the ladder, nearly laughing at the piercing look he was giving her butt. He seemed particularly enamored of her breasts as well as her rear.

She giggled as his muttered "Have mercy," reached her. The sound was filled with hunger, admiration, and warmth. That warmth was what stole her heart. It wasn't just lust. It was something that was just right.

Reaching the small balcony that surrounded the treehouse, Emerson stood and stared out around the forest beneath them. God, it was beautiful here, quiet and peaceful, sultry and warming. She loved it.

"Let's go inside." Pulling up beside her, Macey ducked into the opening and drew her in, and her heart stopped in her chest.

A queen-sized mattress was laid out on the floor, surrounded by tapered candles. An ice chest sat in the back corner, but the mattress held her attention.

It wasn't an air mattress. It was a deep, old-fashioned feather mattress covered with quilts and heaped with pillows.

"You did this?"

"You wanted a treehouse to sleep in." He looked around the small area in satisfaction. "My brothers and I built this when we were teenagers. I wanted to share it with you."

She lifted her hand to her lips as tears filled her eyes. He was giving her so much. So many dreams, so much happiness, and now, he was giving her one of the things she'd longed for as a child. A treehouse.

"I love you, Emerson," he whispered, pulling her to the mattress and kneeling beside her. "I love you until sometimes I think I'm going to go insane if I don't hold you."

She shook her head, a tear falling as she stared into his face. This big tough guy, rough and ready to fight, and here he was kneeling in front of her, love shining in his dark eyes and tough face.

He lifted her hand and she stared down in shock as he slid the ring on her finger. The Ring. She knew what it was. The garnet, her birthstone, gleamed fiery burgundy and curved into a rich, lustrous emerald. Macey's birthstone was emerald.

"They fit," he whispered, his thumb smoothing over the stones inset in the gold band and curving into each other. "Like we fit. Fit me forever, Em. Belong with me forever."

Her lips trembled, and tears fell from her eyes. "I like forever." Her voice shook as she met his eyes and saw all the love, all the hope and joy she could have ever prayed for. "Forever suits us."

"Belonging suits us." His head lowered, his lips taking hers with a hunger that she knew should have shocked her, but instead, it met her own.

She laid back on the mattress, their hands tearing at each other's clothes. Their lips, teeth and tongues devoured every drop of passion and pleasure they could find.

Clothes were discarded. Naked flesh met naked flesh as desperate moans mingled and hungry hands stroked. Sweat built on their flesh, making her breasts slick, heated as his lips slid over them. When his lips covered a nipple and sucked it deep and hard, her back arched in pleasure.

She pressed the mounds together as his lips began to devour both nipples. Sucking and licking as she writhed beneath him in passion.

"I'm hungry for the taste of you," he moaned, moving from her breasts down her body.

His tongue stroked through the narrow slit of her pussy, and before Emerson could make sense of anything else she was drawn into a world of sensual hunger, heat and longing that only built and rose until she was screaming with her orgasm and begging for more. Begging for his cock rather than his lips and tongue, pleading for him to fill her.

When he filled her, he took her with long, slow strokes, worked the pleasure to a crescendo that flung her into the heavens in a burst of brilliant, fiery waves.

It was like this with Macey. Sometimes hard and hot, sometimes slow and hot, but always hot, always building, and always drawing her deeper into the magic of his touch.

Later, as the sun began to cool and shadows began to draw deeper into the treehouse, Macey moved. Champagne and two glasses were lifted from the ice chest along with a platter of cold finger foods.

They fed each other. Drank from one glass, and as darkness descended they loved again. Loved for hours until Emerson knew where she belonged, where her heart lay, and trusted in tomorrow.

In Macey's arms.

# DESERT
# HEAT

CINDY
GERARD

# ONE

"IT'S FOR A GOOD cause. It's for a good cause. It's for a *good* cause." That was Assistant DA Elena Martinez's mantra and she was sticking to it.

Of course, she thought, as she followed Seth King, the sulky Flagstaff police detective, down the steep rock slope under a blazing April sun, the view was almost worth it. And she wasn't just thinking about this leg of their trek into the magnificence of the Grand Canyon.

Her female colleagues in the DA's office called Seth King eye candy of the highest caloric content. Yeah, Elena admitted grudgingly and adjusted her visor to block the morning sun's glare. "Detective Dreamy" was easy to look at; she couldn't deny that. He had the requisite poster-boy broad shoulders, narrow hips, rock-hard abs and thick buzz-cut black hair. Not to mention that his face, all hard angles and intriguing planes, elevated the drool factor to new levels. That amazing face and impressive, bare, oiled chest had launched last year's Flagstaff Police Force calendar benefiting the children's wing at the hospital—and Elena would never think of January as cold again.

Yep, she thought, carefully stepping over a pile of loose stones, easy to look at. He was also a good cop. A clean cop. She respected him for that. Too bad he not only had a great ass, but could also be a monster *pain* in the ass.

King was one of the rare people who made her want to yell—she *never* yelled—and the fact that she'd come close to giving into the urge a few times with him didn't set one bit well.

So why was she here? Simple. She'd needed a break from the constant crunch at the office. This hike could have been a peaceful, energizing experience. Would have been, if the luck of the draw hadn't paired her up with King for this year's annual law enforcement benefit event.

Signing up for the two-day Survival Scavenger Hunt in the Grand Canyon that had started at six this morning and ended at six tomorrow night had been a no-brainer. Elena loved the Canyon. Relished the exertion and the amazing scenery. Plus she needed to get out of the office and see something besides government-gray walls, crime and courtrooms. Since she'd scored her promotion a year ago, she'd done little besides work.

Not backing out after she'd found out Seth was

her partner, however, fell dead center into the "What was I thinking?" category.

And the utterly disarming sensation that she was being watched—which was as ridiculous as letting King shake her—was taking what was left of the fun out of the experience.

"You're awful quiet back there, Martinez," King tossed over his shoulder as he hiked along ahead of her at a comfortable pace. "How'd I get so lucky?"

"Just hike," she sputtered, and told herself she wasn't one bit impressed by the tan muscular thighs visible beneath his drab olive hiking shorts. Or by the way his snug white t-shirt hugged his chest beneath his backpack or by the bulge of his biceps as he dug his walking poles into the steep, downhill grade of Kaibab Trail. Or by the fact that two hours into the hike, carrying at least fifty pounds of water and gear, he hadn't even worked up a sweat. "And save the sarcasm for someone who appreciates it."

"Just out of curiosity, if you didn't want to do this, why did you sign up?"

Elena planted her poles for balance while stepping over a sun-bleached log. "I didn't say I didn't want to do it. I just didn't want to do it with *you*."

He stopped, twisted at the waist and grinned back at her from beneath the brim of his red and blue Arizona Wildcats cap. "Are we still talking about the scavenger hunt?"

Leave it to him to spin her remark into a sexual

innuendo. "You have a highly overinflated opinion of yourself, you know that, King?"

He chuckled and started back down the steep downhill grade. "If that's the case, why are you always checking out my ass, *Martinez*?"

Following him, she grunted, unwilling to give him the satisfaction of knowing he was right. "Get over yourself. And while you're at it, get over the Devine case. I'm tired of your grumblings filtering back to the DA's office."

That stopped him short. Literally. She almost ran into him. When he turned to face her this time, his mouth was set in a line as hard and unforgiving as the Kaibab limestone walls of the canyon at this elevation. She couldn't see his eyes behind his aviator shades, but she had no doubt that pale blue had transitioned to deep indigo. She'd seen that shade plenty during the course of the Devine case. He hadn't been happy about the way she'd prosecuted Joey Devine, the son of Clyde Devine, a bad-ass piece of crap and the head of the local drug syndicate.

She waited while he transferred both of his walking poles to one hand then reached for the tube on his CamelBak. He took a long drink, all the while watching her face.

"Let's just clear the air once and for all, okay?" she pressed, staring him down. She was beyond weary of his anger at her over the case, and she was feeling just enough physical stress over the arduous hike that her guard was down.

"What's to clear?" He recapped the drinking

tube and tucked it away. "I had the little bastard nailed for murder one. The case was solid, Elena, and you copped for voluntary man."

"Yeah," she agreed. "Your case was solid."

"And yet, you, in your infinite wisdom, let him plead to the lesser charge. It was bogus and you know it."

Elena was confident about the job she'd done on the Devine case. On all of her cases, for that matter. It pissed her off when King questioned her. She'd worked damn hard to get where she was and she hadn't moved up in the ranks because she didn't know what she was doing.

"Look. It got Devine off the streets, didn't it? And with the plea bargain he gave up the goods on Evans and *that* put another lowlife behind bars. I'll go for a two-fer any day of the week."

King snorted. "That's bullshit reasoning. Crank Evans was small potatoes."

"Tell that to the parents of the kids Evans supplied," she said, then drew a quick breath to check the disturbing urge to raise her voice around him.

"Tell that to the school district where he'd set up his trade," she continued, back in control. "I think they're damn glad the trade-off of a voluntary man conviction for Devine also netted the Evans bust. As of last week another predator is off the streets."

"Yeah, well," Seth squatted down on one knee to retie the laces on his worn hiking boots, "I guess it's a moot point now, isn't it?"

Elena took the opportunity to readjust the straps

on her backpack and resettle its weight. "What do you mean, a moot point?"

Silence.

The kind of silence that made the hair on the back of her neck stand on end. She saw by the expression on King's face that he knew something vital.

He stood, stretching to his full six-plus feet and cocked his head. "You didn't hear?"

"Hear what?"

He gave her a hard, troubled look. "Joey Devine is dead. Knifed in the prison yard yesterday."

"Jesus," she said, stunned.

He pushed out a grim grunt. "I doubt very much that Jesus was in play on that deal."

Man, Elena thought. Joey Devine was dead. Despite the furnace blast of heat welling up from the interior walls of the canyon, a chill whipped through her. It wasn't that she felt remorse over Joey Devine's death. He was a murderer and a drug lord; the world was a better, safer place without him. But she couldn't help but replay Clyde Devine's whispered threat as she left the courtroom after Joey's conviction.

*"You'll pay, bitch. For taking my son from me, I promise, you will pay. And you'd better hope nothing happens to him in stir or when I come after you, I'll make you wish you'd never been born."*

"Hey—you okay?"

She glanced at Seth. Realized his eyes were full of concern. "Yeah. Yeah, I'm okay," she said with an absent nod.

But she wasn't okay. She was shaken. She'd never told anyone about Clyde Devine's threat. Figured it was just gang-mentality bravado. Now though . . . now that Joey was dead—another shiver rippled through her. Well, now that Joey Devine was dead, she was going to have to watch her back when they got back to Flagstaff.

Head down, focused on the trail, she tried to push thoughts of Devine from her mind as she followed Seth down the rough pass.

She never noticed the glint of sunlight bouncing off a pair of binoculars from the ridge of a switch-back above them.

# Two

SHE WAS TOUGHER THAN he'd thought she'd be, Seth admitted around nine A.M. Who knew that hidden beneath the boring, mannishly tailored power suits she wore to court, interviews and depositions, that pretty, prickly Elena Martinez had an athlete's body. A curvy athlete's body to boot.

Despite the fact that they often butted heads over the way Flagstaff's newest assistant district attorney prosecuted his cases, Seth had often wondered about her hidden assets. Well, he didn't have to wonder anymore. She'd started out the cool morning with a long-sleeved red jersey shirt and long pants tucked into her hiking boots. Hadn't taken long for the sun to warm the canyon walls and she'd zipped the legs off the pants to make shorts and packed the shirt away in favor of a sweet, yellow tank top.

*Thank you, sun.*

Her arms and legs were a sexy honey-colored hue, slim yet surprisingly well-toned. The lady apparently lifted something other than stacks of legal briefs. The lady had also been carrying concealed. Nice rack. Sweet little ass. While that heavy mass of chestnut hair was still twisted up in a snug, prim knot on top of her head, he had a feeling that when she let her hair down—*if* she ever let her hair down—it'd be silky and sleek and sexy as all hell.

A vivid image of that thick, lush hair trailing over his belly played through his mind like a wet dream.

"You're a dirtbag, King," he muttered under his breath as he rounded yet another switchback and maneuvered over some dead fall. She already thought he was a pig. If she knew what he was thinking, she'd shove him off a cliff. Lord knew she'd have plenty of opportunities before this scavenger hunt in the canyon's desert terrain was over.

The trouble with Elena was she was too smart and too stubborn. He generally preferred a woman who wouldn't be such a challenge, although, on too many occasions, he'd wondered how she'd be in the sack.

The truth was, he grudgingly admired the hell out of her professionalism—as well as the package it was wrapped in. She just pissed him off sometimes was all—especially when she pulled something like she had in the Devine case. As far as he was concerned, the DA's office made too many plea bargains and let too many scumbags back on the streets. He'd seen one too many murderers find a way out of prison only to kill again. That's why he was determined to make it difficult for the DA to do it with his cases—even if the DA, or in this case, an assistant DA, tripped the kind of triggers Elena Martinez did.

"Let's take a breather," he said when he rounded the next switchback and discovered an overhanging ledge that would provide them with a nice little pocket of shade. "You need to rehydrate and we could both use some salt and protein."

Without a word, she ducked under the ledge, found a "comfy" rock to perch on and shrugged her pack off her back.

"So—what made you decide to enter this year's charity event?" Seth asked as Elena worked her shoulders free of the stiffness he knew she had to feel. He was feeling it too. "It's not exactly for the faint of heart."

She smiled to herself as she dug into her pack then opened a bag of trail mix. "I ever give you any reason to believe I was faint of heart?"

He couldn't help but grin as he tugged off his cap, wiped the sweat from his brow with the back of his forearm and resettled the cap. No. She never had. In the cases the two of them had been involved with, she'd proven to be a tough prosecutor; she was thorough, accurate and didn't back down to even the most experienced defense attorneys. She didn't back down to him, either, when she took a tack that pissed him off. Like with the Devine case.

Faint of heart? Not this woman—emphasis on woman.

"Nope." He fished an apple out of his pack and sliced it in two with the blade from his Leatherman. "You never have."

Just for the hell of it, he offered her half of the apple.

She regarded it, then him, with a wary look over the top of her open water bottle.

He laughed. "It's a peace offering, all right? You might tick me off with some of your decisions, but hey, that's not my call. You're doing your job. And from where I sit, you do it damn well—even though I don't always agree with your methods."

She shoved her dark glasses up on the top of her head, her coffee-brown eyes still distrustful. "Okay . . . now you're being just plain rational— which is scary. What's the catch?"

He laughed again, bit into his half of the apple. "No catch, Ms. Assistant DA. Figured maybe it was time to bury the hatchet is all. So this is just me, trying to be a nice guy."

She smiled another one of those secret, amused smiles. Secret and sexy.

"And that's funny because?"

She bit into the apple. White teeth, lush lips, and pink tongue. Holy God, he definitely had to quit looking at her mouth.

"Because it surprises me to know there's a 'nice guy' side to your persona."

He grunted. "I'm a surprise a minute. And I think I've just been insulted."

A sexy dimple dented her left cheek. "We haven't exactly seen eye to eye on the last two cases, and you don't exactly conceal your resentment."

"Yeah, well, I'm competitive. So sue me."

They lapsed into an almost comfortable silence as they drank, finished off the fruit and took in the vast and stunning beauty of Canyon buttes, high plateaus, mazes and crannies stretched out around, above and below them. The Colorado meandered in a long, thin silver ribbon half a mile below, yet still several miles away via the trails.

Five teams of two participating in the scavenger hunt had spread out this morning from the South Rim of the Canyon. The other four teams had taken Bright Angel Trail down then fanned out on varying side trails depending on their individual maps.

Seth and Elena were the only team to draw Kaibab Trail, which was further down the rim. The first couple of miles were the hardest. The chalk-colored limestone passes were steep as hell, hard on the knees and not for the weak of body or heart. You had to be a serious hiker to do the Canyon's desert climate or it would eat you alive.

It had been over an hour since they'd seen any other hikers. Seth knew from experience that not many made it this far into the "big hole." It was just too rigorous. As they progressed even deeper, traversing thirty thousand years of the Canyon's five-million-year history with each downward step, the chances were they'd seen their last human until they climbed back out tomorrow afternoon—hopefully in time to see the condors fly in to roost in the jagged cliffs near the Canyon Village compound.

"So why *did* you enter the hunt?" he asked again.

She offered him her bag of trail mix. "While it may seem that I prefer the courtroom to anything else, I love the Canyon. I love hiking. And I love the idea of helping out for a good cause. How about you? Why'd you enter?"

He shrugged and poured the mix of nuts and raisins into his palm before handing the bag back to her. "Same reasons, I guess. My dad was a teacher so he had summers off. He and I used to camp somewhere in the Canyon three or four times a summer. I love it here. Never get to see it these days."

She nodded then smiled again.

"Okay. What's funny this time?"

"Us. Sitting here talking like civilized people instead of yelling over points of law."

Seth scratched his head. Grinned. "It *is* kind of weird, huh?"

"Yeah. Weird. Best not get used to it. We're in a bubble here. Two days from now it'll be back to business as usual and I imagine we'll be butting heads again."

Business as usual? *I don't think so,* Seth speculated to himself when she stood and brushed off her butt. It was all he could do to resist offering up his services to handle that chore for her.

Elena Martinez might tick him off sometimes, but she'd always intrigued him. Fascinated might be the better word. He'd never get a better chance than now to capitalize on this close proximity to the dishy assistant DA. They'd be spending a lot of time together during the next forty-eight hours. Alone time. He planned to make the best of each and every hour. Anything could happen if he decided to give in to a little carnal curiosity and she did the same. She was curious, too. He could tell. Just like he could tell she didn't want to be but her resistance was slipping.

"No less than five, no more than twenty." She shouldered her pack, adjusted its weight. "We've been here a little over fifteen minutes."

Nope. The gorgeous Elena was no panty-waist, Seth thought again. She knew her stuff. Knew that less than a five-minute rest was worthless and more than twenty would cause their muscles to stiffen up.

He tugged a map out of a zippered pouch on the leg of his shorts. "If this map is accurate, we should be getting close to our first item on the list. That means we'll be veering off the maintained trail soon."

There were only thirty-three miles of maintained trails in the canyon, so any off-trail path was always an added adventure.

"A pair of waxed lips?" she asked, looking over his shoulder at the list of treasures. She stood close enough that he could get a whiff of something fresh and flowery. Her shampoo, maybe. Or maybe it was just her. Whatever it was, it was workin' for her. Workin' *on* him.

"Who thought of these things?" she asked with a shake of her head. "And who came out here and planted them?"

"You ever met Sergeant Wayne?" He refolded the map and tucked it back in his pocket.

"Tater Wayne?" She laughed—a husky, sexy sound he'd never heard from her before. He liked it. Liked how it softened the lines around her mouth and the tension in her shoulders and knocked the stiffness out of her entire bearing.

"Yeah. I know Tater." She fit the straps of her walking sticks over her wrists. "And enough said."

Seth heard the affection in her tone. Shared it. The sergeant's love for french fries had stuck him with the Tater handle. His warped sense of humor was responsible for the odd items on their list.

"Didn't peg him for a hiker." She sounded surprised.

"Leads a troop of Eagle Scouts. He and the boys were busy last week planting little treasures for the hunt."

"Since they worked so hard, what say you and I get busy? Maybe we can make it out of here with our booty in record time."

*Record time? Fat chance.* Seth was in no hurry to climb back out of this magnificent hole. Not with the delectable *booty* of Elena Martinez to occupy his thoughts.

# THREE

"WAX LIPS—RED. KITE string—long. A romance novel—hot. Guess you could say we had a pretty good day."

On her knees, rolling out her sleeping bag, Elena looked over her shoulder at Seth as he stretched out on his side of his own sleeping bag, checking the three items off their list.

She turned back to reorganizing her backpack. He was right. It had been a long but good day—in spite of her recurrent, niggling sensation of being watched.

They hadn't had to search too long for any of the "hunt" items and had been able to knock off early. While, as the crow flies, it was only a mile to the bottom from the South Rim, they'd hiked over six miles to get to within fifty yards or so of the Colorado. She was beat—in a good way—and ready to rest her feet.

Taking advantage of a lone pinion and a hulking

rock formation that formed a shelter of sorts, they'd made camp for the night a hundred or so yards off the main trail on a ridge overlooking the river. At noon they'd both eaten premade PBJs for protein and snacked on more fruit and trail mix. Tonight they'd have real food. Seth had promised to cook.

For now, he lounged in the shade of the lean-to he'd erected from a lightweight survival blanket. He'd rolled his sleeping bag out beneath him, stretched out on his side, propped himself on one elbow and now he was lazily thumbing through the romance novel.

"Hoochie mamma." He grinned, stopped on a page that caught his interest. "Listen to this. 'Even in the pale glow of the campfire, Lance could see the fire in Victoria's eyes. He moved closer—' "

Elena held up a hand. "Spare me."

He affected a look of puzzled amusement. "What? You don't like this stuff? I thought all women loved a good hot romance novel."

"I didn't say I didn't like it. One of my best friends is a romance novelist. I love her stuff. I just don't want to hear it from you."

"Ah . . . gets you all hot and bothered, does it?"

The full lips that pulled back into a smile revealed teeth that were straight and white—a stunning contrast to his tan face made even darker by a heavy five o'clock shadow that had started showing up around four.

She grunted, failed to suppress a grin. "In your dreams, cowboy."

He slanted her a considering look. "So, it's a cowboy fantasy you like. Well, then, Miz Elena, I reckon this cowpoke's got a yarn or two and a move or two under this here ten-gallon hat that could turn that sassy little head of yourn."

She laughed. He was ridiculous. And funny—something she was just learning about him. He'd never given her a glimpse of his sense of humor before and it made her feel a little off-balance. He was also sexy as hell with the long, strong length of him reclined on his side on his sleeping bag, grinning over the novel.

He was also too damn charming for his own good. Hmm. Who'd have believed that? Elena Martinez thinking Seth King was charming. In a cheesy, adolescent, bad-boy-up-to-something kind of way.

"You're in a mood." She sat down cross-legged on her own sleeping bag facing him.

He smiled—the kind of smile that could melt even the coldest, most cautious of hearts. And, she realized, surprised to admit it, it was a smile that could turn into a problem before this camp-out was over.

"It's been a good day," he said simply. "We found three of our six items, the weather's great, company's good and tonight I'm going to do my most favorite thing in the entire world."

She shot him an arched look.

"Stargaze," he clarified with an evil grin. "You thought I was talking about something else, didn't you?"

"Hey—what a man does in the privacy of his own sleeping bag is no concern of mine."

She was really getting addicted to that laugh, she thought as his deep baritone rumble caressed the air. "Why didn't I know you had such a bawdy sense of humor?"

"Maybe because you're usually in my face and roaring over something I did that you didn't like?"

"There is that," he agreed with a sage nod, then, grinning like that little boy again, he opened up the novel. He cleared his throat dramatically. " 'Moonlight danced across the gentle rise of her breasts—' "

She reached across the distance and snatched the book out of his hands. "Haven't you got a fire to start or something?"

"Darlin' . . . that's what I'm trying to do if you'd only cooperate."

Sporting a grin that should be illegal, he rose and dug a lightweight portable camp stove out of his pack then set out the makings for their dinner.

Definitely illegal, Elena thought as she dug into her own pack for dinnerware. So were those devil blue eyes that danced and teased, flirted and tempted.

Despite his obvious and outrageous flirting, like it or not, as the day had progressed, she'd started seeing him in a whole new light. If he'd come on to her all heavy and macho—and he *was* coming on to her— she'd have dismissed him and his frequent smiles out of hand. But he was having fun with it. Even making fun of himself. Reading from a romance novel, for God's sake. Just to make her laugh.

And yeah, to make her hot.

Which, unfortunately, he had, Elena admitted as she checked her water supply. Of all the reactions she'd expected to have to Seth King on this trip, the last one she'd seen coming was attraction, or that, considering their history, she might actually like him.

Oh, well. She was a big girl and this was a short camp-out. A bubble, she reminded herself, which would pop the minute they climbed out of this canyon tomorrow night.

Didn't mean she couldn't look a little in the meantime, though, did it? So she did. She indulged in a little guilty pleasure and watched the play of light and shadow dance across his handsome face as he hunkered down to start the burner on his camping stove. Enjoyed the hard angle of his jaw, the lush mobility of his lips, the thick dark lashes that hid his eyes as he struck a match and lit the flame.

Two flames, she admitted reluctantly, as a warm flush spread low in her belly.

*Lord.* She dragged her gaze away from all that man who had ignited all this heat. *Save me from myself*.

"AND HE COOKS, TOO," Elena said, tasting her pasta.

"In and out of the kitchen," Seth agreed, digging into his own dinner.

She didn't say anything, but Seth got the reaction he wanted. A reluctant grin. A roll of her eyes. A little shake of her head.

Yeah, she was trying her damnedest not to find him funny and maybe a little cute, but he could tell he was starting to get to her.

"This is the life, huh?" he observed with a nod toward the canyon walls stretching out for miles around them. This deep in the Canyon, every color from bone to red, to umbers and rich sand colors decorated the striated canyon walls.

"Yeah," she agreed with just the right amount of awe in her voice to tell him how much she really loved it here. "Peace. Perfection. Unequalled beauty. It's daunting. Humbling to face the elements and the isolation."

She glanced at him, the wonder she felt for the Canyon coloring her voice and her expression. "Did you know that over four and a half million people visit each year and less than one percent ever make it off the rim?"

"Don't know what they're missing." He waited a beat then decided to chance it. "I'm beginning to think I've been missing something too."

When she held his gaze, he knew she recognized his look and his statement for what it was. He wasn't referring to the Canyon. He was referring to missing out on something with her. Instead of an instant rebuff or a "Cool your jets, cowboy," she just looked thoughtful.

That encouraging reaction made something other than his heart swell.

*Down, boy. You don't rush a woman like Elena*

*Martinez.* Yet all he could think about was the possibility of ending this evening with a kiss—maybe a little something more.

Maybe a *lot* more.

"I think I'll clean up a little," she said after washing both their plates and forks and handing his back to him. "Thanks for dinner."

He watched her dig around into her backpack for soap and a washcloth then pick up an extra water container. "My pleasure," he said quietly as she walked toward a small stand of scrub growing around a boulder. "Don't wander off too far."

He cleaned up too while she was gone. Wished he'd brought a bottle of wine. God. Listen to him. Thirteen hours ago he'd been dreading spending time with her and now he wanted to put the moves on her.

Things change.

Things changed a lot more when she came back.

The sun set like a curtain coming down. There was light. Then there wasn't. Only a purple-blue sky in a dark gray dusk playing against the craggy silhouette of the vast North Rim stretched out for miles across from them. Suddenly the evening turned as cool as the day had been warm.

Seth snagged his wind-up flashlight, turned it on and set it in the middle of their campsite for a little light. Then he shrugged into his long-sleeved shirt. As he tugged it down over his head, he saw her. A graceful silhouette walking back to the campsite. Tall, lean, curved in all the right places.

"Thought I might have to send out a search party," he said, surprised by the gruffness in his voice.

"Sorry. Didn't realize how late it had gotten."

He watched her carefully. She seemed tense. Even a little jumpy.

"Something wrong?"

Looking preoccupied, she glanced at him. Shook her head. "No. I don't know. It's . . . probably nothing."

"*What's* probably nothing?"

She rubbed her arms against the sudden chill. "I've just had this creepy feeling on and off all day. Had it again just now. Like someone's watching me."

"Have I been that obvious?"

He'd wanted her to smile and she did, but it was a reluctant smile. "Someone other than you, Detective. You haven't . . . noticed anything?"

"I've noticed that you are an amazingly beautiful woman."

She rolled her eyes but she smiled. "Do you ever quit?"

"Quit?" He shook his head, held her gaze. "Not so much, no. Not until I'm absolutely, positively, indisputably certain that I've been beaten."

Another reluctant smile. Then she turned serious. Thoughtful. "Beaten? So what game are you playing, exactly?"

He watched her for a moment, judging her mood—assessing his own. "That's the thing," he said, surprised by his own reaction. "I'm not so sure it is a game."

That was God's honest truth.

Something was happening here. Something he hadn't planned, hadn't counted on and didn't quite know how to handle.

Her gaze held his for a long moment before she looked away, shaking her head. "Look. This . . . You and me. It's not such a good idea. You know that."

Ah. No beating around the bush. He liked that in a woman. She knew where this was headed and she'd decided to call him out. Fine. He was ready for the challenge.

"A little early in the . . . game . . . to make a decision that important, isn't it?"

"Yeah . . . see . . . there's that word again. Game. It keeps coming back to that. And *that's* the problem." She reached up and pulled a few pins out of her hair. He held his breath and felt the impact deep in his gut as she shook her head and all that chestnut-colored silk untangled around her face and shoulders.

He knew she had no idea what effect letting her hair down had on him as her dark eyes met his.

"I don't play games, Seth."

No, she didn't. He understood. Silent seconds ticked by before he answered, knowing he was speaking the truth and a little rattled by it. "Like I said. I'm not sure this is one."

He saw the answering spark in her eyes. Felt a sudden electricity in the moment that compelled him to close the distance between them.

He searched her face, back-shadowed by the night and the canyon rim. Touched a hand to her hair. Gently fisted his fingers in the thick, luxurious weight of it and drew her toward him.

"I'm not sure what *is* happening here, Elena, but whatever it is . . . it damn sure isn't a game."

Then he kissed her. Open mouth, seeking tongue, and a suddenly desperate need. Hadn't realized how much need until he'd been within touching distance. Hadn't realized how much desire until she responded to his deep, throaty groan with an answering sigh and wrapped her arms around his neck.

*Holy God.* The woman could kiss. The woman could reduce him to a puddle if he wasn't careful. But careful wasn't in him at the moment. He felt reckless and hungry and the way she responded to the demands of his mouth told him she felt exactly the same way.

He deepened the kiss, tasting, exploring, welcoming her lush responses and inviting more. He filled his hands with her hair, tilting her head to change the alignment of their mouths and experience another amazing angle of Elena.

With a groan, he let his hands wander down her slim back, cupped her hips with splayed fingers and drew her against him. She gasped when she felt his erection pressing against her belly, did an amazing little shiver thing that ground her even closer and forked her fingers into his short hair.

He could have stood there kissing her like that forever. Feeling all of her pressed against all of him. Learning her curves, the satin feel of her skin as he tunneled a hand up under her shirt. Fire. She was on fire and he wanted to bring her from a blaze to a raging inferno.

He cupped her breast and she moaned. Flicked his thumb over the peak of her erect nipple and she cried out. Then stiffened. Broke the kiss.

He didn't fight her. Hell. He had to catch his breath. Clear his head.

"Wow." Breathless, he cupped her head in his hands and pressed his forehead to hers.

She pushed out a tight laugh, gripped his biceps and hung on like she needed his strength to steady her. "In a word."

He struggled for a deep breath, still holding her that way, forehead to forehead, his hands in her hair, her fingers wrapped around his biceps—like she couldn't decide whether to push him away or pull him back against her.

"That was . . . um . . . that was intense," he whispered, both of them struggling for a steady breath.

She pushed out a tense laugh. "There's another word."

He grinned then pulled back so he could see her face. Her eyes were heavy-lidded; her lips plump and pink from his mouth plundering hers.

"One word that doesn't fit is *game*. No question in my mind, Elena. That was definitely no game. I don't honestly know how long I've been wanting to do that, but from the way my knees feel, it must have been a helluva long time."

She looked sober and stunned and confused. "I . . . I, ah, guess I didn't know it was what I wanted either."

His heart slammed like a brick against his ribs at her admission. "So. What do we do about it?"

She shook her head. Breathed deep. "Taking a step back and thinking it over might be the wisest move."

"Yeah," he agreed with a slow, reluctant nod. "You're probably right. Is that what you want to do?"

She finally met his eyes, sighed in defeat and moved into him again. "Hell, no."

Then she kissed him. On the attack this time, nothing tentative, nothing shy and nothing held back. It damn near knocked him on his ass.

"Elena," he whispered, hearing the urgency in his voice as her busy, busy mouth drove him out of his mind. "If we don't take this horizontal soon, one of us is going to get hurt."

"Oh, you're gonna get hurt all right, lovebirds," a gruff voice growled behind them.

Reflexes honed by muscle memory and practice, triggered by threat, had Seth shoving Elena behind him, automatically reach for his S & W. Which, of course, wasn't there.

Ten feet away, two hard-faced men stood in the

darkening night. One pointed a Glock dead center at Seth's chest. The other aimed the silver barrel of a Ruger revolver at his head.

"You're gonna get hurt real bad."

# Four

"GOT YOURSELF A REAL sweet little piece there don't ya, pig?"

Seth sized up the two men, assessed the threat. They were big. Out of shape, beat up by the trail and mad as hell. Trigger fingers as itchy as dogs with fleas.

He didn't think he knew either one of them. Yet they seemed to know him, or at least they knew he was a cop.

Axe to grind. That was the obvious call. Big axe to have tracked him all the way down here. The question then was, could he convince them they had more to lose if they shot him than they did if they just walked away? The bigger question, how the hell did he keep Elena from getting caught in the crossfire?

"Don't know what your beef is, fellas, but I'm sure we can settle it without the guns, okay? Why don't you just put 'em down before someone gets hurt?" he suggested in a calm, evenly modulated voice. "You look thirsty and beat. We've got water. Food. You're welcome to both."

"Well, that's real generous of you—considering we're callin' the shots.

"You. Lawyer bitch." The guy with the Glock motioned at Elena with his gun. "Get us some water."

Every cell in Seth's body screamed to red alert. Whatever this was about, they knew who Elena was, too.

"Look, guys, whatever your problem is with me, leave her out of it."

"Shut the fuck up, hero!" Glock guy exploded with rage. "And let's get something straight. If it was up to me, both of you would be dead or dying right now, got it? So don't push me."

"What's this about?" Elena asked.

"I think my old man already told you, bitch."

Elena's fingers clutched Seth's arm like a vice. "Oh, God. You're . . . you're Jake Devine. Joey's brother."

*Oh, Christ.*

"That's right. You and this asshole cop are responsible for putting my little brother in prison. Which means you're responsible for him being dead."

*Worse and worse.*

Riled to the point of losing control, Devine closed the distance in three long, angry strides. Got right in Seth's face as Seth shoved Elena further behind him.

"I'd like nothing better than to waste you both right here and now, but the old man wants to save that pleasure for himself. He wants to kill you slow-like. Wants you to know the pain he's going through. Wants you to feel it over and over again."

Jake shoved the pistol hard and deep into Seth's gut. "So don't push me or I might just forget my old man called dibs and start working you over myself."

Eyes still locked with loathing on Seth's face, Devine yelled at Elena. "Now get us some water! And get some goddamn food while you're at it—"

It was now or never. Taking advantage of Devine's attention on Elena, Seth chopped the gun to the side and down before Devine ever knew what hit him. The pistol went off, fired harmlessly into the dirt as Seth wrestled Jake to the ground.

"Elena, run!" he yelled as the two of them rolled over the ground, hitting rocks and brush and sending camping gear flying.

Seth ended up on top, drew his arm back to land a right hook and heard the unmistakable sound of a hammer being cocked. The business end of the Ruger revolver pressed into his spine, directly between his shoulder blades.

"Back off," the other guy said. "Raise your hands now, cop, or you're dead right here."

On a controlled breath, Seth unclenched his fist and raised both hands beside his head in a show of submission.

An explosion of pain stole his breath and his consciousness as something slammed into the back of his head.

"YOU RUN AND I'LL kill him," Jake Devine threatened, rising to his feet. "Then I'll hunt you down and kill you too."

Elena hadn't planned on running. She wasn't leaving Seth.

"Tie 'em up, Benny," Jake ordered the other man.

Elena didn't fight him as the man Jake had called Benny jerked her arms roughly behind her back, pushed her down to a sitting position, then tied her ankles. He made quick work of tying Seth the same way. Then the two men tore into their food supply and gorged themselves.

Seth lay as still as stone beside her, his face ashen where it pressed into the rock and grit of the campsite floor. The blood that soaked the back of his head oozed black in the night. She was close enough that she could feel his breath penetrate her shorts and warm her hip so she knew he was still alive. What she didn't know was how badly he was hurt. Bad, she suspected, for him to be out this long.

"He needs medical attention."

Neither man acknowledged her.

Seth stirred slightly.

"Lay still," she whispered, darting a glance across the shadows, hoping Jake and Benny couldn't hear her. "Just lay still. You could have a concussion."

"Jesus." Seth's voice slogged out, weak and strained. "What . . . happened?"

"He hit you with the butt of his gun. You're bleeding pretty badly."

"Head wounds," Seth slurred. "Always . . . bleed like a . . . bitch."

Elena glanced at the men again. Decided to chance lying down. She rolled to her hip, eased down so she could see Seth's face in the dark.

"How bad?"

He blinked. Tried to focus. "Picked a . . . good place to . . . nail me. Come from . . . a long line . . . of hard heads. I'm . . . fine."

"Yeah," she said, her chest tight with fear. "I can see that, tough guy."

Leave it to him, Elena thought. He could hardly talk, had to be hurting like blazes, and he insisted he was fine.

"What are . . . they doing?"

She glanced toward the sound of gluttony. "Eating. Drinking. Bitching about no-service messages on their cells phones, sore feet and blisters and complaining about the old man and his bright idea to track us out here."

"Must have been looking . . . for a chance . . . to get at us."

Elena nodded. "Probably read about the event in the papers. But why track us here? Why not just wait for their chance and kill us in Flagstaff?"

Seth shifted slightly, groaned. "Think about it."

She thought. Got the connection. "Right. The head-lines would read something like 'Assistant DA and Flagstaff police detective die in unfortunate Grand Canyon hiking accident.'"

"Bingo. They can rough us up real . . . good out here. It'll look like damage from, say . . . a bad fall. No fingers . . . pointing Devine's way."

His voice was so faint, she could hardly hear him over the wild, racing beat of her heart. "So what do we do?"

"Darlin', for the moment . . . we do nothing. Time's on our side until . . . the old man arrives. They can't contact him. No cell tower in the . . . world has enough power to catch a signal from this deep in the Canyon. Gotta figure Daddy won't show up . . ." He stopped, caught his breath. ". . . until morning. He can't hike in, in the dark. Can't chopper in tonight ei-ther. So . . . we wait for these yahoos to fall . . . asleep. They're in no shape for the . . . hike they made today. They have to be . . . hurtin' bad."

"And you've probably got a concussion and we're both trussed up like Thanksgiving turkeys," she pointed out, working hard not to give in to panic.

"Be a pretty . . . dull life without . . . a little chal-lenge now . . . and then."

"You'll forgive me if your warped sense of hu-mor just doesn't cut it for me at the moment."

"Just . . . keepin' it real, babe. We'll get out of this. For now . . . just . . . just watch them . . . okay? And . . . keep me awake. Don't . . . let me fall . . .

asleep. Talk to me. Who's . . . who's the other guy, do you know?"

"Jake called him Benny."

"Benny Cravets," Seth surmised. "Gotta be. He's Jake's watchdog."

The guilt that had been working on Elena since Devine had shown up reached a boiling point. "This is my fault."

"It's your fault . . . that these guys are scum? I don't . . . think so."

"Devine threatened me," she confessed, searching his dark eyes in the night, looking for signs that he was going to pass out again. "After Joey's sentencing."

She told Seth what Devine had promised would happen to her if Joey ended up dead. "I should have told someone."

"Yeah," Seth agreed, "you should have. We should have had . . . a detail watching you. But the bottom line is, this should . . . have been the safest place you could be. No one would have thought Devine would . . . track you here."

"And yet he has."

"Look, we're going to get out of this. Those two . . . they're in a bad way. Out of shape . . . hurting and pissed off about it. In those shoes . . . they probably have bleeding blisters.

"They'll . . . fade soon, okay? Then we'll figure something out. Just don't . . . panic on me. You need to . . . keep it together."

She nodded, shored herself up. "I'm okay. You're the one I'm worried about."

She watched his face as he tried to find a more comfortable position. "I'm fine. Move on over here, though. It's going to get damn . . . cold before this night is over. We need to share body heat since it's . . . obvious who's going to be using our bedrolls tonight."

Elena glanced at the two men. Jake was already settling into her sleeping bag. Benny, evidently, had been tagged with first watch. He sat with his back against a rock, watching them, the pistol clutched loosely in his hand.

As clichéd as it sounded, Seth was right about needing to share body heat. Moving slowly and quietly, she rolled to her other side so her back was facing Seth's front. Then she scooted back against him, pressing as much of her back to as much of him as she could to share heat.

His big body shivered against hers and she felt a sick knot of dread.

"Closer," he said, his breath feathering along her nape. "We've got to keep warm."

"You're going into shock," she whispered, spooning her body back against his.

"No. I'm fine. Just a little . . . chilled. I'm counting on that hot Martinez temper to warm me up."

He breathed deep and nuzzled his face deeper into her neck. "Workin' already," he whispered, and Elena realized exactly what might be heating him up.

Her bottom was pressed tight against his groin. Very tight as his erection grew against her.

"You have *got* to be kidding," she whispered, astonished.

"Sorry, darlin'." Seth rocked his hips closer to her. "It's the adrenaline. But there's good news. It's working. I'm getting warmer by the minute."

Oh, God. She couldn't believe he'd actually made her smile. "Adrenaline, huh?"

"Cut me a break here, Martinez. It's not like I . . . have a lot of control over this."

No, she thought, feeling her own body respond with warmth as his heated up behind her. It wasn't as if either of them had any control. All that stuff about life or death situations and heightened senses were apparently true. She was acutely aware of everything around her—including the raw sexuality of the man at her back.

They lapsed into silence. Above them the sky spread out like a bolt of velvet, littered with millions of stars. A night breeze danced around the canyon walls. It was so quiet she could hear the rhythm of the Colorado cutting its endless path fifty or so yards below them in the base of the canyon.

"Seth? You still awake?"

"Yeah," he said sluggishly. "I'm awake. Talk to me. I need you to talk to me."

A snore drew their attention toward the lean-to.

"One down," Seth whispered. "Which one is it?"

Elena strained to see in the dark. "Jake."

"How's Cravets holding up?"

"Doing a lot of face rubbing and shaking his head. He's struggling."

"So we wait a little longer. Keep talking, okay? Just talk."

"About what? What do you want to hear?"

"What color panties are you wearing?"

She let out her breath on a disbelieving huff. "You are really too much, you know that?"

"Red?" he guessed, a smile in his voice.

Which made her smile, too. Which is exactly what he'd wanted her to do, she realized. "You wish."

"Okay, fine. Spoil my fantasy. Tell me about your family then. Tell me about your childhood. Hell, tell me about your grocery list. Just talk to me."

# FIVE

SETH'S HEAD HURT LIKE a bitch. Elena was probably right. Concussion. Slight, but there. Enough to make him nauseated if he moved too fast. Enough to make him light-headed if he moved at all. Enough that he knew he had to stay awake because if he let down his guard and slept, he might be out for the duration.

In front of him, Elena's body warmed him like a mini furnace. In more ways than one. No problems in that area. And it *was* adrenaline. Plus basic, carnal instinct. A lush, curvy bottom pressed with decided familiarity into his crotch. A pair of soft hands pressed against his belly. He'd like to meet the man who wouldn't have a knee-jerk reaction to that kind of stimulus. His head might hurt, but he wasn't dead.

Dead was exactly what these cretins wanted. For Elena, too. That just wasn't going to happen. Concussion or not.

He'd wait. And he'd find an opening. He just hoped to hell he didn't pass out before the time came.

He tuned back in to Elena. Drifted on the sound of her voice as she told him about her three brothers. All still in Arizona. All professionals. Seemed she came from a family of overachievers. That was all good.

"That why you work your ass off all the time? Not because you want to be . . . top dog in the DA's office but because you want to keep up with . . . your brothers?"

"A little of both, I guess. My father is very old school. He thinks a woman belongs in the home, raising babies and fetching slippers for the man of the house. This is my way of showing him times have changed and I've changed with them."

"I'm sure he's proud of you."

She drew a deep breath. "Very quietly, but yeah. I think he is.

"What about you?" she asked after a moment. "Brothers? Sisters?"

"Yeah," he said. "One of each. My sis is a teacher . . . like the old man. Lives in L.A. Married. Two kids. One on the way."

"And your brother?"

He wondered how much to tell her. Finally decided to spill it all. "My brother is the reason I'm a cop. He'd say I'm the reason he's a screw-up."

She didn't say anything. Just waited, evidently sensing this wasn't easy for him.

"Brian always had a bug up his ass, you know? If

there was trouble to be had, made or gotten into, he was in the thick of it. I don't know . . . don't know why he felt the need."

"Why would he say that *you're* the reason?"

Seth moved even closer to her warmth. "Because I was Mr. Boy Scout. Honor role. Athlete. I guess he felt he couldn't measure up to big brother . . . so he took the low road."

"And you feel bad about that," she said intuitively.

"Yeah. I do. Could never connect with him, you know?"

"What's he doing now?"

"Don't know. He left home when he was seventeen. That was, hell, over ten years ago. Hasn't been in contact with any of the family since."

She was silent for a moment. "That has to be hard. Especially for your mom and dad."

"Yeah," he agreed. "It's been hard. On everyone."

"It's not your fault, you know. He made his own decisions."

"Right."

"So why don't you sound convinced of that?"

"Because I always figured I should have been able to . . . I don't know. Help him. Straighten him out."

"That why you became a cop? To help straighten people out?"

He shrugged, felt the effort in his throbbing head. "Maybe. I don't know."

"I think I do," she said softly. "I think that's

exactly why you do what you do. It's a good thing, Seth. You've done a good thing."

Whatever, he thought, feeling the fatigue and the physical strain of the rap on his skull. Bottom line was, he hadn't helped his brother, the one person in the world he should have been able to help.

"What's happening over there?"

"Jake's still snoring. Cravets is still awake."

"Probably figures he'll go down with us if he screws up and falls asleep."

"As incentives go, it's a good one."

"Still, I don't figure he'll last much longer. They gorged themselves on water and food. It's going to take a toll soon. We need to be ready. You need to do something for me now, sweetheart. Very slowly, scoot down. I'll bring my knees up. See if you can reach in my right boot. My Leatherman is tucked in there."

The all-in-one knife had been a birthday gift from his dad what now seemed like a hundred years ago. It was just one of many things he had to thank the old man for. In his estimation, it was the knife to end all knives.

Titanium handles, pliers, wire cutters, knife, saw, scissors. Hell, it even had screwdrivers and a bottle opener—all packed in less than five flat inches and less than half a pound.

The Leatherman was like his credit card—he never left home without it.

"Oh, thank you, God," Elena breathed when she

realized he was actually armed. "I was certain you didn't really have a plan."

"O ye of little faith." He smiled against her neck then kissed her there. Just a little "trust me" kiss. A little "everything will be all right" kiss before she started slowly moving down.

"Got it," she whispered after several minutes of struggling to remove the knife from his boot. "Now what?"

"Do you think you can work it open?"

"I'll try."

"Take your time," he whispered, encouragingly, when she made a sound of frustration. "Just take your time."

"It's open." She sounded breathless and winded after struggling and fumbling for several minutes.

"Good girl. I'm going to slowly turn to my other side, okay? When we're back to back, you're going to start sawing on the ropes around my wrists."

"What if I cut you?"

"Darlin', cutting me is the least of our worries."

It took everything in him to roll to his back then maneuver to his opposite side. Sweat beaded on his brow and his stiff limbs screamed in protest. His head throbbed like a gong, his vision was blurry by the time he'd settled, exhausted, with his back against Elena's—and she'd actually done most of the maneuvering to push them together.

"What if he sees us?"

"He won't. It's dark. He's already half asleep,"

Seth assured her. "Now start sawing. And don't worry about cutting me. I'll let you know if you hit an artery."

"That is so not funny."

"I'm with you on that one, darlin'. Just get it done. We'll worry about bleeding later."

IT TURNED OUT THAT it was Elena who was bleeding by the time she finally sawed through the ropes binding Seth's wrists. The rope burned her wrists raw from the constant pressure and friction as she worked to free him. She toughed out the pain, knew it would be minor compared to what Clyde Devine had in mind for them.

"You're through," Seth whispered and slipped the knife out of her aching fingers. "Good girl."

Amazed at the toll that small task had taken on her energy, she sagged in relief.

"What's happening over there?"

She lifted her head, looked down the length of her body to the darkened camp area. "Jake's still asleep. Cravets is awake," she whispered. "And fidgeting. Wait. He's getting up."

"Fake sleep," Seth ordered.

Heart hammering, Elena closed her eyes and made her body relax, made herself lay as still as stone as the crunch of Cravets' footsteps on the rough ground grew closer.

She heard him stop at their feet, stand there for a moment, then turn and limp away.

She lifted her head, watched as he walked in

ever larger circles, as if trying to keep himself awake with exercise. Then he disappeared behind a rock—probably to relieve himself.

"He's out of sight," she said, energized by the excitement of a possible opportunity to escape.

Seth sat up, leaned forward and made quick work of the rope around his ankles, then around hers.

"Hurry," she whispered as he moved to her hands and quickly freed her. "He might come back soon."

Her shoulders ached with the sudden release, her entire body screamed with pain as her stiff joints suddenly shifted.

"Are you . . . are you going after Jake's gun?'

"Darlin', the way my head's spinning I'd probably fall flat in his lap. Let's just get the hell out of here," Seth whispered, tucked the Leatherman back in his boot and rolled to his feet.

He immediately dropped flat on his face.

"Oh, God." Elena bent down to help him up. "Can you walk?"

"Yeah," he said weakly, and on a wobbly effort rose to all fours. With her help, he pushed to his feet. Staggered and sagged against her. "I . . . I can walk."

She glanced back toward the boulder, certain Cravets would appear any second and level the gun on them.

"Come on." Seth let her sling his left arm over her shoulder to steady him. "Go, go, go."

With one hand latched onto the wrist hanging over her shoulder, her other arm wrapped around his waist, Elena moved.

He weighed a ton and she knew he was struggling to stay upright but she didn't care. Adrenaline spiked through her body in huge, fortifying waves, giving her the strength she needed to carry not only her weight but a good share of his.

The night was dark, the ground uneven and mined with rocks, spindly clumps of brittle bushes and barrel cactus. More than once, she tripped, caught herself then rushed ahead. She had no idea where she was going. Away. All she could think about was getting away from them.

Then she heard it. A foul curse. The echoing anger of a heated argument and she knew that Benny had returned to the camp, found them gone. Awakened Jake.

"So much for our head start," Seth said, sounding winded. "Head for the river."

Elena swallowed hard. The river. Her stomach dropped like a skydiver in free-fall. She had an awful feeling she knew where this was going.

A gunshot rang out in the dark, immediately followed by the jump of earth at their feet.

She ran faster, ignoring Seth's moan of pain as he struggled to keep up with her.

"Stop right there!" Jake roared and fired again.

Missed again. Cursed and howled like a wild animal.

A series of rapid gunshots followed. Shots in the dark. Any one of which could hit their mark any second, but they jumped in the earth around them, ricocheting off rock formations.

"Move," Seth demanded and somehow found the strength to dig a little harder, run a little faster.

"You can't get away from me!" Jake shouted, sounding winded and pissed and a whole lot desperate. "I won't let you get away from me!"

He was less than a hundred yards behind them now and closing fast. His voice grew closer every second.

Just as the river had grown closer. They'd reached the end of the line. Stood on a precipice overlooking the swiftly running current forty feet below.

"Tell me you can swim," Seth said.

Elena nodded. "I can swim."

The next thing she knew she was free-falling in midair, arms flailing, her scream caroming off the canyon walls as she plummeted off the cliff toward the muddy depths of the wild Colorado.

# Six

THE FIRST THING THAT registered was pressure. On his lungs, in his ears. The next was the current. Swift and reckless and strong. Then the cold set in. And finally snapped Seth to his senses.

Sensing he was about at the end of his capacity to hold his breath, Seth kicked his way to the surface. Burst through on a gasp only to have the current suck him under again.

This time he was ready. He pushed, clawed, muscled his way above the waterline, sucked in air and searched the dark ahead for something— anything—to grab on to as the river propelled him forward at warp speed. He found it in an up-rooted tamarisk tree, snagged a root as the river whisked by, determined to wash him all the way to the gulf—or drag him under again or beat him to death on the rocky rapids in the shallows farther downstream.

Hanging on for his life, fighting for breath, he searched frantically for Elena. Could see nothing but the rush of water and dark shadows stretched out like ghosts along the shore on either side of him. Then one of those shadows moved.

"Elena!" he yelled above the low baritone rumble and hissing roar of the rapids less than a hundred yards downstream.

"Seth!"

She was within a few yards of him, clutching a boulder while the water waked around her like liquid in a blender, trying to dislodge her from her precarious grip and drag her further away.

"I . . . I can't hang on much . . . longer!"

"You can!" he shouted above the rushing water. "You can do it! I'm coming."

Head cleared by the cold and by panic for Elena, he worked his way toward her, grabbing the next root, letting go, hand over hand, floating quickly to her side.

He wedged himself against the boulder, grabbed for her outstretched hand. Missed.

Grabbed again.

And latched on just as her other hand let go.

"I've got you! I've got you!" he assured her, slowly pulling her in while cascading water washed around his head and the current did its damnedest to tug her away.

Finally, he reeled her to his side, shifted until she was wedged between him and the boulder while the cold Colorado washed around them in a swift, deadly caress.

"You hurt?" he asked against her soaking hair, yelling to be heard above the roar of the rapids ahead.

She shook her head, her body quaking with cold against him. "N . . . no. Fr . . . reezing."

Not really freezing, but close enough. Hypothermia was a real possibility with the water temp running a very cold fifty-something.

"We need to get out of here. Hang on. Just hang on."

He searched the shoreline. Less than two yards of wildly rushing water lay between them and relative safety. He reached for an overhanging tamarisk root. Missed. Stretched and tried again. This time he caught it.

"Turn around," he ordered. "And hang on to me."

Very slowly and carefully, her limbs stiff with cold and fatigue, she maneuvered her body against the boulder until she was facing him.

"Atta girl. Now wrap yourself around me like a monkey. That's it. Don't let go. Whatever happens, do not let go, okay?"

Shivering uncontrollably, she nodded, clung.

He paced himself, puffed in several deep breaths and took the plunge. With only the root to hold them both, he swung their weight toward the shore. The root snapped when they were halfway there. They dropped back into the current like stones and the Colorado had them in her grasp again.

The water sucked them under as they swirled

and spun, at the mercy of the river intent on claiming them as her own.

Then he hit solid rock, felt the air burst out of his lungs on a rush, gasped on a spear of pain as his ribs took the brunt of the crash. Never letting go of Elena, he wrapped his free arm around a stone spire that rose out of the water like a tree trunk and saved their lives.

"We're okay, now," he panted into her hair. "We're . . . okay."

Several deep breaths later, he mustered the strength to drag them the rest of the way out of the water and up onto the damp, sandy bank.

Where he collapsed. Flat on his back, beyond feeling pain in his head or ribs. Barely believing he was on solid ground with Elena spread out on his chest. Panting. Gasping. Choking up water and battling to catch her breath.

His hand felt like it weighed a ton as he lifted it, cupped her head. "So . . . that was refreshing, huh?"

She breathed deep. Managed to lift her head. "You've got a . . . strange sense of humor, King."

He smiled into the night. "And you like it."

She made a weak sound of exasperation. "Yeah. I like it."

He wrapped his arms around her, held her trembling body tight. "We're not out of the woods yet, you know that, don't you? They're going to come looking for us."

"May . . . maybe they'll think we . . . drowned."

"Maybe. But they'll still look."

She was quiet for a long moment as she squirmed closer to the warmth of his body. "How f-f-f . . . far downstream do you th-th-th . . . think we rode the river?"

"Hard to say. Half a mile if we're lucky. Less if we're not. Can't figure they'll try to find a path down in the dark. At least we've got that in our favor. Jake and Cravets are not outdoorsmen. They aren't dressed for hiking. They'll lick their wounds until morning. Start their search at first light."

The violence of her shivering alarmed him.

"In the meantime, we've got to warm you up."

"And you're going to d-d-d . . . do that how?"

"You know how."

"Oh, nnnn . . . not that old cliché," she sputtered, but there was a faint smile in her voice.

"Yeah, that one," he said, admiring her grit. "Lucky for me. Can you sit up?"

Her entire body trembled as she pushed herself up and sat on the rocky shore beside him.

"Come on. I'll help you."

She didn't say a word. She just lifted her violently quaking hands over her head and let him strip off her wet shirt. Huddled into herself when he went to work on her boots then tugged them off along with her sodden socks. Lifted her hips after he'd worked the zipper on her fly and let him shimmy the wet cloth down her legs until she was shivering in her bra and panties.

"Hang on," he said gently as he stood and tested his balance. Iffy, but better than he'd expected.

As quickly as he could, he stripped down to his boxers then spread their clothes out to dry on the branches of spindly willow and salt cedar limbs and on rocks that still held the residual heat from the sun. Then he hurried back to her side.

"Black," he said easing down beside her where she sat on a small patch of coyote willows and horse-tail grass in her black bra and bikini panties. "Even better than red."

"One . . . track . . . mmm . . . mind," she stuttered between chattering teeth as he drew her tightly against him, fusing their flesh together so their body heat would combine and draw from each other and eventually increase both her body temp and his.

"Sorry my hands are so rough," he apologized as he briskly rubbed her back, her arms, her legs where she'd knotted them with his in an effort to speed the warming process.

"F . . . friction. Good," she managed and already he felt her skin warming beneath his hands.

"Elena. Beautiful," he grunted back in his best caveman voice.

"Okay. With th . . . at remark you officially hit m . . . my definition of certifiably in . . . insane."

"Why?" He kept up the constant rubbing, relieved to feel a slight decrease in the severity of her tremors. "Because you think you're not sexy as hell—even though you're half drowned?'

"Because not f-f-f . . . five minutes ago, we almost died and you're s-s-s . . . still coming on to me."

He smiled against her wet hair. "A man's got to do what a man's got to do."

"Seth . . . do me a f-f-f . . . favor, will you?"

"Anything."

"Shut up."

He grinned. God, the woman had guts. He hugged her tighter. She could be bitching and moaning and working herself into hysterical tears. Instead, she endured.

"You've got spunk, you know that, Martinez? I like that in a woman."

"King," she said in a leading tone.

"Yeah, yeah. I know." He kissed the top of her head. "Shutting up now."

HEAT. WEIGHT. PRESSURE.

All good. All wonderful.

Elena fought against the pull toward consciousness. She liked where she was just fine—drifting between sleep and wakefulness.

*Heat. Weight. Pressure.*

The force of it reassured her. Warmed her. Stirred her.

*Heat . . .*

*Weight . . .*

*Pressure . . .*

In all the right spots. In all the right ways.

*Seth.*

Holding her. Warming her. Protecting her.

She opened her eyes. To a moon riding high and bright over a broad, bare shoulder and the jutting, jagged peaks of the canyon walls. To the strength of his big body sheltering her in the night.

*Delicious heat.*

*Substantial weight.*

*Exquisite pressure.*

She moved her hand. Across warm skin covering sinew and muscle and bone.

She turned her head . . . and realized he was awake and watching her.

"Hey," he whispered, a gentle query, a concerned hello.

"Hey," she whispered back, that single word telling him much more. *I'm okay. I'm . . . aware. And yeah, I'm probably going to regret this in the morning.*

"Did you get warmed up?" he murmured with a gruffness in his voice that forewarned her of the erection growing long and thick against her belly.

"Um," she murmured and rocked her hips against him, "yeah. But not warm enough."

He smiled. "I'm giving it all I've got, darlin'."

She smiled, too. "Well . . . no. I don't think you are," she said with meaning.

He searched her face in the moonlight. And saw exactly what she wanted him to see. He saw the welcome, the wanting and the urgency there. Recognized the need in her to be something other than frightened and vulnerable and raw. The desire to stall the truth of their situation. They'd almost died.

They could still die and she needed validation that right now, this moment, she was alive and vital and desperate for something other than fear to get her through the rest of this night.

With exquisite sensitivity, he forked his fingers through her still damp hair. "You sure about this?

She held his dark gaze. Nodded. "Very sure."

He lowered his head tentatively. Touched her lips with a tenderness that almost made her weep. Moved against her with an intimacy that damn near made her beg.

Elena didn't sleep around. No time. No proclivities to muck up her life. No illusions about love and romance and sex having anything to do with each other.

But there was something . . . something about Seth that dared her to forget about her own rules, toss caution to the wind and take anything and everything this man could offer her.

When she moved closer into him, he gave up any pretense of hesitation, too. He rolled her to her back in the soft, green grass, caged in her shoulders with his elbows, cupped her face in his hands and claimed her mouth. Claimed and tormented and tantalized. Long, deep strokes of his tongue. Quick, biting nips of his teeth. On her jaw. On her chin. Back to her mouth again where he bit her lower lip until she gasped, then soothed the tender hurt with his tongue.

She loved the way he kissed her. With hunger and greed and a studied self-indulgence that made her feel savored and desired and outrageously sexual. With a total dedication to both his pleasure and hers that overshadowed anything but the moment.

For now, the moment was just fine.

His big hand made quick work of the clasp of her bra, shoved it out of the way and made room for his mouth to cover her nipple. He wasn't rough, but neither was he gentle. What he was was absorbed. Wholly. Exclusively. He sucked and laved and tugged, triggering her flash points, making her writhe with impatience beneath him.

Cupping his head in her hands, she held his marauding mouth against her breast, arching her back, rocking her hips and inviting him to take, pleading with him to give as she spread her legs to make room for him there.

He growled low in his throat—a primitive sound of pleasure that transitioned to throbbing frustration.

"What? What's wrong?"

He lifted his head, searched her face as she gripped his shoulders. "I wasn't prepared for this." He buried his face in the hollow of her neck. "I can't protect you."

*Oh, God. Protection.*

"I'm on the pill," she said quickly. "And I'm . . . it's been, well, months since I've been in a relationship. If you . . . if you're worried about STDs, don't."

He raised his head again, eyes narrowed. "And you're not worried about me?"

She swallowed, let her hands slip down to his lean waist. "Should I be?"

He nipped her chin. Kissed her cheeks. Her brow. "No, darlin'. I'm whistle clean."

She splayed her fingers over the tightly bunched muscle of his hips, pressed his huge erection against her pubis. "Well, then?"

The rough growth of his beard felt erotically arousing and abrasive when he smiled against her temple. "Are you always this trusting?"

She froze, self-conscious suddenly. "You think I'm naïve."

"No. I think you're amazing." He bussed her nose with his. "And I think—despite the current fix we're in—that I'm the luckiest man alive."

"It's probably the concussion," she said, sinking back into his kisses. "It's clouding your perspective."

His mouth spread into a smile against hers. "Or maybe," he whispered, reaching between them to guide himself to her opening and push inside, "maybe . . ." he repeated through clenched teeth as he drove all the way home, "my perspective is finally crystal clear.

"My God, Elena. You . . . feel . . . so . . . good."

She took him in on a gasp, on a sensual rush of blinding pleasure as he filled her, thick and hard and deep. Rocked with him as he pumped and teased and slid in and out of her slick, wet heat.

Lingering thrusts.

Lazy strokes.

Penetrating plunges.

*Heat* . . .

*Weight . . .*
*Pressure . . .*

When she lifted her hips to his, begged and enticed him to quicken the pace, lazy transitioned to hard, grinding plunges. She wrapped her ankles around his hips, held on for her life and plummeted over the edge on a wild and reckless free-fall of acute sensation and desperate, clawing desire.

He moved one final time above her, seated himself deep and took the plunge with her on a panting groan, stiffening, shuddering, spilling hot and thick inside of her.

# SEVEN

THE SUN WAS STILL low on the horizon, its slanting rays barely spearing into the canyon when Seth opened his eyes to a pounding head and little needles of pain tingling through his left hand. The warm weight of the naked woman who had caused his arm to go to sleep more than made up for the discomfort.

The clearing of the cobwebs from a dismal attempt at sound sleep told him they had to get up and get moving.

"Elena," he whispered, caressing her bare hip. "Sorry, darlin'. Time to run and gun."

She buried her face deeper into his shoulder and made a soft sound of protest.

God, what he wouldn't give for twenty-four hours of uninterrupted time locked in a room with her. A room with a bed. And a shower. And a chair where he could visualize her riding him until he couldn't see straight.

Today, he had to settle for a head start from the

bad guys. Very bad guys who would happily shoot them on sight now and damn Clyde Devine's wrath. Their pride had been bruised when Seth and Elena had given them the slip last night. So the boys were pissed. With pissed came double mean.

Very carefully, Seth slipped his arm out from beneath Elena's head. With even more care, he sat up beside her. Immediately lowered his head between his up-drawn knees when a wave of dizziness slammed him.

"Shit." He hoped to hell this was just a temporary bout of weakness, a drop in his BP after being horizontal for so long.

After a few deep breaths, he lifted his head but still didn't do any celebrating when he found he felt steadier. Standing up and moving around would tell the tale.

Finally, he trusted himself enough to stand. Fought off another, weaker wave of light-headedness and decided he might be able to function after all. He worked the needles out of his hand, ignored the raging headache and walked slowly to gather their clothes.

He wasn't surprised to find them dry. The humidity at the bottom of the canyon was minus zilch. The thirsty night air had sucked the moisture out of everything. Only their hiking boots were still damp inside.

He dressed in silence, reached in a zippered pocket for the power bar he knew he'd find there.

"Thanks, Pop," he whispered. It was a lesson his

father had taught him early on. Along with his Leatherman, he'd taught him to never be without food on his person in the Canyon. It was a beautiful but treacherous place. You never knew what was going to happen.

"Amen to that," he muttered and turned back to Elena.

His heart literally skipped.

*Holy, holy God. Would you look at her?*

She was curled up on her side, as naked as the morning, as breathtaking as the spill of sunlight crawling down the canyon walls. It broke his heart that her smooth and flawless honey-gold skin was marred by nasty bruises from her tussle with the rocky river.

Hunkering down beside her, feeling an unaccustomed tenderness, he brushed the backs of his fingers over her cheek, smiled when she opened her eyes and saw him there.

"Morning," he said. "Again."

Totally uninhibited in her nakedness, she made another one of those sexy, sleepy sounds and sat up with a catlike stretch.

"Oh, man," she said around a yawn. "You get the license number of the truck that hit me?"

He grinned. "And here I thought we'd had a good time last night."

She breathed deep, plowed both hands into her tangled hair and dragged it away from her face. Looked at him. "You're dressed."

He handed over her clothes—with a whole helluva lot of reluctance. The picture of her sitting there, naked and glorious with it, would be burned in his brain until the next millennium. "We need to get a move on. Sorry."

She nodded, looked self-conscious suddenly as she reached for her bra. "And I did, by the way. Have a good time," she said quietly when his brows furrowed. "Well, except maybe for the part about being tied up and held at gunpoint, and getting pushed off a cliff and almost drowning," she added with a fatalistic little smile.

*God-all Friday.* He could fall for this woman. Seriously. She had the courage of a lioness and an amazing ability to find humor even in the depths of this very dangerous situation.

"You're something else, Martinez." He was waiting for her when she poked her head out from the neck of her shirt. Kissed her lightly. "One hot, tough cookie."

"You're . . . something yourself," she said, then kissed him back. "How's the head?"

"There. But I'll live."

"Could you live better with these?" She fished into a zippered pocket of her pants and came up with a little waterproof plastic pouch. Inside were a couple of Band-Aids, a tiny tube of antibiotic ointment and a tin of ibuprofen.

"I think I love you," he said, greedily taking the pain tablets she offered him.

"Just wish I'd remembered I had them last night."

She made him sit then carefully applied ointment to the gash on his head.

"Ouch. Easy. And don't beat yourself up about it. You've had a few things on your mind."

Like running for her life, he thought as she gently finished dressing the wound.

Like making love to him with a hot and desperate sweetness he knew he'd never forget—not in this lifetime.

"I have something for you, too." He reached into his pocket then handed her the power bar he'd taken out earlier.

"Oh, my God. Just ignore me if I drool, okay?"

She unwrapped it, broke it in two and handed the big half to him.

He shook his head. "Already had mine," he lied. He'd be fine. She, however, needed some protein.

"Anyone ever tell you you can't lie worth a darn?" she challenged, still holding out the bar to him. "Unless you can show me the wrapper to prove you ate another one, there's no way I'm going to eat this entire thing."

She had him there. Even though they were running for their lives, she knew he'd adhere to the "leave no trace" rules. He'd never have tossed a wrapper in the Canyon—which meant if there was one, it would be in one of his pockets.

"Just eat it. I'm fine," he insisted.

"Okay, we can fight over this and risk letting Jake and Benny stumble onto us while we squabble over a snack or we can share. Your choice, but I'm not going anywhere until you get a protein fix."

"We're not in a courtroom, Elena," he grumbled, reluctantly taking half of the power bar and popping it into his mouth.

"Nope. But I just won my case."

"Only because I know what a sore loser you are."

She grinned, slipped into her shorts then reached for her boots. "Said the pot to the kettle."

He grunted.

"So what's the plan?" she asked, lacing up.

"Oh, yeah. The plan." He made a big show of scratching his head. "Figured you'd want one of those."

OKAY, NOW WAS NOT the time and this was certainly not the place, but all Elena could think about in the moment was that Seth King might very possibly be a man she could fall in love with.

"Whoa. *He's* the one with the lump on his head, not you," she muttered under her breath and watched him walk to the river's edge and scoop water into his hands.

He washed his face and head with the cold river water, then dipped up more and drank from his cupped palms.

Sunlight glinted off water droplets clinging to his dark hair and tan throat as he hunkered there, the hard muscles in his calves and thighs bulging, the broad strength of his shoulders flexing. A heavy stubble darkened his square jaw, making him look even rougher. Tougher.

Raw.

The man was a force. As hard and inflexible as steel when it came to survival.

And yet . . . a thin strip of bare skin where his shirt rode up and away from the back of his waistband peeked at her. There his skin was soft. Soft and smooth and sensitive. Last night, in the middle of the night, her fingers had lingered there. Lingered and stroked, then clenched and knotted when he'd pumped into her with the power of a man on the edge.

Contrasts. Yeah. Seth King was a study in contrasts. And so much more than she'd given him credit for.

She dragged a hand through her tangled hair and thought about last night, in the depth of the night, when she'd lost herself in his arms. They'd both been on the edge. *So* on edge, Elena had opened herself up to him with an abandon that scared the hell out of her in the daylight.

She could think about that later. Later when they got out of this. *If* they got out of this.

For now, she had bigger, badder things to be afraid of. Like angry men with big guns . . .

The *whoop, whoop, whoop* of a distant helicopter had her jerking her gaze skyward.

"Shit," Seth swore and searched the sky with her.

She shaded her eyes with her hand. "I don't see it."

"Not yet."

"You don't think it could be a park chopper?" she asked, reacting to his grim look.

"What I think is that we can't afford to let who-ever it is spot us before we figure out if they're friend or foe."

He hurried across the sandy riverbank, grabbed her hand and tugged her along behind him. "Come on. It's getting closer. Let's tuck in beneath those willows and wait."

They'd just folded themselves into the trem-bling leaves of a clump of struggling willows and tamarisks when a chopper zipped around a rock wall and into view. It flew low and slow along the length of the river, stopping to hover not fifty me-ters from their hiding place.

"They're definitely searching for someone," Elena stated flatly, as aware of Seth's hard body pressed against her back and his warm breath beating against her cheek as she was of the potential danger. "We're not due out of here until later this afternoon so . . ."

"So it's not the park department rescue chop-per," Seth concluded, and pulled her back tighter against him and further from view. "And it's sure as hell not a guided tour."

Elena shivered and tried to make herself smaller. "Which means . . ."

"Which means," he said, steadying her by wrap-ping his arms tightly around her, "that this particu-lar bird is not flying friendly skies. Gotta be old man Devine. Him and the boys must have had a prearranged check-in time."

"Can you tell how many people are inside?"

His jaw pressed tightly against her temple as he squinted against a sun that glinted off the silver and white engine housing. "I'm seeing two heads."

"Devine and the pilot. So he hasn't picked up the boys yet."

"No place to set down the bird around here. Besides, Devine's probably so pissed at them for letting us get away, he's most likely given orders for them to scour the area on foot and find us or else."

"So Jake and Benny could show up any time, too," Elena concluded, feeling suddenly like they were about to be flattened between two slices of bread in a bad-guy sandwich.

"They're pulling out."

She followed the direction of Seth's gaze, then watched with a tentative sense of relief when the chopper did a one-eighty and resumed its search in a slow crawl up the length of the river.

"Another bullet dodged," he said and gave her shoulders a squeeze.

"But for how long? We can't hide from them forever."

Seth rose slowly and helped her to her feet. "Even if we could, we wouldn't."

His jaw was set as hard as the canyon walls when Elena turned to face him. Her heart flipped like a trout in shallow water even before she asked, "We wouldn't hide? Like there's an alternative?"

"The alternative is the unexpected. They'll expect us to hide. So we'll do the opposite. We're going on the hunt instead."

"The hunt," she repeated, unable to hide the trepidation in her voice. "For help?" she suggested, thinking, hoping, he was figuring on the possibility of a boatload of rafters or something.

"There's no help coming, Elena. We're going on the hunt for the hunters," he said with a resolute determination that made her blood run cold.

*Oh God.*

"Okay, um, would now be a good time to point out that they have guns and a helicopter and that you took a really bad rap on your head?"

He managed to look like he was in total control of all of his senses—which he obviously wasn't. "But we have the element of surprise on our side."

"Element of surprise," she repeated, practically choking on her skepticism. "Surprises are for birthday parties . . . and . . . and . . . EPT results. Surprises are *not* for a drug lord with a vendetta."

He actually grinned. "Don't worry. It'll be fine."

Yeah. And she was the Easter bunny.

They were going to die.

# EIGHT

"I KNOW THIS PART of the Canyon," Seth told Elena after the chopper disappeared, resuming its search upriver and around a bend. "There's only one place near here big enough for the bird to set down. Only one place close enough for Devine to rendezvous with Jake and Benny in this area."

He led her to a spot on the bank where soft dry sand gave way to wet. Using a stick, he scratched out a rough map.

"We're here." He pointed to the map with the sharp end of the stick. "The chopper came from here." He indicated a winding path through the canyon. "We last saw Jake and Benny here—about a half mile upstream."

When she nodded, he continued. "While cell towers can't catch a signal, they've probably got radios or SAT phones that work here in the bottom of the Canyon. So they're talking now and Devine knows where we parted ways with the boys. He's not stupid so he'll figure the river took us downstream—just like it did. So he's probably ordered Jake and Benny to scour the area ahead of where we went in while the chopper heads upriver just in case we doubled back."

"Which means, they're most likely around here somewhere."

"But above us. On the cliffs. That way they've got both areas covered. The chopper searches down here, the boys up there."

She shot a nervous glance toward the jagged terrain above them while he continued.

"When they don't find us, they're going to double back, right?" he pointed out. "Keep looking. Only we're not going to be here. We're going to follow the river to the spot where the chopper will put down." He X'd a spot on the sand map. "It's got to be their rendezvous point. We're going to be waiting for them when they get there."

She drew a deep breath. "And we're going to manage this without them spotting us how?"

He touched a hand to her hair. "You like the water, right?"

She closed her eyes and felt herself go pale. "I live for a good near-drowning experience. Can't get enough of it. And dry clothes are highly overrated."

He hugged her hard. "You'd have made a good cop, Martinez. You've got guts. And you've got try."

"Yeah, well, right now, I'm about to get a bad case of the screamingohmygods. That a desirable cop trait, too?"

He turned her in his arms. Squeezed her shoulders. "Lady, there's not a damn thing about you that's not desirable."

She grunted. "Said the man with the concussion."

He laughed. Hugged her again. "Come on. We're going to walk a ways past these rapids before we get ourselves wet again. No use taking any unnecessary risks."

"No unnecessary risks. Right. I would laugh," she said, not sounding one bit amused, "at the incongruity of that statement in the face of the risks we've already taken, but I lost my sense of humor about the time you pushed me off the cliff."

Fifteen minutes later, they'd made marginal progress down the riverbank, sometimes walking the bank, sometimes wading the perimeter when the terrain got too rough. No sign of the boys. No return of the chopper. Not yet at any rate. But Seth knew they'd have another close encounter before long.

On cue, the *whoop, whoop, whoop* of helicopter rotor blades drifted to them on the faint breeze.

"We've risked being spotted as long as we dare," he said when they reached a spot in the river where the water had quieted and the roar of the rapids was behind them.

He'd hoped they would have reached an area on the bank where they could find cover without taking the plunge. No such luck. They were as exposed as electric wires on a frayed cord—and their situation was just as combustible.

"I know," she said when he glanced at her. "Into the deep freeze."

He picked a spot where water washed over rock, stirring up the current, and yet was deep enough for them to submerge their entire bodies.

Even though the sun beat down and warmed the Canyon air to over eighty degrees, the Colorado's average water temperature hovered just under sixty degrees in the main channel even in daylight hours. It was going to be hell. And they wouldn't be able to stay in long.

"Ready?" He wrapped her hand in his.

"As I'll ever be."

With the chopper noise growing dangerously closer, they waded quickly into the frigid river. Her teeth were already chattering as they sank down until only their heads were above water.

"Here it comes," he said. "Head down. All they can see is the back of our heads. Call on your method acting experiences. Be a rock. *Be* the rock."

"You are so n . . . not funny," she stuttered through chattering teeth, totally unimpressed by his feeble attempt at humor.

He drew her tightly against him, gathered her hair in his hand to corral it and started shivering himself.

They waited. Lips turning blue.

Several minutes passed. Several more.

And they still couldn't move.

Hypothermia, Seth knew, would soon become a threat as the chopper continued a slow, low, back and forth crawl less than fifteen yards above the surface of the water.

"You still with me?" he whispered against her hair and clamped her trembling body tighter.

Her response was a weak, "Um."

He'd take that for a yes. They had to get out of here soon. Adrenaline had pumped their systems full of heat last night and kept them from succumbing to the cold. They'd been full of calories and carbs from their pasta dinner. Today, without the benefit of food to fuel them, they were more vulnerable to the stinging cold.

Seth could no longer feel his toes. His thigh muscles ached like deep bruises. It was getting harder and harder to draw a full breath.

Finally, thank you, God, the sound of the chopper drifted away. He chanced a very slow turn of his head. Saw the bird disappear around a cliff face. And didn't waste a second.

Willing legs that felt like dead stubs to move, he half waded, half stumbled toward the bank, dragging Elena with him.

"I know, I know, baby," he crooned when they dropped like bags of sand on the shore. She moaned, her lips blue, her limbs stiff as posts. "Hurts like hell. We've got to work it out."

His heart damn near broke when he rubbed her

arms with stiff hands and she bit back a cry that told him she was hurting as bad if not worse than he was. An ache so deep filled his bones that it felt like the marrow had frozen. A follow-up burn sizzled like fire as nerve endings slowly reawakened and shot heat-starved sensation into extremities ravaged by the icy-cold Colorado.

"Hang in there," he murmured, fighting his own pain and fumbling with clumsy fingers that alternately ached like they were broken and stung like they were ablaze. "Deep breaths. Breathe through it."

Her body shuddered as she forced herself to comply.

"Still with me?"

A determined nod was his answer as she fought her way through the pain.

"Can you stand?"

She clenched her teeth, rolled to all fours and pushed herself to her feet. Where she stood on wooden legs and uttered not a single word of complaint.

It may have been a cliché, but from his experience on the force, Seth knew it was true that you learned a lot about a person when things got tough. His years as both a beat cop and as a detective had taught him that the true measure of a man came to light when he was faced with danger and in how he handled pain.

The men he wanted at his back or at his side sucked it up, stayed the course, got the job done—no matter how they felt about the plan of action. No matter the discomfort.

As they warmed under the heat of a blazing sun, and he helped Elena work her way along the river's edge toward what he figured was Devine's rendezvous point, he was satisfied that she could watch his six anytime.

She hadn't been happy about his plan of turning the tables on the Devine crew. But she accepted that he was making the calls, and after her initial hesitation, she'd tucked away her doubts and protests and put her faith in him to know what to do to rescue her. Hell, to rescue both of them. She'd sucked it up against the pain from submerging herself in icy water like a pro.

Yeah. He'd want her guarding his back anytime.

Ever watchful for the two-legged predators intent on killing them, he pushed her relentlessly on toward the rendezvous point, hoping to hell he didn't let her down and get them both killed.

"DO YOU SEE ANYONE?"

They were hiding behind a natural windbreak of coyote willows and cattails.

Seth shook his head. Scanned the sandbar that time and rain and the relentless flow of the river had carved out of the bank. The sandbar was a perfect landing zone for a chopper. Flat, wide, dry. A well-used put-in for rafter and kayakers.

"This bend in the river provides fairly good protection." They had hiked about two miles downstream from the spot they'd first jumped in. "We can set up and wait for the bad guys here."

"Protection? I guess I'll have to take your word for it. Because right now, I feel about as exposed as a centerfold in *Playboy*. And do *not* take that as an invitation to capitalize on the image," she added hastily, making him smile.

"Can't fault a guy for wanting to visualize that one," he pointed out, and got a halfhearted glare for his efforts.

She was playacting. Keeping it light, keeping it real for his benefit and maybe a little bit for her own. Their situation was grim. She knew it. He knew it. And, bless her, she was doing her part to keep them both calm.

He'd deal with the centerfold image later, though. At his leisure, he hoped. Right now, they needed to get cracking.

"I expect they'll show up before long," Seth said surveying the familiar walls of the Canyon and searching for a likely path the boys would have to take to get down to their level. He found it when he spotted an irregular cutout of stepping stones. That's where they would come down. And that's where he would set his deadfall trap.

"When they show up? What then?" she asked, rubbing the flat of her palm over her forearm and a red and bleeding welt from a scrape with a dead tree limb.

"When they show up, we'll be ready for them.

"Come on." He took her hand, promising

himself he'd make up for all the pain she'd been through when he got her out of this. And he would get her out of it. He was going to make damn sure of it.

Even if it killed him.

"We don't have much time. Let's get you into position."

"Position?" Elena pinned him with a look. "Position suggests you really do have a plan. Would now be a good time for you to tell me exactly what it is?"

He considered her, considered the cliffs above and around then. "Let me ask you this first. How's your arm?"

"My arm? My arm is fine," she said, moving it as if checking for pain.

"What I meant is, can you throw like a guy or do I have to go to plan B?"

"I throw like a girl," she said, squinting up at him. "Like a girl who was the first team pitcher on an all-state softball team."

*Lord Jesus God, how did he ever get so lucky?*

"You're one amazing surprise after another, you know that? Tell me that, when we get out of this, you'll marry me and have my children," he said, hugging her and planting a quick hard kiss on her mouth.

He wasn't altogether certain he was kidding. He'd sort that part out later, too.

"Yeah, sure. We'll elope to Vegas. We'll get an

Elvis impersonator to do the deed. I'll promise you anything if you can get us out of this alive."

"Darlin'. Your golden, all-state arm just upped the odds of that happening by about a thousand percent."

# NINE

THE PLAN, ELENA DISCOVERED, depended a lot on luck, a lot on timing, and way too much on the accuracy of her aim.

Sweat tickled the indentation of her spine as she lay on her belly, still as the stone cliff above and beneath her, praying to God she was hidden from view of the chopper when it finally closed in on the LZ. Praying also that timing and luck smiled down on them today.

Rocks. She was supposed to take down the chopper with rocks. She judged the weight of the stockpile of stones they'd gathered. The rocks were the only thing joining her on her solitary perch on a six-foot-by-three-foot ledge jutting out of a rock wall approximately twenty-five yards above the Canyon floor.

Precarious at best. But the vantage point was perfect. According to Seth.

"A log or two would be better," he had said as they'd scoured the shallow riverbed for weapons.

"A log?" She'd merely stared. "We both know that's not going to happen, right?"

He'd just grinned, selected several big stones, tucked them into his shirt, then helped Elena climb up the cliff face so she'd be positioned above the chopper as it came in for a landing.

"Okay, here's what's going to happen," he'd said, winded and panting, once they'd settled her in. "We're going to hope the rotor blade is made of some fiberglass composite."

"Do you know how often the words hope, luck and maybe have come up in the past twenty-four hours?"

He'd grinned again and went on. "Most rotor blades are made of fiberglass," he stated. "Some aren't. So we're *hoping* with the odds. To pull this off, you need to drop or throw the rocks from above the bird into the main rotor."

"Rocks. At the main *rotor* blade?"

"Yeah. Rotor blade. It's the big blade that lifts the bird."

That's when her heart actually jumped to her throat, making talking—not to mention breathing— damn near impossible. "For God's sake, I *know* what the main rotor blade is. What I *don't* know is how you think I can hit it. And even if I could, how you think I can take down a helicopter with a rock."

"Unless you've got a rocket-propelled grenade

launcher tucked under your shirt, yeah. You can do it. And yes, you can do it with a rock. Look. All you have to do is nick the blade, okay? Just nick it. It could crash even if you don't make a direct hit because the impact will still throw it off balance. That'll spook the pilot. Maybe he'll do something stupid—like crash all by himself."

Sweet Lord.

"Be safe," he said suddenly. Kissed her hard and took off.

So now here she was. Hugging the sun-warmed stone from toe to chin. Seth had scrambled back down the side of the cliff five minutes ago, leaving her here to contemplate the magnitude of what she had to do.

In silence she'd watched him as he'd sprinted across the sandbar, stopped abruptly when something caught his eye. After some digging and fishing around, he dragged a long rope out of the sand.

He'd turned to give her a grinning thumb's up before wading to the other bank then scaling the opposite cliff.

At first she thought he was going to find a hiding place and wait, like her, but instead, he climbed over to a huge boulder, fussed around with some rocks and the rope, and then threw the loose end down the cliff face.

Before he was finished, he'd planted the remainder of the rope along the ground, then hidden his handiwork with sand and dried grass.

Laying a trap, she realized. Like she'd seen her brother lay for a poor unsuspecting rabbit once. Jake and Benny may be unsuspecting. But they weren't cute, fuzzy, harmless little forest creatures either.

If she remembered right, her brother never had gotten that trap to work on a bunny. What were the odds, she wondered, that Seth's trap was going to work on two very ugly, very mean bottom-feeders?

About the same as her odds of taking down a chopper.

With a rock.

And with *hope*

. . . and with *luck*

. . . and a whole lot of *maybe*.

And to think . . . once her world had been so concrete.

SETH KNEW HE WAS running out of time, and just like a cat that had escaped half a dozen close calls, he was running out of lives. He hadn't let on to Elena, but his head had started throbbing again. Double vision came and went like the sun that ducked under, then out from behind a scattering of puffy white clouds dotting a sky so brilliantly blue it hurt his eyes.

He couldn't deal with any of that now. His gut told him the chopper would be setting in to roost soon, and that Jake and Benny wouldn't be far behind.

He had to be ready for them when they came. He

had to get the drop on them or he didn't have a chance in hell of pulling this off.

And he had nothing but his experience to make it happen. Hands on his hips, he scanned the riverbank for something, anything that might help . . .

When his gaze snagged on something half-buried in the silt of the riverbed, he thought he might actually be hallucinating.

But he trotted toward it, waded knee deep into the water and reached down. And damn near collapsed with gratitude for someone else's carelessness.

It was a rope. Probably lost by a kayaking party or a rafting crew, and it was the lifeline he needed.

"Sweet mother of God," he muttered when he'd hauled in the full one hundred fifty-plus feet of it. He was in business.

He tugged his Leatherman out of his boot, flipped out the blade and scanned the rock walls surrounding them for a likely deadfall trap. Thought back to a time when he was ten and he and his dad were camping and he was determined to catch something wild for dinner.

He heard his dad's voice in his head.

*"Son, this is how it works. Imagine a brick, a six-inch long stick and a shoelace. Tie one end of the shoelace to one end of the stick. Point it up with the shoelace-end of the stick on the ground. Prop the brick up on the other end of the stick. When you yank the shoelace, the brick falls, trapping whatever is under it.*

*"Now improvise. No brick. No shoelace. But*

*there are lots of sticks. Why don't you see what you can come up with?"*

He'd come up with a rope from the tent and a cage he'd constructed out of flexible willow twigs woven together with bark. Then he'd propped that sorry-looking sucker up, laid the rope on the forest floor, covered it with leaves and pine needles and hidden in the bushes and waited for his prey.

In his mind, he'd been Daniel fricking Boone. One of the last Mohicans. A trailblazing mountain man. And he'd waited. And waited. Only to fall asleep and wake up snug in his sleeping bag where his father had carried him into the tent several hours later.

No wabbit stew. But the experience had been just as fulfilling.

He didn't have fulfilling in mind today. He had survival. Fortunately, he had the added advantage of Jake and Benny having IQs less than the combined wildlife population in the area. And he didn't have trapping in mind. He was more of a mind for crushing.

He scanned the cliff face—and spotted exactly what he was looking for. A huge boulder, precariously perched on a ledge. Unstable as hell. At least it looked that way.

If he could manage to tie the rope around the base without dislodging it, control the trajectory of the fall by wedging some stones under it to help guide it—he was golden.

He was sweating like a butcher, dizzy and nauseated by the time he finished a series of loops and knots then climbed back down the cliff, dodging beaver tail and prickly pear cactus as he went. There was no way to camouflage the rope on the rock face, but since it could conceivably be mistaken for a long tree root or a vine, he figured he was safe. Once he reached the bottom, he covered the rope with sand and, using grass to cover his tracks, swept his way into the brush.

Then he lay in wait. Sweat running into his eyes, stinging like hell. Head pounding like a jack-hammer.

He'd rested for all of a minute when he heard voices. Then the sound of the chopper.

He glanced up the cliff where Elena lay hidden. Felt his heart slam like a clean-up batter, bottom of the ninth, tying run on third and he was sitting with a three–two count.

If anything happened to her. If . . . Jesus, if she got hurt . . . or . . .

No.

He wasn't going to think that way. She was steady. She was solid.

His vision blurred. He fought it. Fought the pain and the light-headedness.

It was showtime. The boys were just in time for the curtain to go up.

ELENA FELT THE VIBRATION of the chopper's engine clear to her bones. It zoomed in from the west and hovered a hundred yards above the spot where Seth said it would land, and not more than twenty yards north of the cliff where she lay in wait.

The bird started its slow descent and the vibrations increased as dust kicked up by the rotor wash stung her face and her eyes.

Closer. It was getting closer.

She was bone-deep scared. So scared she just wanted to have this over. So close to panic she wanted to start hurling rocks right now! Wildly. Blindly. Just get it over with.

She made herself wait. Made herself lay there. Still as stone. Still except for the trembling in her limbs, her erratic breaths and the staccato beat of her heart in her chest and her ears and her throat.

"Hurry. Hurry. Hurry," she whispered, willing the bird down, down below her.

An eternity passed as it slowly descended. Then an eon as the sound of the blades slammed into her ears and the dust swirled like a tornado stinging her eyes and peppering her skin with grit.

"Hurry!" she shouted aloud, her voice drowned out by the engine roar.

As if her edict actually held sway, the dust settled in an instant. Stunned, she lifted her head.

Below her. The chopper had finally dropped to hover below her, pushing the rotor wash with it, stilling the air above the blades, stirring up a circle of white caps directly below.

Now. She had to do this now!

Reacting with a pure adrenaline rush, she shot to her feet, grabbed the first stone and hurled with all her might.

And missed.

She didn't hesitate. She picked up another. Threw another, another, another.

Missed again.

Yet again.

Roaring with frustration and fear, she dug deep, drew a steadying breath and made one final, powerful throw.

And made the hit.

The sound was unlike anything she'd ever heard. A crunch, followed by a wheezing, whining groan as the bird wobbled, spun, then dipped nose first and plummeted the rest of the way to the river.

Chest heaving, she raked the hair back from her eyes, squinted through the grit then sucked in a breath in horror and triumph and a little bit of despair. The chopper crashed onto the edge of the sandbar and rolled to its side, the rotor blades snapping to a skidding halt in the sand. Fire shot out of the engine cowling as the bird totally upended and lodged upside down, the cockpit half submerged in the river.

She'd done it! She'd dropped the chopper.

And in the process, she'd taken a life.

Two lives.

No reminders that the men in the helicopter had intended to kill her and Seth could stall the sudden nausea that hit her like a roundhouse punch.

She dropped to her knees—just as a bullet whizzed by her head and ricocheted with a sharp, twanging ping off the rock face above her.

"Jesus. Jesus," she muttered, ducking for cover. Someone was shooting at her.

She chanced lifting her head—and saw two figures running along the cliff fifty feet above the opposite riverbank.

Fire flashed from the barrel of the pistol as Jake shot at her again, his aim wild as he half limped, half ran down the uneven path toward the riverbed trying to get to the downed bird.

Survival, not guilt, suddenly jumped to the top of her priority list again.

Seth. Seth was down there. Unarmed. Much less than one hundred percent. She'd noticed. Chosen not to mention how pale he looked, or that his eyes looked a little glazed.

No food, the burning sun and consuming heat and, conversely, the icy dip they'd taken in the river had all taken a toll on him. He'd wanted her to forget that he was dealing with a concussion, though, so she'd let him think she had.

Only now, she couldn't forget it. Now, he was down there trying to face off against two really bad men with really big guns.

She had to get to him, but knew she was as good as dead if she started down the cliff. She'd stand out like a stripper in church if she tried to scale the rock wall now. Jake or Benny would pick her off like one of those little metal ducks in a shooting gallery.

Frustrated, afraid for Seth, all she could do was hug the earth and wait. And *hope* and pray that *maybe* their *luck* would hold out just a little bit longer.

# TEN

ONE SECOND SETH WAS certain the bird was going to make it down without a scratch and he was going to be facing not two but four men and the next the bird jerked, spun, belched out smoke and dropped from the sky like a meteor gone wild.

"Gawd damn," he uttered under his breath and watched it fall, felt the earth shake and the spray of water as the blades chopped and slashed into the river and spat liquid ice in twenty directions.

*She did it. Sonofabitch, she did it!*

He wasn't more than ten yards from the crash site, hiding in the brush, waiting and ready to spring his deadfall trap on the off chance Jake and Benny stumbled into it.

He rose from a crouch, fought a crippling wave of dizziness and steadied himself before heading for the downed bird to see if he could find a weapon when an M-16 rifle floated out of the upturned and half-submerged cockpit.

He didn't think. He just reacted. He wanted that weapon and there was only one way to get it before it drifted downstream and their best chance of getting a jump on Jake and Benny ended up in Lake Mead.

No more than a second, maybe two had passed since the bird dropped when, on a shallow dive, he cut into the river.

The icy shock on his system cleared his head. He rocketed a good ten yards underwater before his head broke the surface and the current started washing him after the rifle.

It took another moment to get his bearings—then he spotted the weapon ahead of him, and thank the fates, the shoulder strap had snagged on a tree root bleached bone white and winter gray by time and sun. He snagged the same root as he floated past, and, fighting the current, freed the M-16. Then he dragged himself along the length of the tree to the shallows along the bank.

He figured no more than fifteen seconds had passed as, shaking from the physical effort, he slogged out of the river, panting and swaying . . . then frantically ducked for cover when he heard a gunshot.

He rolled to his back. Cradling the rifle over his chest, he checked the magazine and found it full. Then he fumbled with cold fingers to pour the water out of the gas system. It took a couple more minutes than he had to spare, but it couldn't be helped. As confident as he could be that the rifle was functional, he rolled back to his stomach.

Jake and Benny, looking battered and bruised and horrified by the site of the downed chopper, scrambled down the far bank . . . and directly toward the deadfall trap Seth had set.

The only problem was, Seth wasn't anywhere near the rope to trigger it.

Strike that. It wasn't the only problem. Jake was firing wildly toward the spot on the cliff where Elena was as good as a sitting duck.

Seth didn't hesitate. He sighted down the barrel—cursed when his vision went fuzzy—and did his damnedest to get a bead on Jake.

He squeezed off a round, then watched as the two men dove behind a boulder and started wildly firing their pistols.

"Not so brave when the odds even up a bit, are you, assholes?" he muttered and, rising, laid down another burst of fire to cover himself as he ran back toward the crash site with the hope of gaining a tactical advantage on the two men pinned down behind the boulder.

"Elena?" he yelled, for the first time close enough to check on her.

"I'm okay!" she yelled back.

If relief had been any sweeter, he'd have overdosed on it. Since he was already dizzy from the damn rap his head had taken, he couldn't afford another hit to his equilibrium.

"Stay put," he ordered. "Me and the boys will have this settled in no time, right, boys?" he yelled across the narrow expanse of river that was linked by the sandbar.

"Fuck you!"

Jake. He recognized the voice. Just like he recognized the sound of his ammo as .45s. Another few rounds flew past him.

"You boys need to work on your attitude," Seth yelled, his tone scolding and intentionally irritating as hell. And, he hoped, not giving away that he felt himself fading.

"I'll give you attitude, pig. You killed my old man!"

Jake wasn't just mad, he was bawling. Any closer to the edge and he'd make a major mistake. Like charging Seth. Which was exactly what he wanted Jake to do. So he goaded him some more.

"Now see, you're just not looking at this right, Jakie boy. I did you a favor. You can be the man now. The man he never let you be."

"You shut up about him! You shut the fuck up about him! This is your fault! Yours! And you're dead because of it! Dead, you hear me?"

"Now, Jake. You keep forgetting, we were minding our own business. You're the ones who came looking for trouble. Well, you found it. In case you haven't figured it out, you can't hit shit with those handguns at this range. On the other hand, this M-16 can take you out like a bad prom date. Now, come on out, fellas, before you force me to do something I really don't want to do—which is waste perfectly good ammo on the likes of you."

Silence.

Spots before his eyes.

Shit.

Seth shook his head. Hurt like hell, but his vision cleared. Just in time to see a shadow move then loom over him from behind.

He spun around . . . and felt his jaw crack when a booted foot slammed into his face. Then all he saw was black.

WHEN SETH CAME TO, pain raged through his swollen jaw, stabbed him behind his eyes and at the back of his head. Clyde Devine stood over him, a 1911A pistol pointed dead center at his chest.

Devine was soaking wet, breathing hard; blood trickled down his temple. Murder fired in eyes as gray as the hair falling out of a gnarled ponytail. Pain furrowed brows etched deep with age and hard living.

On her knees in front of Devine, Elena was silent, her face grimacing in pain as Devine's fist twisted in her hair and jerked her head back hard.

"She goes first," Clyde said, a lethal calmness in his tone that echoed with evil. "She's going slow and screaming. And you're not goin' to be able to do a damn thing about it but watch her beg and watch her bleed."

SETH DIDN'T HAVE TO fake weakness. His ears rang. He fought back the urge to vomit, certain that if he did, he'd probably choke to death. His jaw was so swollen he couldn't open his mouth. Broken, he suspected. Along with a couple of teeth.

But he wasn't dead. He couldn't be. Because if he let these bastards get him, then Elena was as good as dead too.

So he stayed on his feet, tripping and stumbling as Devine marched him toward Jake and Benny, who had come out from behind their hidey-hole and were carefully picking their way down the steep and craggy cliff face.

Hidey-hole . . . Seth thought. Which was in a direct line to his deadfall trap.

Forcing himself to focus through the weakness and pain, he scanned the ground at his feet.

*Where the hell was it?*

*Where the hell was the rope?*

He flinched when a snake slithered across the sand.

No. Not a snake.

He squinted. Fought to focus. Dropped to all fours. Then fell flat on his face. Brain fuzzy. Pain clawing at him with eagle talons.

Sand in his mouth. In his eyes. Rope. Not a snake. A rope beneath his hands.

*Rope.*

He clutched it as Devine kicked him in the side.

Fire screamed through his ribs. He doubled over in agony. Heard himself groan.

"Get up! Get your sorry ass up or I'll take the first slice out of her right now."

"Wait . . . wait," Seth slurred through ungodly pain, struggling to make the words come out. Digging with everything in him, he pushed himself to all fours . . . fought for a sustaining breath . . . then reared back, rope in hand, jerking with all his might.

He felt the rumble, heard the crunch and grind and bass vibrations as the boulder dislodged and roared down the cliff at warp speed times two.

A man screamed. Elena cried out. Devine cursed and kicked him again.

When Seth opened his eyes, the barrel of the M-16 was bearing down, aiming for the spot between his brows.

"You sonofabitch!" Devine roared.

Adrenaline shot through Seth's blood like a fuel injection system pumped gas through a Formula 1 racer.

He grabbed the barrel, twisted and jerked. Heard the burst of fire as Devine pulled the trigger. Felt the burn on his fingers, wrapped in a death grip around the barrel. Jerked when the sharp, cutting sting of the bullet ripped into his body followed by Devine crashing down on him.

It was all muscle memory and blind, raging instinct from that instant on. He fought—not for his life but for Elena's, aware of her screams on a peripheral level. Aware of the pain on an entirely different plane that he blocked as he wrestled Devine to his back, crashed his fist into the drug lord's face with a crunch of bone and spurt of blood.

He hit him again. Straddling his supine body, he kept on hitting him as blood sprayed and Devine's lifeless form lagged like a broken doll with every punch.

He heard his name from a distance. Heard the horror, the pleading to stop, the assurance that Devine was dead.

Still he kept swinging. Wildly now. With no control. No target, no focus . . . no strength.

No . . . light.

No . . . bearings.

Not even a vague idea of where he was, what he was doing, why each breath he took told him to deliver death.

Then he couldn't swing any more. Winded, weak, sluggish with pain and fatigue, he stopped.

Stopped pummeling. Stopped thinking. Stopped seeing. Stopped feeling.

The last thing he remembered was the hesitant touch of a soft hand on his brow. The soothing sounds of a trembling, terrified voice telling him it was over. It was over.

It was over . . .

# Eleven

"HEY, TOUGH GUY. ABOUT time you put in an appearance."

Elena was surprised to hear her voice sound so easy and casual. So . . . unconcerned, when inside, she quaked with relief as Seth struggled to open his eyes.

She'd been so afraid for him. Too afraid to leave his side for more than an hour since the park rescue chopper had evaced them into Flagstaff yesterday.

God. Had it really been yesterday? It seemed . . . well, it seemed that she was still living the nightmare.

But it was over.

Clyde Devine was dead. He'd died as he'd lived. Violently. Brutally. On the wrong side of good.

Jake had two broken legs. Seth's deadfall trap had done its worst. The careening boulder had rolled over Jake as he'd scrambled in vain to get out of the way. He wasn't in great shape, but he would survive long enough for trial. Benny Cravets, however, hadn't been so lucky. A stray rock shot out of the debris of the deadfall trap and had hit him in the temple. Killed him on impact.

Seth, thank God, was alive. And now that he'd opened his eyes, Elena took a life-sustaining breath too.

*Hope. Luck. And maybe.*

Seemed they were enough to get by on after all.

She studied his beautiful, bruised face. As weak as he was, Seth still looked big and dark and strong against the stark-white hospital sheets. And yet she knew how much blood he'd lost before help had arrived and he'd gotten the medical attention he needed.

She knew and she remembered every soul-testing moment as she'd made bandages out of a dead man's shirt. Called for help using a dead man's radio.

She shivered, recalling the lifeless weight and soulless eyes of Clyde Devine as she'd frantically stripped him of his shirt. She'd felt like a ghoul, robbing the dead. But she hadn't cared. Seth had been bleeding out. She wasn't going to let that happen. So she'd done what she'd had to do.

That had been close to twenty-four hours ago and this was the first breath of true relief she'd let herself take since.

His eyes were glazed and unfocused, but they were open as he struggled toward lucidity.

Lord, his face was a mess. His left jaw was swollen twice the size of the right, his mouth was wired shut to support the broken bones.

"Easy, buddy. You're fine. You probably hurt like hell, but you're fine."

Elena lifted her gaze to Lieutenant Dan Gates. The relief in his voice was as palpable as the relief she felt. Seth's superior had been holding vigil by Seth's bed with her for the past few hours. Hours in which she'd caught Dan staring at her with veiled curiosity, obviously wondering about the part of the story she'd left out.

The part that even she couldn't believe had happened. The part about making love with Seth. The part about falling in love with him.

The part that now, under the stark, harsh hospital lights and in the same stark harsh face of reality, seemed as remote and as far removed from the real world as the nightmare they'd both lived through in the Canyon.

"He's awake?"

Elena turned as a nurse walked in. The name tag on the white uniform told them that Lisa, a thirty-something blonde with a big smile and a lot of bounce, was an LPN. She'd slipped into the room to take Seth's vitals and neither Elena nor Dan had heard her.

"Just." Dan moved away from the bed so Lisa could take care of business.

"Fantastic," Lisa said with enough cheer to lead a basketball team to victory. "I'll let the doc know."

"Don't suppose . . . a man . . . could get some water?"

Seth. Voice raspy and weak and garbled by the

limitation of his broken jaw. And so beautiful, Elena
fought tears.

"Not just yet, hero," Lisa said with a chuckle.
"But if you ask real nice, I might be persuaded to
get you some ice chips."

An agitated grunt from the bed. "Pretty please . . .
with pepper on it."

Both Elena and Dan grinned. Lisa too, although
she was already on her way out the door to do
Seth's bidding.

"You had us worried," Dan said, moving back
into Seth's line of sight.

Seth squinted up at Dan. "What the hell . . . you
doing here? And where . . . is here, anyway?"

"Flagstaff. You're in the hospital. You were shot,
remember?"

It took a moment but Elena saw the second that
recognition dawned.

"Elena," Seth said, becoming agitated. He struggled to sit up.

"I'm right here." She moved in quickly, took his
hand in hers to settle him. "I'm fine. I'm fine," she
repeated when he collapsed with a groan of pain and
relief.

He turned his gaze to hers. His features softened through a haze of medication and fatigue.
"Fine," he repeated weakly and his eyes drifted
shut again.

SETH LOOKED LIKE HIS father, Elena realized the
next day when both Bill and Wanda King arrived to

make certain their son was truly alive and going to make it.

Nice people, she thought, watching from the door of Seth's hospital room. Very nice.

But not her people. Not her life. Just like Seth could never be her life. A bubble, she reminded herself as she left the hospital. What had happened, what they had shared—it was just a bubble in time. Now life went on. As it had before.

He was a cop with an attitude.

She was the assistant DA thorn in his side.

Fate had pitted them together. A life or death struggle had remolded their perimeters. Shifted everything out of focus, thrown everything out of place.

Temporarily.

Well. Soon everything would be back to status quo. As much as it hurt to think it, as much as it pained her to accept it, the truth was, business as usual would pit them against each other in court again. Then the reality that they would often be shoring up opposite sides of the fence would take a toll.

Oil and water.

Fire and ice.

Miles apart and passionate about the differences.

So no. Elena would be a fool to think anything had truly changed between them.

They would never again be enemies. But in the long haul, it was not in the cards for them to be friends.

Or lovers, she thought sadly and turned and walked away.

The next day, she put in for a month's leave. She had more than that coming. And it was time.

She went home. Where her mom cooked for her and told her she was too thin and her dad told her she should get married and give him more grandbabies.

Home. Where she could forget about Seth King's kisses and start the process of life as she had once known it without him in it.

# TWELVE

*2 months later.*

"DAMMIT, ELENA, YOU KNOW that's a pile of crap!"

"Order in the court!" The rap of a gavel rang like buckshot through the crowded courtroom.

Elena cringed as Seth, in full uniform, shot to his feet on the witness stand and glared between her and Judge Harrison. It was Seth's third outburst in as many weeks before the same judge. Harrison was at the end of his rope in the patience department.

"He's guilty," Seth went on, his face red with rage. "We all know he's guilty of a felony and she wants to slap him with a misdemeanor!"

"I will have order in my court!" Harrison slammed the gavel so hard Elena was afraid he was going to break it.

The room suddenly echoed in silence.

"Councilor." Judge Harrison's bushy white brows pinched in anger as he glared at Elena. "You will see me in my chambers. Now. And you," he added with a sharp glance at Seth, who sat in the witness chair in full uniform, "you will join us."

Face hard and unreadable, Seth shot a covert glance at Elena as he pushed himself out of the witness chair and followed both her and the judge.

"You are both officers of the court," Harrison admonished without preamble as he closed the door behind them. "As such, it is my expectation that you will work out your differences prior to setting foot in my courtroom. Is that clear?"

Elena nodded. From the corner of her eye she saw Seth, standing at parade rest beside her, do the same.

"He's *your* witness," Harrison went on, a full-fledged scowl darkening his wizened face as his gaze locked on Elena. "It would be my expectation, then, that he would not be hostile. You've got two minutes. Work it out or I'm going to find you both in contempt." In a rustle of flowing black robes, he strode back out the door.

Leaving them alone together for the first time since Elena had left Seth in the hospital surrounded by his family two months ago.

She folded her arms over her midriff, stared at a spot on the floor in front of the toe of her shoe.

She could feel Seth's gaze burning a hole into the top of her head. Knew she should say something. Couldn't make herself speak.

He, however, had no such compunctions.

"This is it, then? This is the way you want things between us?"

More than hard-edged anger. Disappointment. Resentment. Pain. None of it, she knew, had anything to do with the case she was trying. She'd been avoiding him. For his sake as much as her own.

Still she couldn't speak. Except for two words. "I'm sorry."

"Sorry? Jesus, Elena. You skipped. Dropped off the face of the earth."

Of course this discussion couldn't be about the case. It had to be about them. Because whatever was left about them was unfinished.

"So . . . it was nothing? What we shared? What I thought we'd become to each other? Nothing?"

Confusion joined the anger and disappointment in his tone. And almost broke her heart.

"We both knew nothing could come of it," she replied.

He was silent for a long moment. Watching her. Struggling with emotions she was surprised were so strong.

"And we knew that why? We knew that how? How exactly did we know that? You tell me. You tell me why I can't love you. You tell me why you can't love me. Because of our jobs?" He made a sound of disgust. "Screw that. They're jobs. They're not our lives."

So . . . there was this problem with her reasoning. A problem that had been plaguing her since she'd left him in that hospital bed. What if she was wrong? What if . . . what if there was something more? What if . . . what if she could take the chance and love him?

Tears filled her eyes as she met his, and found his eyes misty too. She swallowed back a sob. Let the tears fall, slow and warm down her cheeks. God, she was a fool. "For a supposedly smart woman . . . I made a pretty stupid mistake, huh?"

He searched her face, evidently saw what he needed there. Came to her. Drew her carefully against him. Then he crushed her to his chest where she clung and clutched at his uniform and felt the knot that had cramped in her heart for two long months finally ease.

"Yeah, well. No more stupid than me," he said, tipping her face up to his, "for letting you get by with dodging me for this long."

He kissed her then. Deeply. So very, very sweetly. "God, I've missed you."

"Me too," she managed, although her voice broke.

He kissed her again. Again, feasting on her lips like he was claiming a reward for a long, hard battle of wills.

"Do you really think there's a prayer we can make this work?" she asked, snuggling close against him. "I mean . . . case in point . . . *this* case. We're butting heads like bighorn sheep again."

"What I think," he said against her hair, "is that I'll never forgive myself or you if we don't at least give it a try."

Yes. They needed to try. She only hoped it would be enough.

*One month later*

"DAMMIT, ELENA, YOU can't do this!"

Elena looked up from Larry Olson's desk where they'd been conferring on the fine points of a brief to see Seth—all six long, rangy feet of him—stalk into the DA's office.

He looked lean, mean and mad. Typical.

"Must you always make an entrance, Detective?" she sputtered as every head in the common area turned at Seth's bull-seeing-red stance.

One by one, office doors circling the central pool opened. Heads popped out, saw the thunder in Seth's cobalt-blue eyes and made hasty retreats back to the relative safety of their cramped office quarters.

"I take it you have a problem, Detective King?" Elena straightened and met him eye to eye.

"Damn straight, I do."

"What a surprise."

His eyes burned into hers, all pissed-off male with a bone to pick.

"Fine. Let's take this into my office. No need to disrupt the entire building."

"We can take it anywhere you want to. But we're going to do this now."

Same old Seth, Elena thought, as she turned and

walked with the easy gait of a woman who had all the time in the world. Inside she was quaking. "Follow me."

She received a surly grunt for her efforts but he followed her. He was right on her heels as she reached her private office, opened her door and stepped aside for him to enter ahead of her.

Then she joined him. Closed and locked the door behind her, steeling herself for the confrontation to come.

"You've got a lot of nerve barging in here like this."

He caught her up against him and dragged her into his arms. "Door's closed, babe. You can drop the act."

"You were supposed to be here an hour ago," she murmured urgently, wrapping her arms around him and sinking into his greedy mouth.

"Couldn't be helped," he whispered around long, hungry kisses before finally tearing his lips away from hers. He smiled against her mouth. "Damn, I needed that."

She looped her arms around his neck, content in a way she'd never thought she could be. "That makes two of us."

"You really think we're fooling them?" He backed across the room, walking her with him until his hips bumped the corner of her desk.

He perched on the edge of the desk, made a place for her between his spread thighs and drew her tightly against him.

"Oh, they're definitely guessing. I mean . . . you show up here a lot these days, you know."

He lowered his mouth to her neck, reached up to loosen the pin holding her hair in a neat little knot on the top of her head. "A guy's got to do what a guy's got to do. This suit drives me crazy, you know."

"It's a plain black suit," she pointed out as he peeled the jacket down her shoulders and helped her shimmy out of it.

"That's what I mean. Plain black over a body that's anything but plain. Umm." He worked the buttons on her white blouse. "Take for instance, this bra." He reached for the front clasp and flicked it open, peeled the lacy cups away from her breasts. "It's a miracle of modern engineering."

"We shouldn't be doing this," she pointed out breathlessly as he lowered his head and pinched an erect nipple between his teeth.

"How you spend your lunch break is your business . . . and mine," he murmured.

She sucked in her breath on a gasp when he reached up under her short skirt and skimmed his thumb around the leg of her lacy panties.

"Detective," she whispered breathlessly, trying with desperation to invoke a little protest. Trying and failing when he neatly skimmed her panties down her hips and shoved them to the floor.

"You need a cop, lady?" He nuzzled her hair aside, bit her jaw. "Tell me your problem. I promise, I can fix it."

"For an officer of the court, you're a very naughty man."

"You filing a complaint?"

"No," she let her head loll to the side so he could kiss her there, "but all these ridiculous law-and-order clichés could get me disbarred."

He laughed, shifted their weight abruptly until she was sitting on the edge of the desk, her ankles locked around his waist as he worked desperately to lower his zipper.

"Hurry," she demanded in a husky whisper that changed to a gasp when he freed himself and plunged deep inside of her.

It was always like this between them. The rush. The joy. The unadulterated desire that simmered, then boiled, then fed a need so huge it consumed them.

"Shh," Seth crooned as he gripped her around the waist with one arm and covered her mouth with a big, rough hand. "They'll think I'm attacking you."

She groaned again, then fell back onto the top of her desk and let him take her under.

"Do you have any idea how beautiful you are?" His breath was gruff and raspy as he gripped her hips in both hands, stilled the action of his hips and simply stared at her.

She knew how she looked. Her hair undone and wild around her face. Her arms languid and limp, lying palms-up on either side of her head. Her blouse open, her bra lost somewhere in the tangle, her skirt pushed up around her waist.

And she thought, *Yeah, I know exactly how I look in his eyes. He thinks I'm the sexiest woman on earth.* And with him, she was.

"And do you know how amazing you are?" She met his eyes, watched them fog over as she locked her ankles tighter around his waist and arched her pelvis into his.

"You're going to make me come," he groaned.

"Poor baby. No control. No control at all," she teased, tightened her inner muscles around him and slowly licked her lips.

Another groan as his fingers dug into her hips and he plunged hard and deep. "You're playing with fire here. But you already know that, don't you?"

"I know that I love you," she whispered, lifting a hand to trail a finger down the muscled length of his chest, down his tense abdomen, then lower to touch the root of him where he pressed deep inside of her.

He growled, low and primal and plunged one final time, sending them both over the edge of control in a rush of glorious sensation.

"Will I ever not want you this way?" he whispered moments later as he drew her to a sitting position and held her tightly against him.

"Maybe. But I hope not. If I'm lucky you will always want me." She pressed a kiss against his chest, wishing his uniform shirt wasn't keeping her from touching skin.

Hope. Luck. Maybe.

Words, she'd decided, she planned to live by.

"I love you," Seth whispered against her hair.

Yeah. He loved her. And they would make this work.

With hope. Luck . . . and no maybe about it.

"I love you too, Detective. Now what do you say we clean up both me and this desk before everyone figures out we aren't discussing points of law."

"Which brings me to a point I do want to discuss," he said, helping her with her bra.

"Please," she said with a grin as she piled her hair back on top of her head and went in search of her hairpin. "Not the Bradford case."

"I was thinking more about the King–Martinez case. The one where we make things legal."

She stopped with the pin pushed halfway into her hair. Stared with glistening eyes.

"Marry me, Elena. Rescue me from myself."

Her heart slammed hard, heavy, true, in her breast. She didn't even hesitate. "Yes."

Then she was in his arms again. "Yes, yes, yesssss!!!!!!!"